P9-EFI-468

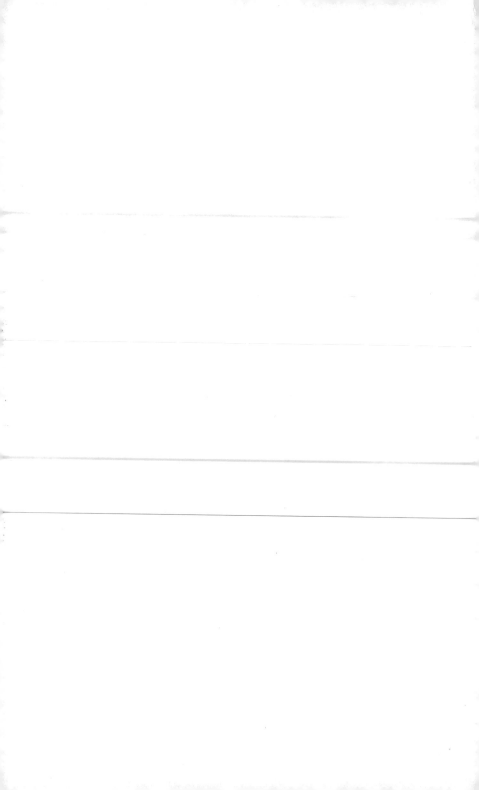

ME AND SAM-SAM HANDLE THE APOCALYPSE

ALSO BY SUSAN VAUGHT

Footer Davis Probably Is Crazy

Things Too Huge to Fix by Saying Sorry

Super Max and the Mystery of Thornwood's Revenge

ME AND SAM-SAM HANDLE THE APOCALYPSE

Susan Vaught

A Paula Wiseman Book
Simon & Schuster Books for Young Readers
NEW YORK LONDON TORONTO SYDNEY NEW DELHI

Boca Raton Public Library

SIMON & SCHUSTER BOOKS FOR YOUNG READERS
An imprint of Simon & Schuster Children's Publishing Division
1230 Avenue of the Americas, New York, New York 10020
This book is a work of fiction. Any references to historical events, real people, or real places are used
fictitiously. Other names, characters, places, and events are products of the author's imagination, and any
resemblance to actual events or places or persons, living or dead, is entirely coincidental.
Text copyright © 2019 by Susan Vaught
Jacket illustration copyright © 2019 by Victor Beuren
All rights reserved, including the right of reproduction in whole or in part in any form.
SIMON & SCHUSTER BOOKS FOR YOUNG READERS is a trademark of Simon & Schuster, Inc.
For information about special discounts for bulk purchases, please contact Simon & Schuster Special Sales
at 1-866-506-1949 or business@simonandschuster.com.
The Simon & Schuster Speakers Bureau can bring authors to your live event. For more information or
to book an event, contact the Simon & Schuster Speakers Bureau at 1-866-248-3049 or visit our
website at www.simonspeakers.com.
Jacket design by Chloë Foglia
Interior design by Hilary Zarycky
The text for this book was set in Fairfield.
Manufactured in the United States of America
0419 FFG
First Edition
2 4 6 8 10 9 7 5 3 1

Library of Congress Cataloging-in-Publication Data
Names: Vaught, Susan, 1965– author.
Title: Me and Sam-Sam handle the apocalypse / Susan Vaught.
Description: First edition. | New York : Simon & Schuster Books for Young Readers, [2019]
| "A Paula Wiseman Book." | Summary: Alternates between the detective work of middle-schooler
Jesse and her new friend, Springer, after her father is accused of stealing, and post-tornado rescue efforts
of Jesse and her Pomeranian, Sam-Sam.
Identifiers: LCCN 2018039713| ISBN 9781534425019 (hardcover)
| ISBN 9781534425033 (eBook)
Subjects: | CYAC: Bullying—Fiction. | Stealing—Fiction. |
Tornadoes—Fiction. | Pomeranian dog—Fiction. | Dogs—Fiction. |
Autism—Fiction. | Family life--Fiction. | Mystery and detective stories.
Classification: LCC PZ7.V4673 Me 2019 | DDC [Fic—dc23
LC record available at https://lccn.loc.gov/2018039713

For Craig Patric Perry II (1978–1993),
who has an amazing sister; for the real Jesse-with-an-e,
who is even more awesome than my Jesse; and for every hero
who has ever needed a Sam-Sam in their lives.

Everybody has their wars, Jesse,
and everybody fights
their wars in different ways.

MASTER SERGEANT CAMILA BROADVIEW
(That's my mom.)
(Looks important when I write it like that, doesn't it?)

Prologue

When the apocalypse came to Avery, Kentucky, I thought Great-Aunt Gustine was out getting a pedicure at Nails, Nails, Nails, that salon with a big pink foot on the door. Dad was teaching English on the senior high side of Avery Junior/Senior High School—AJS for short, and Mom was working with her bomb-sniffing dog near a place called Mosul in Iraq. The person who stole $2,103.15 from my father's desk was pretending nothing bad had happened, and our principal, Ms. Jorgensen, was someplace she had no business being. Again.

As for Sam-Sam, my poor Pomeranian, his sweet fuzzy self was locked in his luxury puppy crate in my bedroom, probably dreaming about becoming a champion bomb-sniffer, since I kept asking him to be good at finding buried treats. People always laughed at Sam because he was so little, but he thought he was massive. I didn't laugh, because people and dogs can be way more than their fur and skin and bones.

I could see the *big* inside of my Sam-Sam. I had been training him for two hundred fifty-two days with mini-tennis balls and pieces of bacon, just to prove to Dad and Mom and Aunt Gus and the whole world that a tiny, fluffy dog could do big things if he wanted to.

Okay, so Sam still couldn't find the containers I hid for him, but he was trying. Hard. Sam might have had trouble sniffing out those buried tennis balls, but he never had any doubts about himself.

I think my little dog always knew he could be a hero.

I just wonder if he knew about me.

1

Monday, Right Before the Train Came

"You gonna shoot that ball or kiss it, Messy?" Ryker Morton leaned toward me on the foul line, grinning so big I could see his ugly pink gums. Chris Sedon snickered, and it kinda sounded like a Madagascar cockroach hiss since his nose had a bandage on it. Trisha Parks roach-hissed, too, even though she didn't have any bandages on her nose. Acting like a nasty insect was just natural to her, I guess.

They hung together like that when they hassled me, Jerkface and his pet cockroaches, a matched set in their green gym shorts and shirts. You'd think after everything that had happened, they'd give this a rest, but noooooo. Same-old same-old.

I didn't think Coach Gray heard them bothering me over all the noise from the skirmish group playing half-court behind us. Plus, she was busy hollering for YOU KIDS to KEEP IT DOWN since Coach Sedon, Chris's dad, was out getting surgery on his hand and she had to do

EVERYTHING FOR EVERYBODY SO SHOW A LITTLE RESPECT!

Four nicer kids from our class stood around the goal—Krista Edmonds, Selena Ruiz, Mark Gopal, and Jake Siddiqi. Nobody but Selena looked at me, and when she did, Chris pointed at her. "What do you want, fly-face?" He put his fingers around his eyes, pretending he had thick glasses like hers. "You think Messy here won't knock you in the nose if you tick her off?"

Selena made a rude gesture at him, and Mark pushed her hand down before Coach Gray saw it. I rubbed the sides of the basketball with both hands and looked at Selena, but she looked away.

A little bit of sad squeezed tight in my throat. I tried to be nice like Krista and Selena and Mark and Jake, at least when people didn't make my brain itch. I mean, I hadn't even smacked anybody in this year's class, unlike Jerkface.

Jake glanced in our direction and said, "Y'all are just a bunch of turkeys."

Great.

Did he mean Jerkface and the cockroaches, or me—or all of us?

"Messy Jesse's a grody pig, not a turkey." Ryker pointed at my tangly hair as Chris and Trisha laughed. "You're never gonna get any better at taking a shower, are you?"

Selena made another rude gesture, sort of at Ryker but maybe sort of at me, too, and she walked off with Krista and Jake and Mark following along behind. Coach Gray tweeted her whistle since they hadn't taken their shots on goal, but they acted like they didn't hear her.

I positioned the ball and tried not to watch them leave. Jerkface and the cockroaches made some more noise, but I ignored them because Dad said ignoring cockroaches and keeping all the lights on was the best way to make them scurry away.

"See, *Jesse-with-an-*e?" Jerkface mocked in my voice. "Jesse-with-an-*e*, like boys spell it. Nobody likes you, Jesse-with-an-*e*."

Did ignoring bugs ever really make them crawl off and bother somebody else? Because it had never worked for me. Breaking Ryker's nose with the basketball so it would match Chris's, now *that* would work for me, but when I turned in his direction, Coach Gray gave me a warning blast with her silver whistle.

As if God agreed with her, it thundered outside.

Coach gave me *the look* and shook her head.

Not fair.

Jerkfaces shouldn't be able to run their mouths if non-jerkfaces couldn't defend their tired ears. What was the problem with violence, anyway? It was effective. Bugs made such a satisfying *crunch* when you stomped on them.

I glanced at the clock. I still had to put up with Jerkface and the cockroaches for seventeen minutes and thirty seconds. That wasn't much. Then again, it seemed like a lot. *Tick-tock.* I hadn't ever heard a clock make *tick-tock* noises. The clocks at AJS just made clicking sounds. Seventeen minutes. 1,020 more clicks. 1,019, 1,018, 1,017. . .

I got a second blast from the whistle and Coach glared like she'd come over to our group and make sure we regretted making her get up off her bottom-bleacher throne, so I forced myself to face the goal. Then I dug my purple fingernails into the sides of the basketball, squared my shoulders, lifted the ball to my chest, and powered it into the air.

The ball fired off to the left like a broken rocket, almost beheaded Coach Gray, and smacked a bleacher step so hard it sounded like an explosion.

Oops.

As everybody ducked and covered, I fake-stumbled and ground my heel into Jerkface's toes.

"Ow!" he hollered, grabbing for his foot, but his cockroaches didn't hear him over the whoops of the skirmish group and the sudden hard rain on the gym roof.

Ryker snarled and reached for me, but I dodged out of his way. Coach got up, caught the runaway basketball, and bounced it toward Ryker for his turn, all the while making her whistle screech at the top of its teeny metal lungs.

Nine hundred clicks to go until I was Jerkface-and-cockroach-free for the day—but at least I felt better enough to stop counting clicks.

The cockroaches seemed to grasp that they had missed

something as Ryker limped to his place at the foul line. They tried to jog toward him, but he waved them off and got ready to make his shot. Jerkface stood a lot straighter than I bothered to do, plus he was taller. His mom had played basketball in college and then gone pro and now she was on the city council, so Ryker thought he was something special every time he touched that ball. Really, all three of the cockroach crew thought they were something special, because everybody knew their parents. Plus, they had muscles and nice clothes and straight teeth and no zits and, of course, the newest phones.

Ryker drew in a breath and managed to side-eye me in the process. I smiled at him, as fake-sweet as I could manage. His cheeks flushed crimson.

Coach's whistle stabbed into my brain over and over again.

Then a strange sound cut under the gym noises, and I thought somebody might be hurt and hollering. I made sure Ryker really was shooting that basketball and not coming after me, then checked the gym to see who had busted a knee.

Everyone was standing or running except Springer Regal, the new kid who had been my new actual friend and fellow detective for a week. Springer hated all things athletic, and he had a note to sit out because he had gotten stomach flu last month, and he told me he planned to ride it for all it was worth. He was tucked in at the very top of the bleachers, resting against the wall with a book as thick as Dad's Shakespeare compendium, but he wasn't yelling or anything.

The sound came again, a distant howl, like a pack of dogs or—wait.

Sirens?

Everybody stopped running and yelling.

Springer lifted his head, gazed in the direction of the noise, then looked at me, dread obvious in his wide brown eyes. He stood slowly, holding tight to his heavy book as another round of sirens wailed in the distance. The hairs along my arms and the back of my neck lifted, and despite the gym sweat dripping down the sides of my face, I shivered.

Coach Gray's whistle punched deep into my mind, followed by her voice, higher-pitched than I'd ever heard it before.

"Hallway!" she shrieked. "Everyone! Hallway now! Go, go, go!"

2

Monday, Seven Days Earlier, Afternoon

I knelt by the metal fire pit in our backyard, careful not to let gravel cut my knees because if I bled on the carpet when I went back inside, Aunt Gus would probably feed me to her bulldog, Charlie. As I finished dropping in dry sticks for kindling, my dog, Sam, who was white and fuzzy instead of bulldog-fat and slobbery, danced around me with his tiny tennis ball. He dropped the ball and arfed, leaning on his front paws and wiggling his fluffy hindquarters.

"Shhh." I snatched up the ball and tossed it, careful to pitch away from the thick trees that bordered the back of our yard. The last thing I needed was Sam getting lost in the Pond River Forest a few hours before sunset. The forest spread around and behind most of Avery, like a comet's tail, reaching between our little town and London, Kentucky, where the Daniel Boone National Forest started. Everybody knew about that bunch of trees. Nobody much knew about ours, except for the people in Avery. Our forest was a lot smaller, but a little dog could still get lost or eaten in there, or maybe go swimming in the muddy pond that was more like a lake and never be seen again.

Sam yapped and shot across the grass, chasing after his ball. While he was busy, I dumped a load of fabric onto the kindling, then checked to be sure Aunt Gus wasn't sneaking up on me.

No sign of her.

Keeping one eye on the back door, I slid the matches out of my pocket—the ones I'd snatched out of Aunt Gus's house shoe in the back corner of her closet. That was where she kept her whole Dad-can't-see-it stash—her cigarillos, some wads of money, and a salt shaker.

Sam reappeared with his ball, dropped it on my knee, and panted happily.

I ruffled his fur. "Go on, now, Sam-Sam. I can't do this and throw a ball for you, too."

Sam kept panting until I threw the ball again. While he was gone, I struck a match, dropped it on the kindling, then scooched around on my butt and glanced at the house, imagining Aunt Gus in the kitchen, watching talk shows while she boiled pasta for dinner. Pasta was supposed to be good for her, except I knew she'd sneak into her room and salt it when Dad wasn't looking.

"Stay inside," I muttered to her. "Please."

Thankfully, it was still early enough in the afternoon that none of my neighbors were outside to see me lighting fires and talking to my house. The brick walls had no opinion, and Aunt Gus couldn't hear me, and my arm was getting tired from pitching Sam's tennis ball over and over, and soon people would start coming home from work— like, Dad—so I figured I'd best get on with it.

As I turned back to the pit, the kindling smoked. I waved my hands over it.

More smoke. Nothing but smoke.

I pitched Sam's ball again, then quickly lit a second match and dropped it on the fabric. Right after that, the kindling blazed. I leaned away from the pit as the whole mess started to smoke and smell like gaggy melting plastic.

Sam ran back to me with the ball, noticed the flames licking across the pit, dropped the ball like it was on fire, and alarm-barked.

"No," I whispered at him. "Shhhhh. Be quiet! Shhhhhh!"

Sam ignored me and barked louder, then started running circles around me and the fire pit. I sighed and used the pit's metal poker to stir the pile and keep any sparks from going rogue. Inside the house, Charlie the bulldog heard Sam's noise and kicked in with his bass woof-snort-woof concerto.

"What?" Aunt Gus hollered from somewhere.

I glared at my dog. "Thanks a lot. You're gonna get me murdered."

Sam grabbed his ball, then ran faster circles. A few

seconds later, Aunt Gus steamrolled out the back door, heading straight toward the fire pit. She had on yellow-striped Bermuda shorts and a white blouse and yellow sandals. With her braided fake-yellow hair, her strands of big yellow-and-white beads, and her big yellow sunglasses, she looked like a fashion ad for people over the age of seventy. All she needed was a beach or a cruise ship in the background instead of Charlie, the house, and the big puff of black smoke floating over our patio.

"Hush," she said to Charlie, then came at me with "What on earth are you—" until screeching tires cut her off.

Sam yapped and danced and Charlie woofed and wuffled and I groaned as Dad came bailing out of his car and ran toward us. In that moment between when I saw him and when he would likely kill me, I had time to think that he really did look a lot like Aunt Gus, only without the glasses and wrinkles—and Dad had a little less hair. I mean, you couldn't braid his, at least not well. He kept it in a ponytail because of the same older-kid dress code that made him wear khaki slacks and blue golf shirts almost every day of his life. Two years ago, the school board passed a "graduated uniform plan" for local public schools that Dad disagreed with, so he insisted on wearing what his students had to wear, "In solidarity, 'cause that's important."

I rubbed my hand over my T-shirt. The dress code

wouldn't hit the middle schools for another two years, at the same time I'd have to go to senior high. One way or another, I was gonna get morphed into a khaki-bot if Dad didn't kill me right here, right now.

"Jesse!" Dad sounded panicked. "I saw smoke—I thought the house—are you okay?" He slowed as he reached us, then stopped and gaped at the fire pit.

I got to my feet and picked up my dancing Sam and held him close. Sam sneezed all over my neck, then licked his dog snot off my skin. "It's all in the pit," I said. "There's no problem."

"You lit that fire?" Dad sounded stunned. "What did you burn?"

"Demonic things that have no place in my world," I told him.

Dad stared.

Aunt Gus studied the fire pit and said, "I think it's clothes."

Dad glanced from her to the pit and back to Aunt Gus. She turned around and seemed to be struggling not to—I don't know. Explode, or something? Finally, she managed to squeeze out, "It's the tank tops. The ones you made her wear even though she said they were itchy."

She snorted and coughed, but Dad still looked confused. Then Aunt Gus burst out laughing so loud it made Charlie wheeze and woof and pee on the patio.

What with all the bulldog grunts and Aunt Gus

cackling like a Disney witch, it took Dad a few seconds to work up to red-faced mad and ask me, "Did you really just light your shirts on fire, Jesse?"

I clung to my squirmy dog and stepped left to stay upwind of the smoke clouding up from white cotton ash and flame-retardant polyester lumps. "They needed to die."

"Shirts aren't alive!" Dad waved his hand at the smoke. "They can't die! They—oh, never mind. Look, we talked about you needing to get used to new clothes."

My face got warm, probably from the fire. "*You* talked. I just got to listen."

Aunt Gus must have strained something laughing, because she bent over and put her hands on her knees, and Charlie started licking her face. Big wads of bulldog drool hit the patio beneath them.

"You!" Dad pointed at Aunt Gus's yellow-striped behind. "Not helpful. And how did she get matches, anyway? Where did you hide them? Did she find your cigarettes, too?"

"Aunt Gus smokes cigarillos," I said. "Those little cigar things. They're cheaper, which I know because I asked the store clerk."

"Always the bad example!" Dad bellowed at his mother's sister. "Keep it up and I'll put you in Happy Acres!"

"Grandma would haunt you," I said. "And Happy Acres is across town, and Aunt Gus couldn't take me to school and pick me up so you can work your own schedule while Mom's deployed, and you'd have to pay somebody unless they change release times between grades, which they won't, because the news said our district budget is over fifteen thousand in the red, and they have to keep the bus schedule staggered."

"Fifteen thousand, huh?" Aunt Gus didn't stop laughing when she talked, but she managed to stand up and keep it to snorts and snickers that Dad might mistake for Charlie's snuffling.

"That's what the news said," I told her. "Fifteen thousand is a big number. Lots of zeros."

Sam-Sam yapped and strained toward Aunt Gus, then Dad, trying to lick the hand Dad put over his own face. After Dad rubbed his eyes, he said, "Jesse, you have to deal with the fact that new clothes can't be perfect, and the world won't change to suit you."

I wanted to kick over the fire pit, but I counted to twenty and imagined puppies doing tricks because I didn't want to set the house or the yard or the forest on fire. "The world doesn't have to change, and my new clothes don't have to be perfect. Just not itchy."

Aunt Gus literally hooted and had to bend over again. Dad put his hand back over his face, and this time, he didn't move it.

I saw my chance and bolted, holding tight to Sam as I ran.

After a few seconds, Aunt Gus hollered my name, but

it was too late. I was already at the edge of the yard, and two steps later, I hit the tree line, found my favorite trail, and vanished into the Pond River Forest.

I turned off the phone in my shorts pocket as I headed to my clubhouse. Dad would send angry messages, and Aunt Gus would try to bribe me, and they might even get Mom to send me a text. Then Dad would shut down my phone until I came back home and got ungrounded, which would be sometime two weeks and five days and ten hours and twenty minutes after NEVER.

Maybe I'd just live in the clubhouse.

I had built it myself two years ago, out of eight sheets of plywood I blackmailed Aunt Gus into buying for me when I caught her smoking in the house. I had hauled the big pieces of wood down the trail with Dad's yardwork wagon, then nailed them to tree trunks to be sure they stayed up even though I didn't really know how to connect the edges despite watching a bunch of YouTube carpentry videos. I had covered the walls and roof with blankets, draped those with plastic tarps and garbage bags I lifted from Dad's tool closet, and nailed pine branches together on top of everything.

Unless people got close to it, my hideout looked like a fallen tree slowly rotting away to nothing. Nobody could see it from the main path, and the forest rangers hadn't found it yet, and neither had Dad or Aunt Gus. The door, really just a propped board held in place with a rock, faced into the dense trees, and it had a note in red nail polish that read JESSE'S PLACE. STAY OUT AND STAY ALIVE, with lots of drips to make it look all bloody.

I kept some of my polish collection in a plastic tote inside, along with a flashlight, some head lamps, bug spray, books and magazines, a dry blanket and pillow, bottles of water, Sam's training containers, and some sealed snacks. The floor had a few big rocks for chairs, but mostly just blankets and dirt.

So imagine my surprise when Sam and I got to my special, private spot and found the door open.

Sam wriggled in my arms, pointed his white nose at the clubhouse, and growled.

"Yeah," I whispered. "I see it."

Then I clamped my teeth together and thought about growling, too.

From inside the clubhouse, a light flickered.

Somebody was definitely in my special, private place— and they were messing with my special, private stuff!

It might be a thief. Or a murderer. Or a bank robber.

I backed up a step, breathing hard.

Should I go home? Wait, no. What would Mom do?

I shut my eyes for two seconds and imagined my mother in her desert fatigues, walking her golden retriever. Shotgun was a war dog with nine years in the field, just like Mom. They both had hawk eyes and stern faces, and

Shotgun had that explosive-sniffing nose. They weren't scared of bombs or bad guys or anything at all. They didn't wait for trouble to come to them. No. My mom and her dog went *looking* for trouble, so that trouble couldn't hurt other soldiers.

When my eyes opened, I wasn't breathing hard anymore. I shifted Sam under my left arm, knelt as quietly as I could, and picked up the biggest rock I could see. Hefting it in my right hand, I stepped toward the open door and hollered, "Hey! Whoever you are, get out of my clubhouse!"

When nothing happened, I moved closer and banged the rock on the wood beside the front door. "Out! Right now!"

Sam alert-barked, adding extra-special ferocity to my yelling.

The light bounced around inside.

"I mean it!" I whammed the rock on the clubhouse wall.

From inside came rustling and mumbling, and somebody said, "Don't shoot!"

Then something big came rolling out of the door.

Like, actually rolling.

All the way out, past me, until it hit a nearby tree trunk.

The boy—it was definitely a boy—stayed on the ground, head covered, like he expected me to beat him with my rock, or maybe turn loose my barking, fuzzy war dog of fury.

I jiggled the war dog of fury. "Shhh, Sam-Sam. Easy. Don't kill him yet."

The boy on the ground—who, I might add, was wearing one of my head lamps and holding my dog-eared copy of *A Wrinkle in Time*—whimpered. I recognized him by his white-blond hair and the fact that he was a foot taller than most people in my grade. Springer Regal, the new kid who had just moved up here from Alabama last month.

"Springer, it's okay." I lowered my rock. "Sam-Sam's a Pomeranian, not a Doberman. See?"

Springer glanced up quickly, keeping both hands over his face. I saw a brown eye peeking between two knuckles. "It can still bite. Don't put it down."

"Sam-Sam is a *he*, not an it."

"Fine. Don't put *him* down. Please."

"A mean person would drop the dog right on your head because you busted into their clubhouse and used their stuff, despite the clear warning on the door. You know, the bloody words saying STAY OUT?"

Springer lowered his hands. "That's not blood. It's nail polish."

"Okay, so maybe you have impressive powers of observation. Nobody with impressive powers of observation should get bitten by a war dog of fury, even a little one." I pitched my rock off into the brush.

Springer flinched when it landed. Right about then, I saw that his left eye was swollen and colored. "Ouch," I said, pointing to his face. "Who hit you?"

He flinched again and didn't answer.

"Sorry," I said. "Maybe that was rude. Dad says I'm not tactful."

Springer studied me for a few seconds, then nodded. After that, he smiled.

I smiled back at him.

With my head lamp hanging halfway to his right ear, he looked like a giant dork who might have gotten lost exploring a bunch of caves. Plus, he had gotten mud on the corner of my *Wrinkle in Time*. I should have sicced Sam on his ankles, but instead I said, "Wanna stay awhile?"

3

Monday, Seven Days Earlier, Evening

Sam-Sam sprawled across my knees and stretched his pointy little nose until he could lick Springer's blue jeans every minute or so. I thought about being jealous, but then I figured Springer needed friends since he just moved someplace new and somebody hit him in the face, and Sam could be a good friend if you didn't mind getting your clothes bathed.

"It really is Jesse—with an *e*," I said as Springer and I munched on Twinkies and bounced flashlight and head lamp beams around my clubhouse, making shadows come to life. "Like boys spell it. Which is a ridiculous concept anyway, boy names and girl names. Why can't it just be name names? You know, everybody names."

Springer blinked at me, looking like he didn't understand.

"It's because I'm named for my mom's brother, who died in a car wreck when he was seventeen," I added.

Springer put down his head lamp, made a shadow-bunny

with his hand, and hopped it toward a rumpled blanket. "That's sad."

"Yeah. Being named for a dead guy can make living a real pain. Especially when Mom wants me to make good grades and act nice like Uncle Jesse did." I snapped at Springer's shadow-bunny with shadow-dinosaur jaws.

"Do you get bad grades?"

"Nah. Not unless I get mad at the teacher."

Springer nodded. His shadow-bird flew over my dino-saur jaws.

I snapped after him, moving my hands closer to his. "Uncle Jesse wasn't just smart, though. Mom says he was good with people, and brave when he played sports, and that if he had lived, he'd probably have been a marine."

"So you don't think you're like him?" Springer asked.

I snorted and snapped my shadow-dino jaws again. "Mom's a hero. Uncle Jesse would have been, too. I'm definitely not hero material. And I can't play sports, and I'm not good with people at all."

Springer gave me a sideways look, like he wasn't sure what to believe.

"I don't tell lies," I assured him. "Dad says I'm honest to a fault. But I'm not sure how honesty could be a fault. It's a virtue, right?"

For a few seconds, Springer looked confused, but then he nodded and flew his shadow-bird over my dino jaws really fast, so I couldn't bite him.

"Who hit you?" I asked him, figuring enough time had passed that we were acquainted now and the question wasn't rude anymore.

Springer frowned. "Ryker Morton."

My dinosaur jaws stopped moving. Sam licked me, and then he licked Springer. "Did he hit you at AJS? 'Cause if he did, there's policies and laws, and you could nail him if you wanted to."

Springer shook his head. "It was over at the park. Little League. My dad made me try out, and Ryker and his friends were there."

He sounded seriously miserable about that, which made me ask, "Do you even like baseball?"

"I hate it." Springer's cheeks flushed red at the tops, and Sam wriggled off me, all the way into his lap. Springer stopped making shadow-animals and petted my dog instead. "But Dad said it would help me learn to be part of a team. Only, the coach told me I had to put this . . . this *thing* on, and that was just the complete last straw."

"Thing?" I reached over and scratched Sam's head as Springer's cheeks got even redder.

"It's part of the baseball uniform."

I waited.

Springer's face turned almost purple. "It's supposed to protect . . . stuff."

I waited.

Springer gestured lower on his body. "You know. Guy . . . stuff."

"Oh. Ooooooh. Like my tank tops!" I clapped and bumped the flashlight, sending swirly shadows everywhere.

Springer looked very, very confused.

I waived my hands in the flashlight beam, making more flitty-floppy shadows. "You're talking about an athletic cup, right? I know an athletic cup isn't a tank top, but what I meant is, it was probably uncomfortable, like those itchy tanks Dad bought for me because I need something to—you know, hold in the girl stuff up top."

"Itchy." His face relaxed. "Yeah, right? That thing Coach told me to wear, it didn't itch, but it pinched. I couldn't stand it. So I went out behind the bathrooms and got it off, and that's when that Ryker guy and his friends caught me alone." He shook his head. "I'm such an idiot."

"You're big enough to bust Ryker's face."

"I don't hit people."

Well, that was a total bummer, because Springer hitting Jerkface would have been something I could get behind. I reached over and collected Sam from Springer's lap and held him to my chest as I scratched his soft doggy ears. "Did you at least throw the athletic cup at him?"

Springer's expression morphed into horrified. "Ew, no. I accidentally stepped on it trying to pull up my pants before he punched me. It cracked and broke, and my parents are ticked because it cost twenty bucks."

"I burned the itchy tank tops right before I came to the clubhouse," I said. "I don't know how much they cost. Dad's mad at me, and he's mad at Aunt Gus, too, because he knows I got the matches from her stash in the back of her closet, and he thinks she's a bad influence. She really isn't. Well, maybe just a little bit."

Springer nodded. Then he asked, "Is your aunt's name really Gus?"

"It's short for Gustine. She's my great-aunt, and she's old, and she has a bulldog and she wears old-people stripy pants."

Springer smiled. "My mom has pants like that, but it'd probably be a bad idea to call her old."

I gazed at Springer from between Sam's tiny ears. "I've known Ryker and his pet cockroaches since kindergarten. He's hit me before, too, lots of times—but believe it or not, he doesn't do it as much as he used to. Last year he punched me in the stomach when we were fighting over a soccer ball and whose turn it was to try a goal kick. He's a jerkface like that. That's what I call him in my head. Jerkface. But I got him back."

"How?" Springer sounded interested.

"About two weeks later, I tripped him in gym and he fell down two bleacher steps and knocked out one of his front teeth. It got me suspended for a week, even though I swore it was an accident."

Springer's mouth opened in an O, like people do when they're shocked. I knew about the O mouth because I got that a lot.

"My folks would ground me until I'm forty if I got suspended," he said.

"I'm gonna be grounded for weeks, no doubt." I pushed my face into Sam's neck.

"For burning itchy tank tops."

"Yeah."

"Well, I'll probably be grounded for cracking that pinchy guy thing."

That made me smile. "Is your house near here? I mean, most every neighborhood in Avery backs up to the forest, and all the main paths are like a big wagon wheel around the pond, and there are fifteen of them if you don't count the little ones, and—never mind. You live pretty close?"

Springer nodded. He pointed over his shoulder. "That way, down the big middle path."

"Okay. Since you found the clubhouse, you can use it if you'll keep it picked up and bring water and snacks sometimes, and leave Sam's doggy training stuff alone." I shifted Sam back to my lap and pointed to the containers with treats in them.

"Thanks." Springer nodded, then gave me a sideways glance. "Are we . . . friends, then?"

I shrugged. "If you want. People who hate itchy-pinchy things need to stick together."

"I don't have many friends," he admitted. "None up here at all."

"Because you just moved to Avery?"

"Maybe. Mom says it's because I'm shy. Dad says it's because I don't act my age, and that I need to if I'm ever going to make anything of myself—you know, that whole you-need-to-grow-up thing parents do."

I wondered if Springer's dad was a jerkface like Jerkface, but I didn't ask, because now and then I actually did think about that no-tact thing and try to do better, and new kids had enough trouble without somebody being untactful. "I don't have many friends because I've got a big mouth and I hit people sometimes."

"Ryker said—" Springer stopped. Shook his head.

"What?"

Springer lifted his hands and made a shadow-bird. It flew slowly across the clubhouse wall, until it couldn't fly any farther. Then he said, "Ryker told me you were weird because your mom's never home and you're 'on the spectrum.' Whatever that means."

"My mom says Ryker Morton wouldn't know his butt from a pee-hole in the snow." I laced my fingers into Sam's hair, and he started panting, maybe sensing that I felt strange, because usually people thinking I was weird didn't matter so much, but for some reason, it mattered now. "Mom's in Iraq and she has a golden retriever named Shotgun, and he can find bombs. I'm trying to teach Sam to find bombs, too. Do you think I'm weird?"

Springer flew another shadow-bird across the clubhouse wall. After it landed, he said, "No. I think Ryker and his friends need to keep their mean mouths shut. Does it snow much here?"

I blinked.

"You said 'pee-hole in the snow,'" he said, pointing backward like he could touch Mom's words. "A second or two ago." He frowned. "Sorry. Dad says I ask too many questions sometimes, instead of figuring things out for myself."

When his head drooped, I let Sam crawl back toward him again. "Ask whatever you want. We get ice, mostly. But not until February. Before then, it's mostly hot and rainy. And I sort of didn't tell the truth about the pee-hole in the snow."

Springer's eyebrows lifted, and he waited for me to come clean.

"Mom says *piss,* not *pee,* because she's a soldier. I figure soldiers always say *piss* instead of *pee* because *pee* sounds—I dunno. Not soldier-like."

"Maybe I'm 'on the spectrum,' too," Springer said.

I shrugged. "Who cares?"

He swallowed, seemed to decide something, then asked in a whisper, "Do *they* come around here?"

"They? Oh. You mean Jerkface and the cockroaches. Yeah, sometimes I hear them out on the big path. They've never found my clubhouse, though."

"That's good," he said. "I wouldn't have seen it if I hadn't thought—"

He stopped. His head drooped all over again, like he felt bad about something.

"What's said in the clubhouse stays in the clubhouse," I said.

Springer lifted his head. "When I was walking, I thought I heard Ryker talking somewhere behind me, so I ran off the path to hide."

"Smart," I said. "So did you pick *A Wrinkle in Time* because you like science fiction?"

Springer grinned and nodded, and started listing every science fiction book he'd ever read, maybe back to the beginning of the universe. After a while, I started thinking he learned to read when he was two or something. Whatever. I could read when I was four.

"It's way after dark," I said when Springer took a breath. "I better go home before I'm grounded for longer than forever."

Springer nodded.

"You going to leave, too?"

He shook his head.

I wondered if his parents would worry about him, or if he'd be in trouble, but I didn't ask, because this was a clubhouse, and it seemed like stuff should be private at the clubhouse. Dad told me once that I should be nicer to people, because I never knew what they were dealing with on the inside, or what they had to go through in the hours when the world wasn't watching.

Springer made his shadow-bird again, and I watched as it flew around the whole clubhouse and finally landed in front of him as he put his hands in his lap.

"See you at school," I said. "Unless Dad grounds me from school, too."

"Can that even happen?" Springer asked as I carried Sam out into the woods.

"I wish," I called back, then got my dog and myself to the path back home. The rocks and sticks and uneven dirt made it hard to hurry in the growing darkness, but I managed, letting images of Dad's mad expression fuel my feet.

We'd had this fight about me running off when I was in trouble a lot of times, but I couldn't help it. Well, I guess I could, but sometimes it felt like if I stayed in a certain place at a certain time, dealing with certain things, I'd burst into flames and burn up like those itchy tank tops. Or worse, I'd come all apart, like I stepped on a bomb.

Sam whimpered, and I realized I was holding him too tight.

"Sorry," I whispered as I got to the edge of the woods and rushed out into my yard. I picked him up to my face and kissed him, making sure to keep my grip a lot looser, and—

Flashing lights strobed across my face.

Blue flashing lights.

Wha—oh, no!

Did Dad really call the police on me for running away? He would not do that. He wouldn't. No.

But there they were.

Two police cars sat in my driveway, right behind Dad's car, lights swirling into the night sky.

4

Monday, Seven Days Earlier, Night

Sam-Sam barked and wriggled in my arms as I held him closer. Sweat broke across the back of my neck.

Police could arrest kids. I'd seen them do it at school. I bet the handcuffs would hurt. They'd be all metal and cold and terrible.

As I stood in the back of my yard shaking and hugging my dog, I could feel the icy cuffs biting into the skin of my wrists. I'd seen lots of arrests on television, and that one at AJS after this kid in fifth grade got mad and hit his teacher with a stick. I'd been mad plenty of times, but I never hit a teacher with a stick. I hadn't ever hit anybody with a stick. Pictures of different sticks went flashing through my brain and I couldn't stop seeing them.

The back door opened, and two officers, one light-skinned with red hair and one dark-skinned with really short black hair, came out with Dad and Aunt Gus trailing right behind them, hollering, "This is beyond ridiculous! You people have lost your minds. Who trains you, anyway?"

"Call Stan," Dad was saying to her as he walked with the officers.

Sticks. Stan? Sticks, sticks, sticks—Stan. Oh. Stan Lewoski, Dad's friend who was a lawyer. Sticks! For a few seconds, my brain kept refusing to do anything but see sticks, but I finally shook my head until my ears buzzed and I processed that I wouldn't be wearing handcuffs, because Dad was. And Dad wasn't walking with the officers. They had him by his arms, and they were walking him, and he was telling Aunt Gus to call a lawyer.

"No!" I ran forward. "Stop! Where are you taking my dad?"

The redheaded officer let go of Dad and turned toward me.

"His wife is deployed," Aunt Gus was saying. "How can you take him away like this? His little girl needs him."

"Stop it!" I yelled as loud as I could. Sam wriggled out of my arms and burst ahead of me, barking and barking and setting off Charlie, who woofed and snorted and bashed himself against the closed storm door.

The redheaded officer seemed to focus on Sam, and his hand drifted toward his hip.

My aunt jumped in front of him. "Are you a monster? She's just a little girl—and that's a Pomeranian, for God's sake. That dog can't even bite through your boot."

The officer raised his hands in the air, like he was surrendering.

Sam screeched to a halt in front of him, all fur and yapping and dancing, and Aunt Gus snatched him off the ground, opened the back door, and scooted him inside with Charlie. They both kept barking like the world was ending.

I stormed right past Aunt Gus and launched myself at the dark-headed officer, swinging both my arms, because I agreed with Charlie and Sam that the world might be ending, and no way were they taking my dad anywhere even if I had to bark, too. My fists connected with fabric and metal and somebody was talking but I couldn't hear anything because somebody was screaming, and I punched and punched and punched and realized it was me making that screamy sound and I felt like I was three and seeing monsters everywhere and my thoughts couldn't stop and couldn't even slow down and my teeth ground together and I screamed anyway, right through my teeth.

"Jesse, no. Honey, stop." Aunt Gus, from a thousand miles away. "Let me get her. Don't touch her! She doesn't know you and that'll just make it worse."

"Please!" Dad's voice. "She has issues. Just let me talk to her."

Dad. My father. The man in handcuffs. The man these ridiculous, awful people were *not* taking away. I swung again, twice as hard, both fists, but I hit air.

"Touch coming!" Aunt Gus shouted.

Then fingernails dug into my shoulders, pulling me back.

The world changed. Black, then red, then yellow, then hazy light. Outside our house in the dark, just the porch lights, and blue lights flashing and flashing and flashing. Sobs tore out of my throat even though I didn't feel like crying. No sad, no happy, no good, no bad, no mad—just tears, and hot. My face felt so hot. My ears rang. My throat closed. My hands ached, and I uncurled my fingers.

The two officers stood pressed against the outer wall of the house as Charlie the bulldog and my Sam-Sam yapped and dug and tried to tear down the universe to get outside to us. I didn't see Aunt Gus but realized she was holding my shoulders and talking to the dogs.

My father, hands behind his back, dropped to one knee in front of me, staring into my eyes. For a moment, I stared back, then my brain itched and my stomach lurched and that was too much and I let my gaze slide to the side, until I was focused on the top of a shiny black police boot, reflecting the porch light. That glowing yellow orb in his boot reminded me of a distant sun in some faraway galaxy, all black and quiet and perfectly peaceful, with no wars or jerkfaces or bombs or handcuffs or anything bad.

I took a deep, slow breath, and my chest shuddered. "Is this because of the fire? Is it illegal to burn tank tops in your own backyard? I can pay the fine. I can clean up from any smoke."

"Listen to me, Jesse." Dad's voice came out low and sad, but steady. Not shaking, like me. "This is not your fault, it has nothing to do with you, and these officers are just doing their jobs."

"Then their jobs are ridiculous!" It felt really good to yell that.

Dad cleared his throat. "Some money went missing from the library fund last week. Well, a lot of money. All of what I hadn't deposited this month."

He stopped and waited for me to catch up, which was nice, but it also irritated me, because people had to do that, wait for me, especially when I was upset. Aunt Gus kept a firm grip on my shoulder, but she massaged gently, like she was trying to feed the facts straight into my head through my neck muscles.

"The library fund," I repeated. "Oh. The thing you've raised money for—three years, to buy more books and computers, right?"

"Yes, about that long." Dad nodded, and I pretended his arms weren't pulled around behind his back, and that those cold, awful handcuffs weren't biting into his wrists. "I put in some donations Friday morning, and all the money was there. Later, though, when the principal went to my desk to get the donations and take them to the bank, he found the collection box empty."

I wished I had Sam in my arms, but he was inside barking, probably standing on Charlie's fat, square head to see out the door. "But how did the money go missing?"

"Somebody must have taken it out of my desk." Dad

tried to look into my eyes again, but I had to look away, because staring into his brain when something was wrong made my soul hurt and I couldn't think and I wanted to crawl out of my own skin.

"It wasn't you," I told him, sort of loud, so the police officers would hear it, too.

"It wasn't me, honey, but I'm responsible for the money. Since it's over a few hundred, the principal had to report it missing. That's AJS policy."

I thought about all the detective stories I read. "It looks like you took it, because it was in your desk and now it's gone."

Dad nodded.

"He knows how to recite Shakespeare," I said to the police officers. "Men who recite Shakespeare don't steal library money."

When the officers didn't say anything, I wanted to kick them, but Aunt Gus didn't let go of my shoulders. The dogs in the house growled for me, at least.

"Jesse, I need you to stay with Gustine and I need you to be safe and okay," Dad said.

Aunt Gus's fingers pushed harder into my shoulder muscles, applying pressure like a therapist taught her to do a few years ago. Only she didn't really do it right, so it felt like she was trying to alien nerve-pinch me into being quiet.

"How long will you be gone?" I asked Dad.

"I'll try to be home tomorrow. Stan will help, but it takes time to get papers processed and bail paid." He got slowly to his feet.

I pulled away from Aunt Gus, grabbed him around the waist, and hugged him, letting my fingers touch the cold handcuffs behind his back, and willing the metal not to hurt him. My brain flashed pictures of handcuffs and sticks and bombs and Shotgun and shadow-birds flying across the walls of my clubhouse.

"Go with Aunt Gus and help her look after the dogs," Dad said, gently moving back from my hug. "It's time for Sam's dinner."

Sam. Sam's dinner. I held my breath, waiting for the officers to grab Dad's arms again, but they didn't. Sam-Sam needed his dinner. No matter what I said or did, the police were going to take Dad. But Dad would be home tomorrow. He said so. Sam-Sam. I had to get his dinner. Sam-Sam needed me. Dogs couldn't fix their own dinner. Poor Sam-Sam. He sounded so stressed. All that barking.

Keeping their eyes on me, the police officers edged down the back wall of the house, taking Dad away. The dark-headed man put his hand on my father's back, but nice-like, as if he only wanted to keep Dad from stumbling.

I watched every movement, every step. My hands curled into fists. I felt small and fuzzy-headed like my dog, who needed dinner, but I wanted to feel tall and full of muscles and looking for trouble like Mom and Shotgun.

Mom and Shotgun wouldn't get shaky and their heads wouldn't fuzz out and they'd be heroes and go find the bomb, not wait for some lawyer to help Dad.

My fists uncurled, and my stomach started to ache. I was no hero. I couldn't be a hero. Not with . . . whatever was wrong with me. There was nothing I could do to keep these people from taking my father away.

The police officers eased Dad into the backseat of the police car at the end of the driveway, and the blue lights showed me people's faces in the dark, neighbors on their porches, in their driveways, watching as men in uniforms stole my father, even though Mom wore a uniform, too, and people in uniforms were supposed to always help each other, because Mom said that a lot.

As the police pulled out of the driveway, taking the blue lights with them, sweeping headlights over the ghostly figures standing in their yards, Aunt Gus warned, "Touch," then gave my shoulder another squeeze.

"Come on inside, Jesse," she said. "I've got to make some calls."

She let go of me then, and my skin burned where her hands had been. Her voice echoed in my head, the words barely making sense. My legs twitched like they wanted to jump off my body and run after the red taillights of the police cars, run until they could climb in next to my father.

"No hero," I whispered, my voice ragged in the night air.

"Jesse," Aunt Gus said again, and I turned around and grabbed the door handle.

Off in the distance, at the dark edge of the woods, shadowy tree branches moved in a way shadowy tree branches weren't supposed to move.

When I turned my head to squint at them, I saw something tall with light hair, something probably named Springer, pushing back into the Pond River Forest.

5

Monday, When the Train Came

Three minutes after the town sirens blared, we were on our knees in the corridor between the gym and the main office, heads covered, matching green-shorted butts in the air.

Usually schools actually let out before tornadic thunderstorms. Except when the weather person completely missed the boat and those tornadic thunderstorms happened all of a sudden, apparently. I blew air out between my lips to keep myself calm, then lifted my head so my arms wouldn't fall asleep.

"Jesse Marie Broadview," Coach Gray hollered from my left side, where she was making sure Ryker couldn't pull my hair and I couldn't punch him in the shoulder so hard his neck cracked. "If you don't keep your head down, I'll suspend you even if we're all flattened by this storm!"

I barely heard her over the roar outside. At first it seemed far away, but with each breath I took, the roar got closer, and soon I felt it in my knees and elbows, and even in my teeth.

The school seemed to shake.

The school *did* shake.

Cool.

Okay, maybe a little bit scary, but I didn't get scared about much, except Dad having to go back to jail, but Springer and Sam and I, we were going to be like Mom and Shotgun and sniff out anything that could blow up and hurt my father. Even though we hadn't had much luck so far, we were going to figure out the whole stolen-money thing, even if the police couldn't.

I turned my head to my right and yelled to Springer, "Tornados really *do* sound like trains."

"We're gonna get blown to Oz!" Springer didn't pick his forehead up off his book. "We're all gonna die!"

I put my head back under my arms, and waited and wondered if the train that really wasn't a train would run over all the green butts in the hallway.

Would that air-train knock us down? Suck us up and spit us out five miles away from here? I'd probably wake up next to a cow.

I didn't much like cows.

Nope. No cows.

And Sam-Sam—he was home alone with nobody but old grunty Gus for company, and he probably didn't even know tornados sounded like trains, and those sirens probably scared him. I lifted my head and started to get up.

"Stay down!" Coach Gray grabbed my arm and pulled me back where I had been, pushing my head toward the floor.

The train-not-train roared like a dragon and made my teeth and eyeballs and bones shake along with the school.

As soon as Coach Gray let me go, I reached over and tapped Springer's knuckles so he'd know it was okay to hold my hand.

He whimpered and squeezed my fingers.

The ceiling fell on top of us.

6

Tuesday, Six Days Earlier, Morning

I was supposed to be in school, but I wasn't in school because I couldn't even think about school because Dad wasn't home like he was supposed to be and the world wasn't what it was supposed to be, and no. When the alarm beeped at five and five thirty and five forty and five fifty and six and six ten, I pulled the covers over my head, and I counted out loud up to fifteen and back down again, because fifteen was a good number, and it was three sets of five, and fives were pretty nice, and I liked how the word *f-i-v-e* looked when I wrote it.

Aunt Gus didn't try to get me out of my room, and she must have heard me counting and called the counselors at Fort Campbell, because a few minutes later, my phone that never got taken because Dad got arrested made a Skype tone. I pushed my covers into a cave and lay on my belly over my pillow with Sam-Sam beside me, talking to Mom.

"I'm not having a meltdown," I told her, which was mostly but not totally true. "I'm too old for meltdowns now and that therapist from last year taught me how to count and use pictures in my head and I do that instead, usually."

"That's good," Mom said. "But Gustine said you were counting really loud, and you're not at school like you're supposed to be, so I figured you were upset."

I tried to look Mom in the eyes over the phone, but I got that itchy feeling behind my forehead and my thoughts went fuzzy and I had to stop. "I'm too old for meltdowns but I'm not too old to kick jerkfaces in the knees and get arrested like Dad. I can't do jerkfaces today."

Mom looked like a military painting in her desert fatigues, with nothing but a brown canvas wall behind her. That was all I ever saw, since the soldiers had a special communications tent with talking stations, and the army made sure nobody could see anything they shouldn't.

"Is that little snot still bothering you?" Mom asked in that tone of voice she probably used to announce bombs being located, serious and dangerous, every syllable pronounced so clearly it was hard to believe she was 6,500 miles from my bed cave, and not on some movie set right down the road.

"He bothers everybody," I said, "but don't call AJS."

Sam edged up next to me, licking my cheek as Mom asked, "Why not?"

I worked on giving Mom my best mom face, as stern and soldiery as I could make it. "Sam-Sam and I can do it. We'll handle Jerkface and his cockroaches like you and

Shotgun handle bombs so they don't hurt soldiers. It'll be like hero practice."

"Shotgun and I have a lot of help," Mom said. "And I don't mind helping you, Jesse."

"That's Private Jesse Broadview to you," I said. Sam licked my chin until I nosed him aside. "What would Uncle Jesse have done with bullies?"

Mom didn't even hesitate. "Well, he would have tried to joke them out of it, and if that didn't work, he probably would have cracked their jaws."

"I really can take care of myself, Mom. Just like Uncle Jesse did. And sorry Aunt Gus bothered you so early about all the Dad stuff, and me not going to school."

"It's not early here," Mom said, her face so tiny on my phone's screen, even though I could imagine her full-sized if I shut my eyes, but I didn't shut my eyes, because I didn't know when I'd get to see her again.

Mom brushed a fly off her shoulder. "It's afternoon. Can't you see the sweat on my face?"

"No," I said, but when she winked at me, I saw that, and told her so.

"I know it's bad right now, baby. I mean Private Broadview." Mom pulled off her desert camo cap, adjusted her dark hair into a better ponytail, tucked it on top of her head, then put the sand-colored camo cap back in place, leaving not a single hair scraggling out, even around her ears.

I hovered my finger near the screen, careful not to

touch it and pause Mom. I mean, I knew I'd just be pausing the Skype call, but it seemed weird in my head that the screen would freeze and Mom wouldn't, and part of me always worried that she would just be sitting there outside Mosul, Iraq, like a Mom statue, even if the bad guys came to shoot at her.

Sam licked my finger.

Mom nodded toward Sam. "Hello, littlest soldier."

Sam-Sam's curly tail thumped against my side. He stretched his body out longer and panted at the phone screen, his head right next to mine.

"I swear that dog knows how to smile," Mom said.

"He's talented."

"How's the training going?"

"Great! Um, well, I mean, okay. Actually, kinda awful. He'll fetch any ball I throw, and he eats bacon whenever I hand it to him, but he stinks at finding the bacon-rubbed tennis balls in hidden containers. Last week, he was at two out of twenty. And I think he only found those because he tripped over the plastic and knocked the lids off."

Mom winced. "Hunting hidden items might not be Sam-Sam's special talent in life."

"I'm not giving up." I rubbed Sam's fuzzy ears. "I haven't tried it since Springer broke into the clubhouse—do you think Springer might mess up the bacon smell and confuse Sam even more? Maybe I should rub bacon on Springer, too."

Mom held up a hand to stop me. "Who is Springer?"

"He's this boy who moved here from Alabama, and he hates athletic cups and understands why I don't want to wear itchy clothes. He doesn't smell like bacon, though. At least I don't think he does. I haven't sniffed him."

Mom reached down beside her leg, and I knew she was running her fingers through Shotgun's fur like I ran my fingers through Sam's soft coat all the time. I wondered if it made her feel better, like it did me.

"Sniffed—itchy—wait. Did you say athletic cup?" was all Mom could manage. "Explain that one immediately, Private."

"They're both uncomfortable," I said. "The cups and those tank tops Dad bought and made me wear until I burned them. Ryker punched Springer in the face, too, but Springer is big enough to hit Ryker back, only he won't."

Mom took all this in without comment. After a few seconds, she asked, "Is Springer your friend now?"

I shrugged. "Sort of."

"That's great! But I'm not sure how I feel about you talking to a boy about athletic cups, even if he is your friend."

"I talked to Dad about girl underclothes and he's a boy. Clothes are just clothes, Mom."

Mom smiled. "Good point."

I put my chin on the pillow and held the phone up so Mom was perfectly level with my nose. "Do your uniforms itch?"

"Sometimes, but I wear them because people expect

it of me, and it's a sacrifice I can make to keep everything in order."

I thought about that, wearing itchy clothes to keep stuff in order. It made sense. I liked things in order. But itchy—I didn't know if I could handle that, because if something itched, I couldn't think about much else and it made me want to scream and it made it so much harder not to punch jerkfaces, and itchy things even made people who weren't jerkfaces seem like jerkfaces.

I told Mom that. She opened her mouth. Closed it. Shook her head and petted her dog.

"It's your decision," Mom said. "For now. Maybe for always, depending on what jobs you choose." Then, before I could start talking about jobs or arguing more about itchy things, she added, "This thing with your father, it'll be okay. We know he's innocent."

I pressed my chin deep into the pillow, so Mom was probably looking at my hairline. "But the police think he's guilty."

"Stan will get your father out on bond, and the police will figure out who really took the money."

"I don't understand why they didn't look at, I don't know, surveillance cameras or something."

"You watch too many television shows." Mom kept petting Shotgun. "Avery's a little town. AJS probably doesn't have cameras. Plus, I know your father. He doesn't keep things very secure. Half the senior high might have been in and out of his classroom the day the money went missing."

I lifted my head. "So half the senior high needs to be on my suspect list? Which half?"

"Nobody needs to be on your suspect list, Private Broadview." Mom's army voice. "The police and Stan and your dad will handle this."

"Dad's too nice to handle this," I told her. "Solving crimes isn't for nice people."

Mom thought about that for a second, then said, "Explain."

"Dad doesn't say what he means, and he never thinks bad about anybody. And he doesn't notice stuff if it's not about Shakespeare and books and teachering."

"Teachering?"

I rolled my eyes. "It should be a word, especially for people like Dad."

"You're right about your father," Mom admitted. "But Stan's a good lawyer. And the police—"

"Might not do what they're supposed to, since they already think Dad is guilty." I shifted on my pillows, feeling hot all of a sudden. "And Dad's too important to leave it all up to other people. I want to help."

Mom's face softened, and for a few seconds, she looked like at-home Mom instead of at-war Mom. "Jesse, the best thing you could do to help is go to school tomorrow, like you're supposed to."

My shoulders sagged as some of the air went out of me because I knew that she wasn't right, and that I needed to do something for the good of my family. What, I didn't know. But something. But, since I was talking to Mom, who was definitely looking at-war again, I said, "Okay."

Mom frowned. "That was too easy. What are you plotting, Private?"

"Nothing." I hoped I sounded innocent and offended. "Can't let Jerkface think he's winning, right?"

Shotgun put his head in Mom's lap. His nose looked bigger than my whole little white fuzzy Sam-Sam.

Sam yapped at Shotgun.

Mom jumped, and so did I.

"Fierce little monster." Mom laughed and pushed Shotgun out of the picture. "I have to go, Private. This bigger monster and I need to get back to work."

"I love you," I said.

"When it gets bad," Mom said, "when you get mad and lonely, remember I love you this much." She stretched out her arms big enough to hug all the space between Mosul, Iraq, and Avery, Kentucky.

Then she waited.

"And I love you this much." I blew her a giant kiss, sloppy enough to splash across mountains and fields and oceans and deserts, with enough love to fly thousands and thousands of miles.

Mom caught the kiss, put it on her cheek, then waved at me. She was about to punch the Off button but hesitated. "Jesse?"

"Yes, ma'am?"

"Don't rub bacon on your new friend."

"Oh. Okay."

She tapped the button.

For a moment, she was frozen there, the Mom statue in Mosul, Iraq. And then she was gone.

For a while, I stayed in my blanket cave staring at the Skype screen. Mom and I had talked for thirteen minutes and forty-two seconds. Eight hundred and twenty-two seconds. That wasn't many seconds out of the 86,400 that made up a day. Or the 31,536,000 in a year. Or the 39,420,000 seconds Mom had been gone this time.

"When I was younger," I told Sam, "I threw fits just so the counselors would send Mom a message to call me and some of my eighty-six thousand, four hundred seconds each day could be with her, even if it was just on a phone."

Sam licked my wrist.

"I know. It was an awful thing to do." I glanced down at Sam's face. He really did smile, just like a person. "But I'm older now, and I can count and think about puppy pictures. And I don't want to worry Mom, and Dad needs me. And when I think about puppy pictures, I think about you."

Sam licked my wrist some more, then smiled again.

"Come on," I told him. "Let's get the room picked up. Then we've got work to do."

7

Tuesday, Six Days Earlier, Afternoon

Eleven thousand, seven hundred and sixteen seconds later, after I made my bed and brushed my dog, when Aunt Gus was watching her shows and smoking a cigarillo inside with her bedroom window open and her hand hanging out over the patio, I borrowed our most recent AJS yearbook from Dad's desk, snuck out of his bedroom window, and took Sam to the clubhouse.

When I pushed open the door, Springer was wadded up in the blankets, curled around one of the totes of supplies. He was still wearing the same clothes he had on yesterday, and his eye still looked all dark and puffy.

I felt surprised, yet not really.

He lifted his head and one sleepy eye and one puffy swollen eye in my direction, and I said, "You didn't go home, and you didn't go to school, either."

"I didn't go home and I didn't go to school, either," he echoed, which made me smile, because usually I was the one echoing things, and it was nice to hear somebody else do it.

"I messaged my mom so she wouldn't worry, though," he added. "And your dad got arrested."

"Dad got arrested," I echoed, because I didn't know what else to say, and it made me relax some that I didn't have to figure out any other words.

Springer sat up, pulling a blanket over his legs. I took Sam to him and told Sam to stay with Springer, and I handed Springer the yearbook. "Get a pencil from the tote by your right elbow. Look through this book and circle anybody who looks suspicious, especially if they're in senior high and Dad might teach them."

Springer petted Sam-Sam quietly for a second or two, then asked, "Suspicious for what?"

"For stealing money out of my dad's desk last week and making everybody think Dad's a thief."

He glanced from the yearbook to the tote and back to me. "Okay," he said, still petting my dog.

"Does your black eye hurt?"

"A little." He touched the edge of it and winced.

"Okay, then. Take care of Sam, and I'll be back in a few minutes."

Before Springer could answer, I left him in the clubhouse with Sam and went back to my house. I didn't sneak inside, just let the doors bang and did what I had to do. And that was making sandwiches and packing chips and drinks, and putting ice in a baggie. I got Springer a washcloth and took one of my dad's T-shirts and a stick of his deodorant, too, and told Aunt Gus to never mind when she asked me what I was doing.

Once I got back to the clubhouse, I turned on my phone and played games while Springer ate and got cleaned up and changed shirts. I had a lot of messages, from Dad and Aunt Gus and then phone numbers I knew were Jerkface and the cockroaches. They liked to do that, send me mean texts. I usually didn't even read them.

Springer wrapped the washcloth I brought him around the baggie of ice and pressed it to his black eye. He didn't say anything, but the look on his face told me it helped. That made me happy. I glanced through Dad's messages, and Aunt Gus's. Just stuff from last night. Nothing new or important.

There was a message from a number I didn't know. It said, *Good job answering that question in math. You saved us from extra homework.*

Huh. That must have been from yesterday, too, when I solved the daily equation.

I looked up, feeling my eyebrows pull together as I wondered who had sent it. I wasn't good with "tone" and humor and stuff. But it almost seemed like a nice message. Maybe even from one of the nice kids that had fourth period math with me.

Heard your pops got arrested. Perfect. Making you was a real crime. Ryker. Not nice, of course.

Bad genes, Messy Jesse. Maybe you'll be next. That one was Chris.

For whatever reason, Trisha had given it a rest for a night—and she was usually the worst one of all on social media, before I deleted all my accounts.

I went back to my games, and for a while, Springer and I just played on our phones. Then I ate and stayed not cleaned up because not cleaned up was less itchy, because soap made my skin tight and dirt made it soft and clothes were lots softer when they weren't just washed, even though some of my brain kept hearing Jerkface call me Messy instead of Jesse.

When we got tired of the phones, Springer held Sam inside the clubhouse while I hid Sam's favorite ball and his favorite bacon treat in a plastic container and tucked it behind a rock, then covered it up with pine needles. I put five other containers near the clubhouse, making sure to get my scent on all of them, and I even half-buried one at a tree base.

"I thought dogs couldn't smell through plastic," Springer called from inside the clubhouse.

"Not really," I admitted as I made my way back to the door and took my now very wiggly dog out of Springer's hands. "But plastic containers aren't as solid as people think. Smells get through."

"Porous," Springer mumbled.

When I looked at him, he said, "I love science words."

"One-third of a dog's brain is made to sniff stuff," I said. "Mom says they smell five thousand times better than we do."

Springer smiled.

I pulled Sam close to my face, until we were nose to nose. His curly tail bounced back and forth so fast it fanned the air. "You can do this, right?" I asked him.

Sam-Sam's tongue fell out of his doggy mouth, and he doggy-smiled at me.

"Seriously," I said, "I know you can. It's not that hard."

More doggy smiles.

"You like tennis balls, and you love bacon. So just find your favorite things."

Sam wiggled and tried to lick my face.

I kissed him and lowered him to the ground.

He danced around my ankles.

"Sit," I instructed.

Sam sat.

"That's impressive," Springer said.

Sam fidgeted. Sat. Fidgeted some more, yapped twice, got up, ran around my legs, and sat back down, dancing from front foot to front foot.

"He has trouble with the waiting part," I told Springer.

"Me too," Springer said.

"Okay, Sam-Sam." I raised my hand.

Sam tried to keep sitting, but he popped up and danced and sat and then popped up again.

"Go!" I yelled, and dropped my hand to my side.

Sam shot off like I'd fired him from a slingshot. For a few seconds, he seemed to follow my scent toward the first

buried container. My heart beat a little faster. Springer shifted his ice bag and leaned in Sam's direction, even his bruised eye opened wide.

Sam stopped near the turned-up earth where I'd hidden the plastic with the ball and treat. So close. If he turned toward it, if he sniffed or dug at it, I could praise him and count it as a hit.

Sam sniffed the air and danced in a circle that sort of took him away from the container's hiding spot.

Springer looked at me, eyebrows raised. "Isn't he supposed to sniff that out and, I don't know, point, or something?"

"Yeah, he is. But we're early in our training, and he's a Pomeranian. That dancing-in-circles thing is what they do when they find bombs, probably."

This seemed to surprise Springer. "You're training him to find bombs?"

"Right now, I'm training him to find stinky tennis balls, but later, maybe, yeah, I'll train him for bombs like Mom's dog Shotgun in Iraq. They find a lot of bombs."

Sam strolled around in the brush, no doubt picking up lots of different types of burs in his coat.

Springer didn't say anything, and he didn't look at me, and I felt my face get warm. "I know, I know," I said. "He might have a little trouble with the finding stuff part, too."

Springer glanced in my direction, his expression sympathetic. He nodded once, then went back to watching

my dog, who had started to wander aimlessly away from the mound of dirt, sniffing the ground and wagging his poofy tail.

About a second later, a squirrel skittered by, and Sam shot off after it, barking and barking.

"Sam?" I stumbled forward, breath catching hard in my chest. "Sam-Sam! Hey, come back!"

Off in the distance, brush and leaves crackled. Pomeranian yips filled my ears, getting farther away with each second.

From somewhere in some other galaxy, Springer said, "Oh. Not good."

One bark. Two. Three. Four, five, six—deep in the woods. Deeper. Cold dread splashed across my insides.

"Sam-Sam!" I ran toward the distant noise.

Woods had coyotes. And hawks and eagles. And owls. A good-sized crow could pick up Sam and carry him away. Even that squirrel he was chasing could probably take him in a fight. "Saaaaaaammm!"

Trees got closer together, and branches smacked at my face. I batted them away with both arms. "Sam-Sam! Sam-Sam!"

My feet ground against leaves and rocks and twigs. My dog. My little fuzzy dog. Tears crammed into my eyes, blurring the world into greens and browns and blues, and I kept trying to breathe, and smelling bacon and dirt.

"Sam!"

I burst out of tree cover and teetered on the bank of Pond River Forest's actual pond. The wide, muddy expanse stretched out before me in all directions, the dark surface rippling in the light breeze. My cheeks stung. My chest hurt, but not from running. All around me, the woods had gone quiet. There was no sound except the quiet *tap-lap* of water against some rocks below me.

"Sam-Sam?" My voice came out in a whisper.

And then I heard the *crunchity-crunchity-crunchity* of something pelting through the underbrush. And the *thumpity-thumpity-thumpity* of something bigger thundering down the path behind me. Off in the distance on a side trail, right where I had to squint to see it, a white fuzzy blur popped into view.

Sam.

He was racing back to me, as fast as his tiny paws would carry him.

He hit me from the side right about the exact second Springer stumbled past me and almost hurtled headfirst into the pond. He managed to stop himself just in time.

I scooped Sam off the ground and kissed him and petted him and kissed him some more. "Good dog," I whispered, pretending I wasn't crying and wiping my face in his fur. "You scared me. But good dog for coming back."

"Good," Springer wheezed from beside me. "Good."

He mumbled something that sounded like "Puppy," then threw up off to the right.

"Sorry," he added. And then, "It's not from the running. It's—I thought—I worried—"

"Thanks," I said, and I wished I could puke instead of scream and hit things when I got totally freaked out. That skill could come in handy in dealing with Jerkface and the cockroaches.

We stood together, Springer and me and Sam-Sam, until I could breathe all the way right again, and Springer stopped looking green around his mouth and eyes, and Sam had licked all the tears off my cheeks. Then I hauled my dog back up the trail to the mound where I had buried the container. Springer followed along until I set Sam gently beside the mound. Sam-Sam nosed at the dirt. Using three fingers on each hand, I slowly dug up the container, hoping he would get the idea.

He didn't.

I opened the container and pulled out the treat and the ball.

Seconds later, Sam rolled around on the ground, joyous and bacon-treated, with a mouthful of tennis ball.

"Good, good, dog," I told Sam-Sam again, so happy that he hadn't vanished into the Pond River Forest forever, chasing that squirrel.

Springer sat beside me on the ground, and the smell of vomit wafted through the air. It didn't bother me much, since I knew it meant Springer had been as worried about Sam as I was.

"I'm glad he's okay," Springer said, rubbing at his bruised eye.

"Thanks, me too."

We stopped talking, and we watched Sam toss his own ball, then chase after it, and he seemed like the happiest dog on the planet. Sometime later, Springer gave a sigh and asked, "If you get him to find the treats, how will you get explosives for him to learn to smell those?"

"I don't know. I thought about ordering some on the Internet, or making some, but I got afraid the FBI would come take me away and Sam would freak out."

"No explosives," Springer said. "No FBI."

I took the ball Sam offered and tossed it for him. "Springer, why didn't you go home last night?"

From the corner of my eye, I saw his shoulder shrug. "Figured Dad needed time to cool off after the baseball failure thing, and me getting a black eye," he said. "Mom agreed. He came home so late from work he didn't notice anyway."

Sam ran over to him with the tennis ball. Springer tossed it, and the dog tore after it. "Dad wants me to hit back like you told me to do, see?" he said. "And I don't. And he doesn't really understand why. He thinks that means I can't take care of myself, that I won't make something out of myself and be successful."

"What about your mom?"

"She doesn't say much when Dad's going on about how

I need to toughen up if I ever want to achieve anything in life. But later she tells me I'm good, and smart, and I shouldn't listen too much when Dad's going through his you-have-to-do-better-if-you-want-to-succeed routine. She says I need to be my own kind of man, and define success for myself."

I nodded. "Messy Jesse."

"What?"

"It's what Jerkface calls me, 'cause sometimes I come to school without a shower. Like if Dad and I were late getting up, or Aunt Gus couldn't get the laundry done, or Sam-Sam gets hair on my clothes, or maybe we all stayed up late talking to Mom, or I just needed not to be itchy and tight-soap-skinned for just one day." I had to stop and scratch my neck, just because I was talking about itchy tight skin. "Sometimes I feel successful just because I got myself to school, but Ryker and the cockroaches don't understand that. Kinda like your dad doesn't understand that there are lots of ways people can make something of themselves."

Sam carried his ball to Springer, and I felt jealous, but only a little.

"Does your mom call you from Iraq on the phone?" Springer asked.

"She Skypes. That way we can see her. I talked to her this morning."

"Because your dad got arrested."

Sam brought the ball to me, and that made me feel better. I tossed it. "Yeah. Why did you follow me to my house last night?"

"I wanted to see where you lived," Springer said. "How close it was to the clubhouse, and stuff."

Another round of ball-throwing, and I made myself look at Springer. "Are you a serial killer or a creepy stalker, like from scary movies?"

"No," he said.

When Sam-Sam brought back the slobbery tennis ball, I rubbed it on Springer's jeans, even though Mom told me not to rub bacon on my friend. "There. Now you smell like bacon and tennis ball and dog drool, too."

"I wanted to be sure you got home safe," Springer admitted. "Last night."

Sam nudged at the ball in my hand and wagged his tail. I held it just above his black button nose. "You wanted to be sure I got home safe because I'm a girl?"

Confusion flickered across Springer's face. "No, because you said we were friends, and friends are supposed to look out for each other."

I handed Springer the ball.

His face lit up, and by the time he threw the ball, he was smiling. While Sam was gone, he pointed toward the clubhouse. "You know that yearbook you gave me? When you left to go get food and stuff, I circled some people. Maybe a lot of people. And I started us some lists we can work with. But yearbook pictures make faces look weird, so technically, everybody looks suspicious. I don't think circling pictures is the best way to start if you want to find a thief who stole money from your dad's desk."

"Where should we start, then?—Oh."

Springer nodded.

"We should start at the desk," I said.

8

Tuesday, Six Days Earlier, Evening

Dad hugged me so tight I couldn't get a breath, but I didn't care. I hugged him right back until I made him grunt. Aunt Gus and Sam-Sam and Charlie bounced around both of us. At least Aunt Gus didn't pant and drool. She just kept saying, "Thank goodness, thank goodness, Derrick."

The setting sun through the windows made our living room look like the end of a movie. Dad smelled like pee and sweat and old clothes, but he was here.

Rustly noises came from the kitchen, and I hoped Springer had the good sense to stack up the lists of teacher names and student names we had been working with all afternoon, since we couldn't investigate the desk right away. When I leaned back from Dad and glanced toward the kitchen table to double-check, Dad seemed to notice there was someone else in the house. His grip on my shoulder got firmer.

"Who is this, honey?" he asked as Springer came into

the living room holding our papers up against his chest like they might be homework assignments. "And why is he wearing one of my T-shirts?"

"This is Springer," I said.

Dad glanced from Springer to me to Aunt Gus.

"He's, ah—" Aunt Gus smoothed her pink shirt against her white capris. "He's Jesse's new friend."

Dad's eyes widened. He looked at Springer again. Springer fumbled with the papers, then stuck out his right hand.

Dad hesitated, then took Springer's outstretched hand and shook it, slow-like. Dad seemed to be trying to smile, but mostly he studied Springer like he was a big piece of illegally salted pasta destined to wreck Aunt Gus's blood pressure.

"Glad you're home from getting arrested, Mr. Broadview," Springer said as Dad let go of his hand. "We know you didn't steal any money."

"Uh, thanks," Dad said. His gaze shifted to me. "He really is wearing one of my shirts. And the boy has a black eye, Jesse."

"I gave him the shirt, but I didn't hit him," I said as fast as I could. "It was Ryker."

"Ryker hit you at AJS, son?" Dad asked in his teacher voice.

"No, sir," Springer said. "He hit me at Little League tryouts."

Dad frowned. "I see. Well, I'm sure the league has rules, and the park—and there's always legal charges. Are your parents handling the situation?"

Springer looked confused and maybe about half freaked out, so I said, "Yes," for him, so Dad would stop. That just made Springer look relieved and then slightly more freaked out.

Dad didn't seem to know what to do or say next, so he went with "Jesse, maybe Springer should head home? Everything that's been going on—this is family business, really."

"Springer knows all about it because he's my friend, and because he saw what happened last night." I stepped over to Springer's side and rescued the papers from his shaky hands. "When they took you away, he was watching. He followed me home from the woods to make sure nothing got me on the trails, because that's what friends are supposed to do."

"I wanted to walk her home," Springer said. "But she got going too fast and I couldn't catch her."

Aunt Gus adjusted a strap on her pink sandal and said something about checking on dinner. Then she bolted around us for the kitchen, even though I was pretty sure she hadn't started cooking anything. The dogs hopped after her, obviously expecting treats.

Dad was still staring at Springer, like he wasn't totally sure Springer was a real boy. "You tried to walk Jesse home from Pond River Forest? Just to be sure she was safe?"

Springer nodded.

For twenty-two seconds, Dad didn't say anything at all. Neither did Springer.

I started to wonder if they were ever going to talk or move again, but finally Dad said, "Thank you for looking after my daughter, Springer. I think I need a shower and a good meal. Will you be staying for supper?"

Before I could go to the kitchen to ask Aunt Gus, she called, "That's fine. I'll add more tuna to the casserole."

"I said I needed a *good* meal," Dad muttered.

"My mom says any meal you don't have to cook is a good meal," Springer said. Then he covered his mouth.

Dad smiled again, bigger this time. "Good point." Then he sort of wiped the smile off with both hands, pursed his lips, and added, "But I'm sad to say, Jesse, we have some unfinished business from when you ran into the woods yesterday."

"Da-ad," I said. "You just said you needed a shower."

He held out his hand.

I sighed, took my phone out of my pocket, turned it off, and plopped it into his palm.

"Thank you," he said. "I'll get the charger out of the kitchen. And now, yes, I do need to go clean up."

As he left the living room, Springer whispered, "You can use my phone if you need one. And I like tuna casserole. Is that weird?"

"Thanks, and maybe a little." I shrugged. "Come on, let's put these lists in my room."

Springer followed me without arguing, and Sam caught up with us, carrying a cloth squeaky bone that had stuffing poking out of one end. When we got to my door, he plopped on the threshold and chomped on it, making it shriek over and over as I stacked the papers on a table between my two rocking chairs.

"Can I sit in one?" Springer asked, running his fingers down the soft brown arm cover of the chair nearest to him.

"Sure," I said. "I rock to relax. That's why Dad and Mom got me these fabric chairs, because when I had wooden ones, I scratched the floor, and the back slats wore out."

Springer eased himself into the rocker. He closed his eyes and rocked, and he started smiling, a lot like when he threw toys for Sam-Sam, who did not need a toy thrown for him right now, since he was squeaking his cloth bone totally to death on my bedroom floor.

"Do you have chairs like these in your room?" I asked Springer as I sat in the other rocker and pulled my weighted blanket off the floor, enjoying the pressure on my hands and legs and arms.

"No," he said, keeping his eyes closed. "I had one for a while, but Dad said I spent too much time in it and not enough time going outside."

Sam squeaked and squeaked his toy. Springer and I rocked for a while, and then I said, "Here, try my blanket."

Even though I didn't want to, I pulled off the weighted blanket and passed it over to Springer, who didn't complain that it was bright yellow. He just ran his fingers along the satin binding, then settled it on his legs. His eyes fluttered closed again, and he rocked faster.

There. Take that, Springer's dad.

Springer finally opened his eyes a few minutes later, sighing like he'd never been happier in his life. His gaze strayed to my dresser, to the silver frame with a picture of Mom when she was fourteen, and Uncle Jesse when he was seventeen, sitting on their front porch acting goofy. It had been taken a few weeks before he died.

"Is that guy in the photo the one you're named after?" Springer asked.

"Yeah," I said. "Uncle Jesse and my mom."

"They look alike," Springer said. "The dark hair and brown eyes, and they have big smiles. You kinda look like both of them."

I raised my fingers to the corners of my mouth, wondering if I could ever smile like that, big and not nervous and totally, completely happy. It made my brain itch to think about it too much, so instead, I picked up our lists and shuffled through them as I rocked without my blanket, feeling nervous but also sort of happy that I had shared my blanket and the picture of Uncle Jesse with Springer. Then, on the papers, I studied the names of the kids in senior high, then realized Springer had added some names from junior high, too—Ryker and Chris and Trisha.

"Why did you put Jerkface and the cockroaches on our list?" I asked. "They're junior high like us. People would ask questions if they were in Dad's hall—especially if they were in his room."

"Maybe," Springer said. "But they're bullies, and bullies always do sneaky bad stuff."

I thought about that for a few seconds. "Mom said Jerkface is a bully because his father never thinks he does anything wrong and pushes him to be some big sports star. She said Chris's dad has issues, and Trisha's along for the ride since they all live next to each other."

"Do you think they know they're bullies?" Springer asked.

"Maybe. Probably." I shrugged. "They used to get in trouble a lot more than they do now. Chris has gotten detention a lot this year."

"I don't think I could ever be a bully," Springer said.

Another few seconds went by. I tried to imagine what it would be like, to be mean and ugly to people all the time. If I acted like that, my parents would be unhappy. I would be unhappy. My dog probably wouldn't even like me, and Uncle Jesse would probably show up as a ghost and haunt me. I glanced down at Sam-Sam, who was busy shredding the rest of the fabric off his exploded squeaky toy.

"It would suck to be a bully," I said.

Springer nodded. "Yeah."

"I'll leave them on the list. But this is, like, seventy people."

"Seventy-three." Springer nodded his head as he rocked. "There are a lot more people in senior high, but those are the ones who looked the sneakiest."

I stared at the gigantic scrabble-gabble of names, which seemed to swim back and forth, running together and pulling apart. So many letters. The first name had twelve letters all together. The next name had twenty-two letters. I could count for an hour. There were probably thousands of letters on this list. I had to close my eyes, or I'd just keep counting. Even after I closed them, my head still counted anyway. So many people. And yet—

"Well, there's the janitors and teachers," I muttered. "And the office staff. Like Mr. Chiba at the front desk, and Principal Jorgensen. I mean, they could come and go from Dad's hall, and Ms. Jorgensen called the police about the money, so really, she's the one who had Dad arrested."

"Then she needs to be on the list," Springer agreed. "Maybe they all do."

"More letters," I said as I opened my eyes. Then I wrote down Principal Jorgensen's name, right underneath Springer's neatly printed letters. I printed neatly, too. Sort of like echoing, only not out loud. Right as I finished, Sam jumped into my lap, spilling papers in every direction. I glared at him for exactly three seconds, then petted his soft fur. He felt warm on my lap, not very heavy, but blankety enough to make me relax. "We'll have to go early and stay late to figure all this out. At least on some days. I'll have to explain it to Aunt Gus, convince her somehow. Do you have to convince anybody?"

"Mom," Springer said. "That's easy, though. I'll tell her I'm working on a project with you."

"Project. Good idea."

"Thanks. If we're really late, we can walk home or something, right?"

"I—" I started, but stopped. Dad and Aunt Gus had never let me walk to school or walk home from school before, so that was maybe a no.

Huh.

Why hadn't they ever let me walk to school, or walk home from school? I mean, seriously, they might flip out if I even asked—but why? They shouldn't flip out. I was old enough. And it wasn't like we lived in some big, dangerous place. There were some busy roads, but I knew to look both ways and all that stuff.

Sam nuzzled under my chin, and I ruffled his long fur.

"I'll stay late after classes to help you whenever you want," Springer said. "It's pretty easy to walk to your house from mine if I use the trail by the clubhouse."

I moved my cheek away from Sam's licking and smiled at Springer. Well, at the side of his face, because he was still rocking with his eyes closed, snuggled under my yellow blanket.

My muscles felt jealous, so I rocked with Sam-Sam. "I'm not sure what to look for when we get to Dad's desk."

"I don't know what to look for, either."

I snuggled Sam into my chest. "If I were a real detective, I'd ask if AJS had security tapes, and if they did, I'd demand to see them so I could figure out who went near Dad's classroom."

"Security tapes would be great, but they won't show them to us, even if they exist, and you said your mom thinks they don't have any." Springer stopped rocking. He opened his eyes but looked out my window instead of looking at me. "What about your dad's lawyer? Would he tell us anything?"

"Probably not, but that was a good idea." I glanced at Springer's face. He looked peaceful as he ran his hands over my blanket.

His eyes drifted to mine, stayed a few seconds, then darted back to the window. "Who does your dad know best at school, grown-up–wise?"

I leaned back so Sam could stretch out across my lap. "He knows lots of people."

"Yeah, but which ones would come in his room a lot? You know, so nobody would notice much?"

"Oooh, yeah, that's a good question." Sam's fur tickled my fingers as I buried my hands in it. "But I have no clue."

Springer leaned over and picked up one of the papers, and pulled a pen from his pocket. "Any students your dad talks about a lot?"

I shrugged. "That changes from year to year. I guess I don't pay attention."

"So really, the desk is the only starting place we've got, unless you want to question Ms. Jorgensen or Ryker and his friends."

I started to pass on that but stopped.

"What?" Springer asked. "You had a thought. I could almost hear your brain working from here."

"It's weird, but—" I stopped, trying to organize my suddenly itching brain and make it think in straight lines.

Springer didn't say anything, which helped a lot.

I let out a breath. "They all send me mean stuff online, Ryker and the cockroaches. I deleted lots of accounts so they'd leave me alone, so they started sending text messages."

"That's evidence, right?" Springer's voice sounded sad. Or maybe mad. I couldn't tell. "You could turn them in."

"I've showed their messages to people before, but they don't curse or threaten me," I explained. "They just poke and tease. Dad says it's kid stuff. Mean kid stuff, but nothing illegal. I've blocked them before, then they get spoof programs that go around the blocks, you know, with fake numbers and stuff. So now I just ignore them. That works the best. But this morning—"

I stopped again.

Springer quit rocking. He turned his face toward me, but I couldn't really look at him as he said, "They probably really needled you about your dad, didn't they?"

"Yeah. Ryker and Chris did," I said. "But Trisha didn't send me a message. And she's the meanest one of them online. So that's what's weird."

When I glanced at Springer, he was chewing at his lip. "Maybe she's grounded from her phone?"

"Maybe, but I don't think her parents ever ground her from anything, like Ryker's parents don't ground him for being a jerkface to the universe."

"Is Trisha being nice?"

That made me laugh. "She doesn't have much nice in her, after growing up living in between Ryker and Chris. So no. I don't think she's being nice. More . . . weird, like I said. Maybe we do need to question them. Well, not question them, because then they would bust us in the face— but, you know, observe them. Listen and see if they say something incriminating. Collect evidence and stuff, and see if we can get a clue about whether or not they know something. From a distance."

Springer made a grunty noise like Charlie. I figured that meant he agreed.

For a quick few seconds, I imagined us detecting all over the place, and maybe stealth-observing Ryker and the cockroaches, and then my dog helping me confront our final suspects, both of us standing there serious, like Mom and Shotgun. "Sooner or later we'll have to talk to a lot of people. And we'll have to make them talk. *Explain.* That's what Mom always says to me when she wants more information."

"Okaaay," Springer said. "Is your mom as scary as she sounds?"

"Yes," I said. And then, "No. She's—she's just Mom."

"I guess all soldiers can be scary when they need to be," Springer said.

"Is your dad as mean as he sounds?" I asked, then thought it didn't sound tactful, and added, "I mean, not letting you have a rocker and stuff, and making you try out for sports you don't like."

"He's not mean," Springer said. "Stern, I guess. And really stressed a lot lately. He wants me to be a good man. And be good at stuff so I'll be able to make a living. He's . . . just Dad."

"So I don't need to call him Mr. Jerkface?"

"Nah," Springer said. "Not right now, at least. I'll let you know if that changes. And I think we might be good at this detective stuff. My mom says I notice things other people don't, that I'm observant."

"My mom says I notice freaky things nobody else cares about, and that I'm weird. In a good way, though."

Springer grinned. "We could call ourselves the Observant but Weird in a Good Way Detective Agency. OBWIG for short? That would work if we have to speak code. Detectives need codes and secrets, right?"

We looked at each other, then cracked up laughing.

"OBWIG," I said. Then I giggled all over again.

Springer pulled off the weighted blanket, handed it to

me, and said, "Here. This was great, but it's probably your turn now."

"Thanks," I said.

And for a while, OBWIG rocked.

I had never had anybody to have codes and secrets with before, or anybody to rock with, either, other than my dog. It really was kind of neat, doing fun things with a person, too.

9

Monday, Right After
the Train Came

My ears buzzed.

I couldn't see anything but white swirly dust and some smoke.

The train-not-train—so loud.

I think I yelled.

Crumbly plaster fell into my mouth. I spat it out and then I got up, and it was raining on my head because I was outside but I wasn't supposed to be outside. I was at school. Not outside. I was still standing in the hallway. Only some of it was gone. And the roof was gone. And a wall.

"Class is outside now," I said, but I couldn't hear myself, because my ears—and that not-train, still close. Everything seemed so dark. And weirdly green, like the air had turned the color of spring grass.

Something hit my leg. An arm. I stared at it. Its fingers wiggled, then the plaster carpet underneath the arm moved, and Springer sat up, all covered in white dust. He looked like a zombie from a scary movie. He leaned forward, and I thought he was coughing, but he threw up. Then he looked at me.

My ears kept right on ringing. I wanted to laugh and then cry because Springer was okay, but my feelings were mushed flat like the gym. Run over by a train. Yes. That was it.

I looked around. Lots of the plaster was moving. And then people seemed to be everywhere. Teachers. Students. Some covered in plaster. Some covered in cuts. There was blood. Too many bright things. Too many moving things. Too many hands and arms and legs attached to crying people. I couldn't count them all. I couldn't keep looking at them.

It kept raining. The rain seemed cold. I wiped it off my face.

Springer got up and stood beside me. His cheeks had little cuts on them and his eyes were wide like moons. My eyes felt moony, too, and my cheeks stung like they were cut. I leaned toward him to be sure he was real and not just me dreaming that Springer was fine and that I was fine and that we got run over by a train and lived.

Springer's lips moved. I couldn't hear what he said, but I knew the words.

Okay to hug?

I nodded, and he hugged me with one arm. It sort of hurt, like I was made out of bruises.

Coach got up next, and Jerkface, and other people, too. I squinted through the dust and the gray and the rain.

"Toothpicks," Springer said, and the word drifted into my brain along with all the buzzing and buzzing and buzzing and I knew what he meant.

Looking out at Avery, Kentucky, from the hallway of our busted school, everything looked like toothpicks, pushed on top of each other. Big giant toothpicks made of tree pieces and building pieces and car pieces and dirt pieces and other stuff I couldn't even name. That's what was left of the town. A big black cloud swirled and swirled, from clouds to the ground, and it was still moving.

Dad . . .

But Dad was probably okay, because the not-train hadn't come from the direction of the senior high, and it was moving away from us, away from the place where Aunt Gus got her nails done, too.

It was headed more toward—

I froze, staring at the way the busted stuff made heaps on either side of a weird, twisty path of wet dirt. Springer got hold of my hand, and he looked where I did, at the new sort of road made by the train. The tornado.

The tornado was headed more toward—it was headed—

"Straight toward your house," Springer said.

"Jesse?" Dad's voice called from somewhere behind me, but I didn't answer.

I let go of Springer, already moving, stumbling and falling over moving plaster and moving people, because my house, I didn't care, I really didn't, not about the house, let it all be gone, all of it, every brick, every fork and spoon and curtain, just not—

Tears streamed out of my eyes and washed away in the rain as some teacher tried to grab me and hollered, "Stop! You can't go running out there!"

"Jesse!" Dad again.

I pushed the teacher trying to snatch hold of my wrist, and then I was running before anybody could grab at me again, before Dad could get to me, and Springer was running beside me because he knew why, he knew, he knew, and I knew, and I cried, and I said it over and over and over and over.

"Sam-Sam! I have to get to Sam!"

10

Wednesday, Five Days Earlier, Early Morning

Your face looks better," I told Springer.

"Thanks." He tapped three fingers against the edge of the now brownish-green bruise. "I looked up the real name for the bruise. Periorbital hematoma. That's cool-sounding, right?"

"Well, yeah." I fiddled with the grapes in my hands. "Especially compared to *black eye.*"

Morning sunlight worked its way into the September chill as Springer and I walked down Oak Lane, heading away from my house. I shifted the straps of my school-color green backpack. We hadn't made it two blocks yet, and my shoulders already burned under the weight of my books, OBWIG's investigative papers, an extra sweater, a throw blanket, several pairs of socks, snacks, and four bottles of water. It was only a mile or two to AJS, but since I had never walked to school before, and Springer was with me, I wanted to be prepared in case we needed anything.

Springer didn't seem as worried. He had on a blue

jacket, and his backpack was a Darth Vader head. It didn't look too full. When we got to the corner of Oak and Cedar, we stopped in front of a redbrick house that had fourteen flamingos and six gnomes in its sidewalk garden. I pointed ahead to our right. "We take a right on Cedar, left on Maple, then left on Spruce."

"Where the school is," he said as I handed him a big, fat grape. "We should get there by six thirty. That'll give us an hour to investigate before first bell."

Springer stared at his grape while I ate mine, savoring the sweet juice as it ran across my tongue. I loved fruit, any fruit. I ate another, and another, then realized Springer was still staring at his, to the point I had to grab his arm to keep him from veering off the sidewalk and strolling into traffic. Well, into the road. We'd only seen two cars since we left.

"This isn't a Frankenfood, right?" Springer managed to look up and keep himself on the sidewalk. "Mom doesn't want me to eat genetically engineered stuff."

"It's just a grape," I assured him.

"A big grape." He touched it to his lips but pulled it back. Then he bit into it and chewed. When he swallowed, he held out his hand immediately. "Okay. It was great. Can I have another?"

I pulled off a cluster and handed it to him.

After he ate a few more, Springer said, "Dad was glad I was walking today. Said I was showing initiative."

"Okay." I shivered, even though I wasn't that cold. "Whatever that means. My dad and Aunt Gus . . . we have a deal that I won't go more than a mile in any direction, which I guess I'm technically breaking this morning, since school is farther away from home than that."

Springer gave me a quick glance, then went back to staring straight ahead. His voice seemed a little too quiet when he asked, "You didn't tell your dad and your aunt we were walking this morning?"

"I left a note on the kitchen table," I said, doing my best to sound like it was no big deal, only it was starting to feel like a big deal, especially since I'd had to give Sam lots of extra treats when I crated him early, and all of a sudden I missed him a lot and wished he were in my arms, except my backpack was really, seriously too heavy, so it was probably good I wasn't carrying a dog, too. "Dad probably won't see the note until he heads to my room to wake me up. That'll be about half an hour from now. And he'll still have to get dressed before he drives to school. So even if he wants to holler at me and ground me, it'll take him a while."

Springer ate his grapes and didn't say anything.

Powered by the best purple fruit in the world, we walked fast. At least, I thought we were walking fast. I wasn't sure what was normal for speed when people walked to school, since nobody ever let me do it. The air smelled wet, and like grass, too. Sometimes I caught a sniff of something like spice. Cinnamon, maybe, or wintergreen. Was that Springer smell? People had scents, or at least most of them did. I wondered what I smelled like. Was that something I could ask Springer, or would that not be tactful?

Hanging out with other people was complicated.

When we got to a wooden house that had twenty AJS-green shutters on the front and no flamingos anywhere in the yard, I stopped. I figured the house had windows in the back, but I couldn't see them, so I couldn't count those shutters. It bothered me that I didn't have a definite green shutter tally. It had a lot of cars in the driveway, though. Seven. Some were parked on the grass.

"It's weird I never noticed flamingos and gnomes and shutters when we drive," I said.

Springer glanced from me to the house, then looked up at the street sign. "This is Maple. We're supposed to turn left here, right? And yeah, I always see different things when I walk than when I'm in a car."

"Right, left," I said. "Wait." I closed my eyes and took a deep breath. Then I opened my eyes. "You are correct that we're supposed to turn left here, but I have to take my pack off for a second."

I fought to lift the strap off my right shoulder enough to wriggle out of it, and I saw Springer look confused. He leaned over to help, then said, "Jeez. What did you put in here, Jesse? Rocks?"

"Not gnomes." I blew out a breath as Springer slid the

weight off me. "Not flamingos. Not shutters. Springer, do I smell like anything?"

He gave me another confused look as he lowered the pack to the ground, opened it, and stared inside. "A little like cigar smoke, and your dog, but mostly . . . cherries." He poked around in the pack. "Four waters? Those are really heavy."

Cigar-Dog-Cherries.

Well.

As human scents went, that wasn't all bad, right?

"I thought we might need the waters," I said. "I've never walked to school before, and I don't really know why. It's not that far. Why would Dad and Aunt Gus always use the car? I mean, half the reason Aunt Gus lives with us is so I can sleep a little later and then come home when our grade lets out instead of having to stay in after-school care and wait for Dad, since he always works late grading stuff and doing his lesson plans. I could have been walking all this time."

Springer took off his pack and handed it to me. "Here. You wear this one. I'll wear yours." He didn't wait for my answer, but instead worked on the strap length until he could get my pack over his shoulders.

I picked up Darth. Compared to my pack, Darth felt like his black-metal-print head was stuffed with feathers. "Do you think it's because they thought I'd get lost, or all, I don't know, absorbed in counting flamingos and gnomes and shutters?"

Springer centered my heavy pack on his back. "Maybe

they're worried you'll get mugged or hollered at or something. My mom says neighborhoods aren't what they used to be, even in little towns like this one. She says people can be mean, and that money problems push even good folks to make bad decisions."

"Money problems." I had heard people talking about stuff like that. We weren't rich like people on television, but we didn't really have money problems. At least, I didn't think we did.

"Yeah." Springer looked at the house with all the cars, then pointed. "Like, maybe those people have a lot of people living with them so they can pay rent—and that helps them pay for the house. If they can't pay for the house, a bank could take it away."

"I didn't know banks took houses."

"Before we came here, a bank took ours," Springer said. His cheeks colored up a little. "It made Mom upset, and Dad got really mad they wouldn't wait for him to make money again after the bottom fell out of the construction market where we lived."

"The bottom fell out," I echoed. "What does that mean, exactly?"

"It means Dad didn't get to design and build houses anymore, because nobody could pay for them, so we lost our own house."

I wasn't great with feelings, but I heard all the sad in Springer's voice. "Did you like that house?"

He shrugged. "It was the only place I had ever lived. For a while I was scared we wouldn't get another home. But then Dad said the construction market was good here, and we moved. Our new house isn't as big as the one we had to leave, but I like it okay."

"I'm sorry you had to move," I told him. "But also glad, since I got to meet you."

"Same," Springer said. Then he jerked his thumb toward the house with all the cars. "So if I weren't with you, would you have gotten absorbed in counting all that stuff?"

I shouldered Darth. "Probably I'd definitely go around behind all the cars and count the shutters, so I'd get the real number of shutters, and not just the front half number."

As if to show me why I liked him better than most people I'd ever met, Springer didn't ask why having the real number mattered, and make me have to explain when I really didn't understand it myself. Instead, he said, "Well, it's probably good your dad and your aunt didn't let you walk alone, because you could have gotten arrested and charged with trespassing for going into people's backyards without asking. And if you were in kid jail, you wouldn't be able to help your dad this morning."

"Trespassing," I said. "I should have thought about that."

We started walking again, and I asked, "Why didn't I think about getting in trouble if I went into somebody else's yard? Why don't I remember—you know, normal stuff like normal people?"

"Maybe because it's not important to you right then," Springer said. "That's why I don't remember normal stuff sometimes. When we get to AJS, can I have the Jelly Fruit Bites? Grape is my favorite."

"Sure." I squinted ahead, because I knew we didn't stay on Maple for very long. Our last turn was coming up. "According to the map I looked at, the Spruce stretch is the longest."

"Is that house, like, yellow?" Springer muttered, nodding his head forward.

I looked toward the next corner, and—

Wow.

"Yeah. Really bright. It doesn't look that bright from car windows." Already, I was noticing no flamingos, no gnomes, no green shutters, but instead there were little bushes along the front sidewalk, twelve on each side, so twenty-four all together. By the time we turned left on Spruce, I had counted every little bush in the yard, coming up with thirty-seven. If it were my yard, I'd plant one more to get thirty-eight, but it wasn't my yard, and I never, ever needed to go in it.

Even though Springer and I made good time on our walk, AJS already seemed busy. When we got close to the drive-around, cars lined up and cycled through, spilling out kids who headed into the junior high side of the complex for before-school care and breakfast. Teachers wandered in different directions, wearing yellow traffic caution sashes and carrying stop signs, motioning cars and trucks and vans into different lanes.

Without talking about it, Springer and I kept our heads down and skirted the traffic area, hoping nobody would notice us or talk to us as we edged toward the senior high entrance. The outside lights were still on at the senior high building, but people moved around on the other side of the glass panels that bordered the metal doors, and a few groups had already gathered near the big school sign, talking and gesturing.

I glanced around the big sloping front lawn, at the cars and kids and parents and teachers behind us. Springer slowed, studying the senior high door, then the groups near the entrance. My breath caught in my throat as I realized that the person who stole the library money and let my father take the blame might be in the senior high building already, maybe even standing close to us.

"Oh," Springer muttered. "Not good."

My heart skipped, then sped up. "What?"

When I looked at him, I could tell he was trying not to glance in the direction of what had bothered him. "Coach Sedon's already here," he said. "He's talking to Ms. Jorgensen over there, by the sign."

I kept my face turned toward the senior high door, but I could see them from the corner of my eye. Until it got cold, Principal Jorgensen always wore blue slacks, a short-sleeved white blouse, and a blue scarf. After it got cold, the sleeves got longer and she added a suit jacket. She was tall, but not as tall as Coach Sedon, who used to play basketball in college just like Jerkface's mom. Coach, who had short brown hair just like his son, was almost taller than the sign he was leaning against. He had on AJS-green shorts that reached to his knees, and his long basketball shirt was green, too. A whistle hung around his neck, and he pulled at it and looked annoyed as Ms. Jorgensen, who seemed red in the face, pointed in the general direction of my neighborhood and fussed at him about something.

"Come on," I whispered to Springer. "Let's just get inside."

"But—" Springer started.

I ignored him and walked away, squeezing the black straps of the Darth Vader pack until I heard him shuffling along behind me.

The senior high entrance wasn't locked, so we slipped in without attracting any attention. Dad's hall was to the right of the big center room called the study hub, and it was the middle corridor of three options. About fifteen kids were in the study hub, which was sort of the senior high version of before-care, with one teacher at a desk far away.

Looking around for possible surveillance cameras, I led Springer across the edge of the study hub to the middle hallway. I didn't see any cameras, but as soon as we got about halfway down the long hall, I did see a big problem, and I stopped.

Springer came up beside me. "What? You know where your dad's class is, right?"

"Yeah," I said, gesturing at the long row of closed rooms. "But the doors are still shut. They'll be locked. We'll have to go to the office and see if we can talk Mr. Chiba into letting us in."

"Listen," Springer said. "What I was going to say outside about Coach Sedon—"

"Oh, look," came an all-too-familiar voice from behind us. "It's Messy Jesse and the beached whale from Alabama."

Springer clamped his mouth shut. His bruised eye twitched.

So did my whole body.

Why was Jerkface at school so early?

"What I was going to say outside," Springer said very quietly, "is if Coach Sedon's here, probably Chris is here, too. And maybe the rest of them."

I wanted to groan, because if one cockroach was in the hall, they all were.

And when I turned around—yep. Ryker, Chris, and Trisha blocked the open end of the corridor. They had on jeans and pressed button-up shirts, blue for Ryker, yellow for Chris, and green for Trisha. No backpacks. They looked sharp and tall and . . . older. If the senior high side didn't have to wear their khaki uniforms, these three would fit right in with the ninth graders, at least.

I held on tight to the Darth Vader straps on my shoulders and glanced at the green pack Springer carried for me. We weren't very stylish. I usually didn't care, but for some reason the packs and my rumply jeans and my black T-shirt with Happy Buddha on it made me feel soooo . . . junior high.

Springer still hadn't turned around. He kept facing the far end of the corridor, probably staring at the doors to the outside—which would be locked this time of day, just like the classroom doors.

"What are you two losers doing on the senior high side?" Trisha asked, her voice flat and dangerous-sounding. "Little kids might get hurt in these hallways."

"Where's your dad, Messy?" Chris asked, almost at the same time.

"At home," I muttered before Springer elbowed me and I realized I should have lied.

"Not in jail?" Jerkface looked fake-sympathetic. "Because by now, everybody in Avery knows he got arrested."

Springer slowly turned around, easing closer to me as he did.

"Wow, big guy, that's a heck of a shiner," Chris said. "Did you trip over something? You know, like maybe a plastic . . . cup?" He snickered, and Jerkface and Trisha laughed even louder.

Then Jerkface walked toward us.

I backed up.

"What, not so brave without steps to shove me down?" Jerkface spread his arms wide. "Come on, Messy. Give me your best shot."

"I don't get you," I said as I reached over and unzipped the green pack on Springer's back and pulled out two bottles of water. "Why do you have to be so horrible all the time?"

"Why do you have to be weird all the time?" Jerkface shot back.

"We're not horrible," Trish said. "That would be you two stains on humanity."

I handed a water bottle to Springer, then got another for myself. He looked at his bottle, then looked at me, obviously confused and scared. The bruise on his face seemed twice as big and twice as dark, now that he was likely to get a matching one, and it would be all my fault.

"Ooooh," Chris said, his face twisted in a sneer as he came closer, too, with Trisha right behind him. "They're gonna give us a shower. I'm so scared."

"Hate to break it to you," Trisha said, "but I can fix my hair and makeup if you get me wet."

They stopped. Laughed. Took another step toward us. Stopped again. Each time we backed up, they laughed more. They were moving together now, and I knew they liked seeing us scared.

"Are you sure about this no-hitting thing?" I asked Springer.

The question made the cockroaches hesitate, but Springer just kept staring at his water bottle. I thought I saw a tear leak out of his hurt eye. My pulse thumped in both my ears, and my mouth went dry. I forced myself to look at the cockroaches, straight in the face. I tried to focus on one of them, but they blurred together, probably because I had tears, too.

"Leave us alone," I said, my voice whispery and small. "We just came here to look at my dad's classroom. His desk. We need to see the desk."

Jerkface and Chris and Trisha laughed some more. I couldn't decide which one I hated worse.

"We need to see the desk," Ryker echoed me in a high, silly voice. Not a nice echo. Not a nice Ryker.

"Wait," Chris said. "I get it. I bet they're playing detective. Isn't that cute?"

Trisha's eyes narrowed, and her mean grin flattened. "Seriously? Is that what you're up to, Messy?"

Jerkface shook his head. "That's twice as sad as usual."

I gripped my water bottle tighter, the plastic making crinkly sounds as I dented it. I tried to think about Mom and Shotgun, and how they were soldiers, and got scared but fought anyway, because other soldiers and the whole country counted on them to do their jobs. Well, Dad was counting on me, even if he didn't know it. And Sam-Sam would be sad if I got my face broken and couldn't play with him for weeks. And Springer—they'd hurt him again, and Springer was too nice to get hurt, and nobody should have to deal with Jerkface and cockroaches and a mean dad who yelled at him for not fighting back.

When Ryker took his next step, I reared back and threw my water bottle as hard as I could, right at his face. He tried to move, but he didn't dodge fast enough. My bottle smashed him in the cheek.

He spun around, grabbing for his jaw and saying ugly words as he staggered toward the wall. The bottle hit the floor and burst open, spurting water up the leg of his jeans.

"Hey!" Trisha yelled, and I threw my second bottle at her. It bounced off her shoulder, smacked the floor, and drenched her shoes.

As she screeched hatred at me, Springer threw his bottle so high and hard that if it actually bashed Chris, it might knock him out. Chris hollered and hit the deck, but the water bottle sailed way above him, on and on down the hallway, and out into the study hub. It hit the ground with a huge thump, exploding and spraying water everywhere.

Kids shouted.

Ryker was still saying ugly words, and he swung around to face us.

Somewhere off in the distance, I heard grown-up voices. Too far away. The cockroaches were pulling together again, and all three of them had murder in their eyes. Three sets. Six eyeballs. Clenched teeth. I couldn't count the teeth.

I imagined I had on desert fatigues and they were the enemy, coming for me and my dog. My hands shook. My legs shook. But I stepped in front of Springer.

"Jesse," he said, but I wasn't listening.

Instead, I filled up my lungs and screamed like the world was cracking straight down the center, like I'd seen a house-sized spider or a snake big enough to eat people, like I was having the kind of meltdown I hadn't had since I was five or six years old. I imagined the sound coming out of my toes and shooting through the air like daggers, ripping up cockroach ears and melting their brains.

Ryker and Chris and Trisha froze.

Chris covered his ears.

I screamed even louder, and lots of people came running toward us then.

As senior high students and Coach Sedon and Ms. Jorgensen and Mr. Chiba from the office ran into the hallway, the cockroaches finally scuttled back, arranging themselves in front of nearby lockers.

Little by little, I ran out of air. When I finally stopped screaming, the hall rang with quiet. For a second, everybody seemed to be staring at me and holding their breath. Then Trisha helped Chris to his feet and started pointing at me and saying how I hit them with water bottles.

"She was trying to kill us," Trisha wailed to Coach

Sedon, who glanced in our direction with something like a worried expression. "They both were! That big kid almost took Chris's head off with a water bottle!"

"That's enough." Ms. Jorgensen held up both hands. "Settle down. Everyone, please. Jesse, she's—well, just, let's talk about this in the office. Can everyone clear the hall? Clear the hallway, please."

Ryker glared at me. He still had his hand on his jaw. I couldn't see a bruise, but I hoped I'd made one.

Oh, wait. No. That was seriously mean. Did that make me a bully like him? New tears swelled into my eyes, and I said, "Touch coming," and grabbed Springer's hand and sort of dragged him to my father's classroom door.

"Let us in," I told Mr. Chiba, each word hurting my throat after that scream. When he didn't move, I got louder. "Let us in, let us in!"

I saw him get afraid I was about to have another meltdown, a way worse one, and I sort of felt guilty, but then I didn't, and I yelled, "Let us in!" one more time.

Mr. Chiba hurried forward, and he unlocked my father's door, and I took Springer inside, where it was safe, and I closed the door behind us.

11

Wednesday, Five Days Earlier, Morning

I can't believe you screamed like that." Springer stood inside my dad's classroom and rubbed his ears. "I think you popped my brain."

"Hush," I told him. My hands shook. I figured all the grown-ups had gone to take Jerkface and the cockroaches back to the junior high, and to find my dad before I went off like a screaming bomb, like I used to. We probably had five minutes, maybe just four before they came back.

"You sounded like a banshee," Springer went on. "Maybe half the school will be dead by morning, and—"

"Please hush?" I realized I was sort of growling through my teeth. It took me a second to unlock my jaws, and another second to realize that Springer seemed afraid of me. I held up both hands, palms out, fingers still trembling. "We won't have another chance to look at Dad's desk, so we should—you know, do it. Or something."

But Springer didn't answer. He was too busy drifting toward the shelves lining the walls. He stopped in the middle of the classroom, gaping at the literary and movie posters, at the figurines dotting flat surfaces, at all the books—*The Hundred Thousand Kingdoms*, *Harry Potter*, *The Lord of the Rings*, *Akata Witch*, dragons of unknown origin, warriors, old guys with bears who looked like they came from Shakespeare's time—Dad had just about everything a book person could want.

"I—" Springer started. "Wow. This—" and then he just couldn't.

He sat on the floor.

I'd had my own floor-sitting moments in life, so I didn't bug him. I figured he needed to calm down, just like I did. For a few long breaths, I squeezed my fingers into fists and counted to twenty, then back down again. I thought about dancing puppies and wiggling puppies, and Sam-Sam's cute little smile.

Jerkface and the cockroaches made me *so* mad. And they were so mean! And I'd busted Ryker in the face with a bottle of water, and I'd hit Trisha, too.

Did that make *me* mean?

"No," I mumbled out loud. "Self-defense is different. Right? It sort of has to be. I hope it is."

My gaze flicked back to Springer, who had defended himself and me, too, without hitting anybody at all.

Blowing out a breath, I turned to the desk, which was a lot easier to stare at than Springer. It seemed sort of weird that it wasn't wrapped in yellow police tape or something.

Had the police already investigated the crime scene? I was pretty sure they should have, especially since they'd put Dad in awful metal handcuffs, but I didn't know.

As school desks went, Dad's was medium-sized. It was made of dark wood, and people had etched things into the grain, small letters and symbols, sometimes in ink. I couldn't make out most of the carvings as I walked around it, trying to take in the details. On top of the desk, Dad had a cube of Post-it notes, a big planning calendar, a daybook, and a gigantic coffee mug labeled ROCKET FUEL. Class textbooks were lined up across the front, held in place by two bookends shaped like Shakespeare's head. Dad had a pencil holder made to look like an open novel, and beside that, a tape dispenser. The desk had five drawers, two on either side of where the chair went, and one wide, thin one in the middle. None of the drawers had locks. The drawer on the bottom right had a label on it reading LIBRARY FUND DONATIONS.

"Good one, Dad." I sighed. "Just make it easier for the thieves next time, okay? Leave the money on top with a sign reading STEAL ME."

"What?" Springer asked. He was still sitting on the floor.

I ignored him and sat in Dad's rolling chair. My eyes went to the big calendar, to the day the money got stolen. Dad—or somebody—had circled it in red. *Staff Meeting 2:30–4:30* was the only thing scribbled onto the lines.

"Huh," I said out loud, mentally making a note that Dad would have been out of his class the afternoon when the money was taken. In fact, all the senior high teachers would have been in that meeting, right? "Unless some of them missed it . . ."

I needed something to take notes on, since Dad had taken my phone. Dad's Post-its were good enough, so I pulled a blue square of paper off the top of the cube. Then I picked up a black pen with a raven on top and wrote, *Check to see if any teachers missed the staff meeting.*

After I put down the pen, I decided to open the drawers. The top left drawer had lesson planners and boxes of pencils, and a small stack of blank white paper. Bottom left had stacks of opened mail, some bags of little candy bars, and three board games—It Was a Dark & Stormy Night, Bookopoly, and Trivial Pursuit, Book Lover's Edition. The thin middle drawer had pens, pencils, paper clips, scissors, change, and a funky broken ruler with a feather on it labeled HALL PASS. In the top right drawer, I found peanut butter, crackers, and a partially eaten sleeve of Oreos.

The bottom right-hand drawer had nothing in it but a ledger and an empty lidless box. I started to reach for the ledger, then stopped. "Springer, do you think the police took fingerprints from this drawer already?"

"Nah," he said from behind me, spooking me so badly I almost fell out of Dad's chair.

"Sorry I scared you," he said. "I don't think fingerprints

would help on that drawer. There would be too many, you know? And the police couldn't make everybody in the school give them fingerprints to try to match."

"They could if it was a murder," I said. "They'd fingerprint everybody who was even near the school that day."

"Maybe, but this wasn't a murder. It was a theft. They won't take it as seriously."

I pulled the ledger out from beneath the empty box. "It's really serious to me. To my family. I wish they would do a real investigation. Um, whatever that would be."

"OBWIG is investigating," Springer said. "That'll have to be enough."

"OBWIG," I said.

He smiled. "OBWIG forever."

As I thumbed through Dad's ledger, Springer pulled out his phone and snapped pictures of the desk from different angles.

"At first it looks like Dad or Ms. Jorgensen made deposits every week," I said, scanning through the ledger pages, "but this last year, it's more like every month." I ran my finger down the last page of the record, noting BAKE SALE and a total, and WRAPPING PAPER AUCTION and another total, then DONATION a bunch of times, with different initials by each one. The donation lines were small numbers, just a dollar, or a few dollars, like maybe people gave Dad their spare change.

So many numbers. I could spend hours adding them.

I'd need to rewrite them in neater columns. But the thought of spending hours with the ledger made me dizzy, in a happy sort of way.

I wasn't sure how long I'd been sitting there comparing the size of 5s and 4s and 6s Dad had written when Springer put his finger on the ledger and carefully slid it away from me.

I blinked.

He smiled at me.

"You were counting out loud," he said. Not mean or anything.

I smiled back at him. More an echo of his expression than a real smile, but that was okay. He didn't mind. When he was sure I wouldn't grab all the numbers back from him, he photographed the page I had been looking at, then the few pages before it.

"So," Springer said as his phone went *click-click-click*, "we know the theft had to happen during regular school hours, or your dad's door would have been locked."

All the numbers that had been swirling through my mind went poof, like popped balloons. "Yeah. You're right. And we know it would have been pretty easy to swipe the cash, since Dad *labeled the drawer where the money was.* Sheesh. Oh, and Dad said it happened in the afternoon, so he would have been in this staff meeting." I pointed to the calendar, then the blue Post-it. "I made a note for us to check that all the other senior high teachers went, because if they were at the meeting, we can take them off our list."

"Good thinking!" Springer snapped a picture of the Post-it. "Too bad the police won't take your father off the list if he was at the meeting."

"They think he did it." I shrugged. "The police would just say the money could have gone missing anytime."

"Yeah," Springer said, studying the page through his phone camera. "Guess they wouldn't take his word for the last time he saw it in the drawer, like we're doing."

"I wonder if he writes down the little donations right when people give them," I said, my eyes going back to the ledger. "Because if he does, these last few people would have seen how much money was in the drawer."

Springer moved the phone aside and leaned toward the ledger. "KA, JS, MK, NN." He raised the phone. "I've got the snapshot, so we can use a yearbook to figure out who these people are, if there aren't too many with those initials."

I wrote down *Match initials to students in the yearbook* on my Post-it, just so we had backup in case Springer got grounded from his phone, too. Too bad we hadn't seen RM, TP, or CS. That would have made life easier for basically everyone in the universe.

"Can I see your phone?" I asked Springer.

"Sure." He handed it to me.

I got out of my chair and stood next to the donation drawer. I raised the phone and snapped a picture of the door from the angle the thief probably would have taken to get into the drawer, after they snuck into the classroom. "If the door was open," I told Springer, "I'd be able to see into the hall from here, and people in the hall could see me— but not many. I wonder if anybody in the other classes could see me right where I'm standing?"

"Let's find out." Springer went to the classroom door and pulled it open.

I raised the phone to take a snap of the view, but as the door swung wide, a crowd of people surged inside.

Click.

Aunt Gus's great big eyes and open mouth.

Click.

Ms. Jorgensen, pulling at the ends of her scarf.

Click.

Mr. Chiba, looking worried.

Click.

My father, red-faced, arms folded, all of a sudden standing *really* close to me.

The phone's battery died, which was probably a good thing. A few more seconds of Dad's laser glare might have cracked its screen.

We got marched straight out of the senior high back to the building where we belonged. Ms. Jorgensen had an office in both places, and Mr. Chiba had a desk, too. For now, at least, we had the junior high office to ourselves. Sort of. It had big glass windows with words like STRENGTH and HON-ESTY and EFFORT stenciled on the glass in white paint that looked like silver frost. I couldn't help thinking as I sat next to Springer under KINDNESS that the words didn't hide very much. As they walked by on their way to class, every kid in our grade could stare at us sitting in the chairs in front of the main desk, and most of them did.

Or maybe they were staring at my father, who was pacing. Or at Ms. Jorgensen, who was sort of following Dad. Or at Aunt Gus, who was sitting on my other side wearing a cherry-red zip-up bathrobe and matching red house shoes. Her hair was tied back with a red scrunchie, and she didn't have on makeup, and I couldn't remember ever seeing Aunt Gus with no lipstick, unless she had just gotten out of bed—never mind being out in public in her pajamas. Poor Mr. Chiba was definitely staring at Aunt Gus while he sat at the desk trying to call Springer's parents.

Or maybe, just maybe, he was staring at me.

"Jesse, of all the irresponsible, impulsive . . ." Dad ran his fingers through his hair as he marched up and down in front of where we sat. He had on last night's jeans and a blue T-shirt, not his khaki senior high stuff. Before he ever finished his sentence to me, he started hollering at Ms. Jorgensen. "And you—my child is being bullied. Her friend Springer here, he's being bullied, too. Look at his eye. What are you doing about it?"

Ms. Jorgensen stopped walking and leaned against the main desk with arms folded. She spared a glare for me and Springer, too, before she nodded to my father. "It's a problem. But that eye didn't get punched at school, from what I've been told."

"So?" Dad and Aunt Gus and I swear Mr. Chiba, too, said at the same time.

"I can't address what doesn't happen here," Ms. Jorgensen said. "But honestly, Jesse and Springer came out on the better end of the deal in this morning's scuffle."

"This morning's *scuffle*," Aunt Gus grumbled.

"It wasn't just a scuffle." Dad's voice got louder. "That was full-blown bullying. Those three have been at it for years, and they need some consequences."

"As do these two." Ms. Jorgensen nodded toward Springer and me. Her gaze came to rest on Springer's black eye, which still had a little purple in it, and her sure-of-herself principal smirk turned down at the edges.

Springer's head drooped, and that was more than I could stand even if I got grounded forever. "He didn't do anything," I said as loud as I could manage given my sore throat. Ignoring Aunt Gus's hand on my knee, I stood. "I hit Jerkface and the cockroaches with the water bottles. Springer threw his over everybody's heads to get us some help."

"The boy came to school early with you just to do— whatever it was the two of you were up to," Ms. Jorgensen countered. "Neither of you should have been on the senior high side."

My mouth dropped open. "You're kidding, right? We had to investigate. Besides, Jerkface and the cockroaches came to school early, too, and they were at the senior high."

"They had to ride in with family," Ms. Jorgensen said. "They have permission, mornings and some afternoons. And investigate? What are you talking about?"

I started forward, but Aunt Gus grabbed the hem of my shirt and yanked me back into my chair. I thought about getting up again, breathed through it, and said, "My dad didn't take that money from the library fund. Somebody has to clear him. Yeah. Clear him. That's what police detectives on television say."

Ms. Jorgensen's eyes narrowed, then went wide. A lot of the color faded out of her face, and she straightened herself, walking away from the main desk as Mr. Chiba plugged one ear with his finger, pressed the phone against the other side of his head, and said, "Hello?"

My eyes darted to Mr. Chiba and the phone as Springer covered his eyes with his hands. My stomach cramped as I wondered what kind of trouble I had gotten him into. No doubt his cover story to his mom didn't include launching water bottle missiles in the senior high.

Don't start yelling, I reminded myself. *Yelling never helped anything. One, two, three, four—*

"I know your dad didn't take the library fund money, Jesse," Ms. Jorgensen said.

That snatched my attention straight back to her. "I—you—what?"

"Your father is an honest man." Ms. Jorgensen nodded at Dad, who finally stopped pacing. "That's why I didn't suspend him longer than a day. But policy is policy. He had charge of the library fund, and a substantial sum is missing. I had no choice but to report it, and law enforcement made their own choices after that."

"Wait." I shook my head to clear my thoughts. "So you didn't press charges against Dad? The school didn't?"

"Of course not." Ms. Jorgensen looked genuinely surprised. "I know it seems bad right now, but this is just—" But I couldn't let her finish.

"It's not *just nothing*—or whatever you were going to say. Police put my dad in handcuffs. I had to watch them take him away to jail! You knew that, right?"

"I did, yes." Ms. Jorgensen's voice dropped, and her expression shifted to something a lot like sadness, or maybe . . . guilt? To Dad, she said, "I'm sorry, Derrick. You know this will get cleared up really soon."

"I hope so," Dad said. "My kid needs me."

The look on Ms. Jorgensen's face got even weirder, and I wondered if Springer saw it, too, but Springer still had his head down.

The room got very quiet as Mr. Chiba said, "No, no,

Springer's not suspended. No, not injured, either. He's a smart young man, and he did a very good job getting staff's attention, and—oh. I see." He glanced at Springer, then at me. "A project. Yes, I understand he's new to the area and the school. Of course, Ms. Regal. I'll explain the boundaries to him again. If you don't want to come get him, he'll be home at the regular time."

Springer's chin lifted off his chest a few inches. His eyes seemed glazed, but I caught a hint that he was coming back to himself as he—as both of us—realized that Mr. Chiba had been talking to his mom, not his dad. Even better, he hadn't told Springer's folks there was no project we were working on together before school. Springer wasn't suspended. Mr. Chiba had complimented him, even. Maybe he wouldn't get in trouble so bad he wouldn't be leaving his house until next November.

My gaze moved from Springer to Ms. Jorgensen. "Am I suspended?" I asked her. "Because suspending people for defending themselves would suck a lot."

"Jesse," Aunt Gus warned.

But before anybody could answer, Dad stared down Ms. Jorgensen and asked, "Can we talk briefly in your office? Alone?"

Ms. Jorgensen's weird expression got really, *really* strange. She sort of looked like her face got pinched and she couldn't relax it again. Before I could ask her what was wrong, she gestured toward the little corridor behind the main desk, and she and Dad headed into the principal's office.

"You think she ate something bad for breakfast?" Springer asked me in a whispery-but-really-too-loud voice.

"You saw the pinch-face?"

Springer's right eyebrow lifted. Aunt Gus put a hand over her mouth and coughed, and Mr. Chiba cleared his throat a few times.

"Was his mom mad?" I asked Mr. Chiba. "Because really, Springer didn't do anything."

Mr. Chiba seemed to be trying to look all stern and proper, but his hand slipped up to scratch a spot behind his ear, and the wrinkles around his eyes crinkled more. "I think she was fine. Just worried about her boy."

A coolness filled my chest, something like relief. I sat back in my chair, mushing the fingers Aunt Gus had wound into the back of my shirt. Ignoring her grunt as she pulled her hand away from me, I turned to Springer. "I'm glad you're not in trouble. I was worried."

He patted his chest. "Me too. Now you need to be out of trouble, and everything will be fine."

"Not gonna happen," Aunt Gus offered, massaging her knuckles.

Springer frowned. "She packed a backpack full of food and stuff so we'd be okay walking. She had maps. She even kept me from stepping out in traffic when I got distracted. I think she did a good job—and . . . and we figured out a lot of things."

"You kept him out of traffic?" Aunt Gus asked me, sounding impressed.

A few seconds later, Mr. Chiba said, "What things?"

"Sorry," Springer told her, very seriously. "You're not part of OBWIG, so we can't tell you."

Mr. Chiba looked at Aunt Gus.

"It's not you," Aunt Gus reassured him. "I have no idea what OBWIG means."

"Do you keep records of who goes to the staff meetings and who doesn't?" I asked Mr. Chiba.

"Yes," he said, before he noticed Aunt Gus giving him a frantic cut motion and shaking her head no so hard her brains probably rattled.

The office door banged open behind her, and we all jumped.

Dad strode out, looking half-ticked, half . . . I don't know. Rumpled. Maybe sleepy. He pointed at me.

"Come on," he said. "We're going home."

"She's suspended?" Aunt Gus stood so fast I was afraid she'd go storming to the principal's office.

"Touch coming," I warned, and grabbed her robe just like she had grabbed my shirt.

"No," Dad said. "Just a voluntary cooling-off day. Excused."

His fierce expression turned on Springer, who had also gotten to his feet. "You—er." Dad wiped his hand over his face and managed to look nicer when he finished. "You okay, son?"

Springer's ears turned red, but he nodded.

"Okay, then." Dad clapped Springer on the shoulder.

Springer staggered sideways into Aunt Gus, but that was okay, because I pulled her robe hard enough to keep her from falling.

Dad looked at his hand, then at Springer. "Sorry."

"It's okay, sir," Springer said. "I don't have good balance."

Dad nodded. "Thank you for getting help when those bullies went after Jesse."

"I needed help as much as she did," Springer said. "It was really for both of us, but you're welcome."

Dad acted like he wanted to say more, but in the end, he walked to the junior high office door and pulled it open, holding it so Aunt Gus and I could walk through.

"Tell Sam-Sam hello," Springer called as it closed behind us.

When I glanced over my shoulder, I saw him standing with Mr. Chiba. He had his arm around Springer's shoulders.

12

Wednesday, Five Days Earlier, Afternoon

Dad paced past the kitchen table and turned to me again. "What were you thinking?"

I picked at my cheese and crackers and managed not to groan or even roll my eyes. "How many times can he ask me that? 'Cause I'm counting seven. Or maybe eight."

"Don't look at me." Aunt Gus raised both hands, then smacked them back down on her knees. "I'm not in this."

A pot of chili bubbled on the stove behind her, filling the air with garlicky, tomato-y smells. My stomach rumbled. The cheese and crackers compared to that delicious stuff— yuck. Not hitting the spot. I moved my foot until I felt Sam's fur against my ankle, then rubbed my leg against him. He snuggled into me, happy to sleep on the floor as long as we were together.

I had gone with exploring the universe, having time with my new friend, taking time to smell the flowers and look at yellow houses, and asserting my independence. I had used that one several times, in fact. All of that was true, at least a little bit. It just wasn't the whole story.

Dad positioned himself right beside my chair. "I'm going to ask you why you walked to school without permission one more time, Jesse. I expect an answer. A real one. No more of this asserting your independence stuff."

"Fine. Springer and I were investigating who really stole that money, okay?" I tried to look at him, but I couldn't. "We did it to keep you from having to go back to jail."

Dad made a snorty sound, kinda like Charlie the bulldog.

Sam stirred against my ankles, and I rubbed my leg against him.

"And for this, you had to sneak out of the house, not tell us you were walking to school?" He sat in the chair next to mine. "That could have been dangerous, especially for somebody like you."

"Somebody like me," I echoed. I tried again to look at him in the face, but got that itchy sensation and stared at his cheek instead. His very red cheek.

"I didn't mean anything bad by that," Dad said, his words coming out really fast. "But you know sometimes you don't see danger like other people. You can get distracted."

I wanted to echo *distracted* so bad I had to bite my bottom lip to keep from doing it. Instead, my brain just kept repeating *somebody like you* in Dad's voice, adding mean stuff to it in Ryker's voice, then Chris's, then Trisha's.

Somebody like you. Not like your mom.

Somebody like you. Not like your uncle.

Somebody like you. Not like the nice kids. The strong kids. The mean kids. The smart kids. The kids who can grow up and do important things, brave things. The kids who are normal.

Somebody like you.

Somebody "on the spectrum."

My jaw clenched so hard my teeth scraped together.

"Seriously," Dad said. "I didn't mean that in a bad way, honey. You're—you're you. And that's fine with us. I just want to be sure you're safe."

I rubbed the top of my jaw until I could talk, but I still couldn't really look at anything but his cheek. "We don't live in a war zone, Dad. It's safe enough to walk to school. Besides, if I had asked you if I could leave early with Springer, would you have said yes?"

"No!" he said.

I flinched from the noise but kept my eyes fixed on his cheek. Dad sorta needed to shave. It was all I could do not to start counting stubble hairs. "Then to answer the question you asked a minute ago, yes. Yes, I had to sneak out of the house and walk to school without permission."

Dad looked at Aunt Gus.

Her hands came up again. The edges of her painted nails were chipped, as if she'd bitten them. "Not in this, don't even look at me."

"There's a house between here and school," I said. "It has twenty green shutters on the front, but I don't know how many in the back, because if I went behind the house to count them, that would be trespassing. I didn't go around back, so see? I know how to keep myself safe."

Dad had nothing for that one, but Aunt Gus managed a "That's good, honey."

"That house had a lot of cars in the driveway," I went on, finally able to move my eyes to Dad's chin, his other cheek, then his whole face, at least for a few seconds. "Lots and lots of cars, like maybe they're renting out rooms or running a business or something. Do you think they need money? Do you think the bank is going to take the house away from the people who live in it?"

Dad waited before speaking. Ten seconds, then fifteen. He looked like he was trying to see the house in his head and count the shutters himself. Finally he said, "Yeah, I do know that place. And good for you, not trespassing, especially there. All those cars aren't renters, but I do think yes, they're running a business. Well, businesses. Probably not legal ones."

"What do you mean?" My stomach rumbled again. That chili—I really needed to eat some. "Not legal businesses. What kind of businesses aren't legal?"

"The police have to go to that house a lot," Dad said. "Some of the people who live there, they've gotten in trouble for selling drugs and using drugs and fighting and gambling. So that's not a place I want you to spend time around. And that's what I meant before. The world can be dangerous if you're out in it all alone."

"I wasn't alone," I reminded him. "I was with Springer."

Dad didn't try to argue with that. Instead, he asked, "Why were you wondering about a bank taking somebody's house?"

"Banks take people's houses if people can't pay," I told him. "Springer said so." I didn't tell Dad the bank took Springer's house before he moved, because that seemed like it would be telling a secret. "Will the bank ever take our house?"

"No," Dad and Aunt Gus said at the same time.

Then Dad said, "That's not something you have to worry about, and neither is the situation with the library fund. The police will take care of investigating the theft. It's not that serious."

My eyes snapped to his, no itch at all, because I had fire instead, right in my chest and my throat and my mouth. "You. Went. To. Jail. The police put you in mean metal cuffs and took you away from us and you were gone for one thousand, one hundred and seventy minutes. Do you know how many seconds that is?"

Dad blinked.

Sam licked my leg.

Charlie grunted.

Aunt Gus wrote invisible numbers on the table with

her cracked-polish pointer fingernail and said, "Wait a minute, wait a minute, I got this."

But I couldn't wait. "Over seventy thousand! You were gone for seventy thousand, two hundred seconds and it's a big deal, it's a huge deal, and the police aren't doing anything to find who really took the money!"

"Seventy thousand," Aunt Gus sounded frustrated. "I used to be so much quicker at math, but she puts me to shame."

"Seventy—um. Okay." Dad shook his head. "Of course the police are doing things to find the thief, honey."

"Did they take fingerprints?" The fire in my insides seared my eyes to my father's. It was weird, how his darted back and forth and looked all watery in the corners. Mine were watering too. "Did they look at your donation ledger or your schedule book? Did they question anybody other than you?"

"Um," Dad said again. "Well, I—they looked at my room, and the desk, and they took some notes."

I pushed my picked-at crackers and cheese away from me, and immediately felt both Sam-Sam and Charlie head-butting my legs, hoping for crumbs. "Do the police know the money probably got taken while you were in staff meeting?"

"No—I mean, I don't know." Dad's eyes moved away from mine, then came right back. "How do you figure that?"

And the fire left, and the itchy came back, and I stared at the ceiling. "Because of the doors."

Silence.

Until Aunt Gus said, "Okay, you lost me. Help an old woman, Jesse?"

She had changed clothes when we came home, into her favorite tie-dyed T-shirt and turquoise leggings. I focused on the bright blues and yellows and greens. "Who has a key to your door, Dad?"

"Just me," he said. "And Mr. Chiba keeps the master on his key ring, with an extra in the office safe."

"So unless Mr. Chiba took the money," I said, "or somebody took the safe key, the thief had to be somebody without a key."

"I'm still not following," Aunt Gus said.

I sighed. "The senior high classroom doors are locked when it's not school hours. And Dad said the money was there that morning. And Dad and Mr. Chiba have the only keys other than the one in the safe."

Aunt Gus nodded when I paused. "Okay so far. Keep it coming."

"Dad probably would have noticed somebody getting in the drawer during class," I said. "I mean, somebody could have dived in when Dad was in the bathroom or on break or something—but lots of people would have seen that. The time when the doors would have been open and the halls almost empty, when nobody would have seen—"

I risked a look in Dad's direction, and he finished my sentence for me.

"The most logical time would have been when most everybody was in the staff meeting." He frowned. "That makes sense."

"Who missed the staff meeting?" I asked him.

Dad's brows came together, and I could almost hear his brain cells grinding together. Then his eyes went round. He blinked a few more times.

Aunt Gus and I stared at him.

"Well?" Aunt Gus said.

"I don't really remember," Dad said too fast, and his voice sounded funny.

"Are you telling the truth?" I asked him.

Aunt Gus patted my hand. "Honey, that's not very respectful."

"But it's right," I said, trying not to sound all whiny.

"I don't want you investigating anything—or anybody—else," Dad said.

"What about the students who knew how much money you had in your drawer?" I asked, getting louder with each word. "Who are KA, JS, MK, and NN?"

Dad rubbed both of his hands through his hair. "I—excuse me? What are those initials?"

I couldn't believe my own father sometimes. "The people who donated money before everything got stolen. If you wrote down their amounts in that ledger in front of them, they would have seen the total and known how much was in your drawer. You know, the one you labeled *Library Fund Donations* so everybody would know exactly where to steal stuff."

"Derrick, please tell me you did not label the drawer," Aunt Gus said.

Dad gave her a glare strong enough to laser her words right out of the air.

"We have pictures," I said. "Springer took pictures of the desk and classroom so we could examine them for evidence, but I remember what I saw. KA, JS, MK, and NN are evidence, or they might *have* evidence." I grabbed a cracker and piece of cheese, crunched it in my fist, then dropped the mess for the dogs to vacuum. Charlie's smacking sounded like one of those shark feeding frenzies I watched on Animal Planet. Poor Sam. He probably didn't get much of a bite.

"She has evidence, Derrick," Aunt Gus said, even though she didn't usually echo.

"Don't," Dad warned her.

"Who are those people?" I asked my father again.

Dad didn't answer.

Aunt Gus rolled her eyes.

"Fine. I'll use the yearbook to figure it out." I got another piece of cracker and handed it straight to Sam, who took off with it, probably to tuck it into my bedcovers for later.

"The police can't really believe I'd steal from the library fund," Dad said. "I've only gotten three speeding tickets in my whole life—and I've worked at that school since I was twenty-three years old." He didn't rub his hair this time. He rubbed his face instead. "And what's wrong with labeling the drawer? I've never had anything stolen at school before."

"See? This is where Jesse gets her dreamy thinking from." Aunt Gus folded her arms across her swirly rainbow shirt. "Her mother's more practical. She's a realist."

"What's *dreamy thinking* mean?" I asked. "And can I have some chili?"

"Touch coming," Aunt Gus said, then patted my hand. "Dreamy isn't anything bad. Just something I'm bothering your father about. And no, the chili isn't ready yet."

"You bother me frequently, Gustine," Dad said, sounding sad.

Aunt Gus winked at me. "Don't let him fool you. It's good for his soul. Now, honey. Tell me about this . . . OBWIG your friend Springer mentioned back at the school."

I felt myself go very still, and I swallowed. The words almost jumped out of my mouth just because she asked, but I managed to say, "It's a secret."

Her eyebrows lifted. "Between you and Springer?"

I nodded.

"Another touch." She feathered her fingers through

my hair. "Okay, then. I won't ask. I'm really glad you have secrets with a friend."

"When will the chili be ready?" I glanced at the pot. Because it sure smelled ready.

"A few hours," Aunt Gus said. "Close to six, regular dinnertime."

"Can I go outside awhile then?" I looked at Dad. "Or am I grounded to the house?"

The surprised expression on his face told me he hadn't planned a punishment. Yet. Or maybe this would be one of those times I didn't get one. Hard to say. Sometimes I couldn't figure out the difference between stuff that got me grounded and stuff that didn't.

Aunt Gus patted Dad's arm.

Dad sighed.

Then he waved his hand toward the back door.

I lay on the dirt, nose to nose with my sweet dog, deep in the Pond River Forest, probably somewhere dead center between all the neighborhoods in our town that circled the trees. Sam's tail thumped as I patted the mound of dirt where I had buried his treat container this time.

"All you have to do is sniff," I told him. "Bark at it. Try to dig it up. We came all the way down here to get away from Springer's smell and my smell and I thought maybe you were getting confused about all the holes and stuff."

Sam licked my nose.

He showed zero interest in the dirt mound.

I dug my fingers into the loose topsoil. "Like this, see?"

Sam glanced at my hand but didn't move. When I realized he was waiting for me to pet him, I gave up and stroked his head. It was hard to feel so disappointed, especially when he gave me his brightest, cutest doggy smile. "It's okay," I told him as leaves rustled above us in the light breeze. "Sometimes it takes me a while to learn new stuff, too."

My nose got another bath.

I dug out the container and let Sam have the treat inside. Since we were so far off our home turf, I pocketed the little ball to throw when we got back to the clubhouse. Slowly, sort of hoping Sam would paw at the dirt I messed up, I got to my feet.

Sam wagged his tail and looked at me, doggy smile blazing.

"Come on," I told him, and held out my arms. Sam-Sam jumped into my hug, I picked up the container, and we started toward the big path that was just a few trees away.

Almost instantly, Sam went stiff in my grip and growled.

I stopped.

"You okay?" I whispered, then wondered why I was being so quiet.

Sam pointed his head toward the path, and the black tip of his nose twitched. He growled again, soft this time, like he didn't want to be heard, either. His eyes narrowed like he could see something in front of us. Then the ruff around his neck fluffed, and that made the hair on the back of my neck stand up, too.

I put the container on the ground as quietly as I could and used my free hand to gently cup Sam's nose. "Shhhhhh," I told him, then eased behind the nearest, biggest tree.

Sam let me hold his little muzzle to keep him from barking, but he stayed stiff, almost pointing his whole body toward the path.

Tap-tap-tap.

Shoes on dirt. Somebody walking. No, wait. Somebody running.

Sam's growls made my bones vibrate. He was shaking. I held tight to him, my heartbeat picking up speed.

"Wait!" A guy. "Would you wait?"

Oh, great. I'd know that voice anywhere. But I made sure I stayed away from his side of the paths!

Yet Jerkface was here in the forest, and I didn't have anything to hit him with. Worse, I had Sam. I wasn't sure Ryker knew about Sam, but I wouldn't put it past him to hurt my poor dog just to be a huge donkey turd.

I pulled Sam up under my chin.

If I ran the other way, Jerkface would probably hear me. But if I stayed here, Sam might bark. Dad's voice floated through my head. *The world can be dangerous if you're out in it all alone . . .*

My jaw tightened.

Sam wasn't alone. He had me, and I'd take care of him, just like Mom and Shotgun took care of the soldiers they protected. If she could do it, so could I.

Slap-slap! The running person made it to the part of the path near my tree. I didn't dare look out, but the person sniffed, hiccupped, and sniffed again.

Crying?

Jerkface yelled, "Please wait, Trisha."

Double great. One of the cockroaches, too. I bit my lip and wished I had taught Sam-Sam a command that would make him run home. I'd have to do that if he and I got out of this in one piece.

The *thump-thump-thump* of another person jogging up and stopping near my tree matched the *thump-thump-thump* of my heart. My brain wanted to start counting steps and heartbeats, too, but I kissed Sam's head instead.

As the thumps on the path slowed, Jerkface said, "He didn't mean it."

More sniffing. Then Trisha spoke, her voice shaky and quieter than usual. "I hate it when he's awful like that."

It took my brain a few seconds to really understand that somebody had upset Trisha, and she was actually crying. Who knew cockroaches had tear ducts?

The thought of a sobbing roach made me relax a little, and Sam seemed to sense this. He kept up his whisper-growls, but he gave up alerting toward the path and snuggled in under my chin. I let go of his muzzle and scratched behind his ears to keep his attention.

"He's just in a bad mood," Jerkface said.

Trisha came right back with "Yeah, like all the time?"

Who were they talking about? Who on earth could make a cockroach cry by being awful? Seriously, Trisha was, like, Queen Mean. How bad did things have to get for her to go all boo-hoo-hoo?

"Nothing makes him happy anymore," Trisha said. "Even when we play Pig or Horse, he gets ticked off and ends up bashing the ball against the garage door."

Silence.

More silence.

Ryker said, "We went to the movies night before last, and he got us thrown out. Kept flipping popcorn in people's hair. I mean, I get it, stuff like that used to be a lot of fun—but I paid for that movie myself, and I really wanted to see it."

A breeze shifted the leaves, making afternoon light dance around my tree. Sam cuddled and licked my chin. And out on the path, Trisha said, "I thought it was just me he was starting to hate."

"I don't think he hates anybody," Ryker told her. "I think it's just—you know. His dad's kinda not in a good place right now. I don't even like to go over to their house. It's like Chris can't do anything right. It's like nobody can."

Trisha sniffed. "Does that mean he has to be awful to us?"

"No, but—well, maybe yeah, I guess." I didn't see Ryker shrug, but I could imagine it. "I don't think he means to be a total butthead."

Silence again.

Long.

The breeze blew, and one of them coughed.

"Do you think he took that money out of Mr. Broadview's desk?" Ryker asked, his voice so quiet I almost didn't hear him.

It took long seconds for me to process, to understand that—

Oh.

Oh, wow.

My fingers slipped deeper into Sam-Sam's fur as we both strained to listen.

"No!" Trisha said, her voice harsh. "Why would you even say that?"

"Sorry, I didn't mean—it's just, he was broke at the movies, then he bought a new basketball and some shin guards and a skateboard yesterday—it was weird." Ryker sounded concerned, even though I was pretty sure he didn't possess that emotion. "Plus, Chris got even more riled up after what happened in the hall outside Mr. Broadview's class."

"He just hates that the little weirdo gets special treatment even with all the fits she's had," Trisha said. "You remember kindergarten and first grade, right? I used to think my brain would bleed out my ears from the noise. And last year, she knocked your teeth out."

"Yeah. I guess." Ryker laughed. "I probably hit her first, though."

"Well, she would have deserved it," Trisha shot back. Then her voice totally changed to something softer. "I want it to be like it used to be, Ry. The three of us hanging out together. All of us going to basketball camp for the summer."

"Me too," Ryker said. His voice turned so gentle I couldn't believe it. "I really miss going to camp."

Trisha didn't say anything back.

Ryker gave a really loud sigh. "Come on. Let's go back and see if we can talk some sense into him."

"You go ahead," Trisha said. "I'll come in a few minutes."

"Okay." Ryker's last word sounded distant. He was probably walking, not running, so I couldn't hear him moving away, but at least he was leaving.

I sagged against the tree—and accidently mooshed Sam's foot.

He gave a startled yip.

Everything in my body went stiff, like some kind of fear-freeze. I held Sam close and tried to figure which direction to run. Not toward Ryker. Needed the clubhouse—or better yet, my actual house. I felt too turned around—

"You." Trisha's cold voice froze me even more solid.

Sam growled.

Trisha had come around my tree, and she was standing right in front of me, arms folded. I took in her pulled-back hair, the glitter of her stud earrings, her green blouse and pressed jeans. She was smiling, all teeth and no warmth. It looked more like a snarl.

When I didn't say anything back or try to move, her eyes narrowed. "If you tell anybody what you heard, I'll spend every minute of my life making you miserable."

My heart slammed against my ribs, and I held tight to my rumbling dog, smelling his Sam-Sam scent and imagining I had the strongest muscles in the world, because I absolutely wouldn't let anything happen to him, no matter how bad I wanted to just start screaming and run away.

Trisha stepped toward us, and I finally unfroze. I backed up a step, then circled around a few more, putting Sam and me between her and the path.

"If you hurt my dog, I'll crack your face open," I said, surprised by how low-pitched and loud my voice sounded.

Trisha's head snapped back like I had slapped her. She looked more surprised than I could have imagined, and she shocked me when she said, "Jeez, don't go all warrior princess. I would never hurt a dog."

She honestly sounded like she meant it. But this was Trisha. This was one of Jerkface's cockroaches. I couldn't take a chance on believing her, but . . .

"I would never tell people about somebody having a

cry in private, because I'm not a hateful bully," I told her.

Trisha stared at me. A shadow seemed to pass over her face. Maybe leaves moving in the breeze. Maybe a bird flying overhead. Maybe her witchy, shriveled heart trying to actually warm up enough to kill her.

For a few weird seconds, she looked like she might cry again. For another few seconds, she looked like . . . someone else. Just a normal girl. Just a normal, sad girl. Then she turned her back to me, and I saw her fingers curl into fists.

Her voice came out almost like a growl. "What you heard—Chris didn't take that money. I mean it."

I held Sam against me, protecting him because Trisha had morphed back to the hateful creature I usually dealt with, and I just looked at her.

"Go away, Messy," she said.

And I went.

13

Monday, After the Train Came, I Don't Know When Because Time Stopped Ticking

My sneakers ground into grass and bits of wood and black hunks that looked like pieces of pavement. Something cut my ankle. I didn't stop.

My phone rang in my pocket. Probably Dad. And he was probably following us—but that was okay because Dad was okay and I knew he wasn't hurt, but Sam-Sam—

I reached in and switched off the sound. When it buzzed, I pulled it out long enough to turn it off, and somehow managed not to bust my face in the process.

Springer and I made it to the road outside the school. At least I thought it was the road outside the school. Nothing looked right. Nothing smelled right. The air seemed way too still after all that roaring wind, and my nose got clogged with the stench of dirt and oil and wet and something yuck like sewage.

Cars seemed to be everywhere, but none of them were moving. Some were on their sides and some were upside down. Alarms beeped and blared. Rain drizzled into my face. I kept jogging, even though I wasn't sure, couldn't really figure what—how—

From somewhere seemingly on another planet, Springer said, "Please don't let there be people in those cars."

I glanced at him.

He jogged beside me, eyes wide, cheeks red.

"Which way?" I yelled, using all my willpower not to start counting upright cars and turned-over cars and cars on their sides, because they would all need different totals, right? And then I might need to divide them by color or type or size. My chest ached from panic for my dog. I didn't have time to count cars. Why did my head always try to do stuff that I didn't need it to do?

Springer grabbed my arm and stopped me before he let me go. Together, we breathed really hard and squinted through the rain until he pointed. "There. That's Spruce. That way. Oh, wait."

He took out his phone and looked at it. "Mom. She says she and Dad are fine." He tapped at his screen, talking his message out loud. "Fine, too. Helping Jesse find her dog."

"My dog," I echoed, staring at Spruce. I had no idea how Springer knew the street name, because the sign was gone. Something that looked a lot like it lay about thirty feet away, upside down and stuck through somebody's car door.

We ran toward the corner, dodging around cars and hearing their alarms and not looking, not looking because maybe people—no. I didn't want to see people hanging upside down in busted cars and I didn't want to count the cars or even see what color they were because Sam needed me.

But there were people.

Some in those cars, trying to get out, and getting out, and helping other people get their doors open. It kept raining. The flat air and toilet-mud-oily-nasty smells kept smothering me. We kept running.

When we got to Spruce, the yellow house, it wasn't yellow anymore. More brown-and-black-streaked. It looked like a giant had stepped on the roof and crushed half the house's rooms, then ripped stuff out of the yard and thrown it all over the place. Those bushes, the thirty-seven little bushes I had counted five days ago, there were maybe three left, and they weren't right side up. Springer and I almost tripped over two of the bushes and their roots. We had to get in the road to go around them, and we realized part of the pavement had been cracked.

I caught Springer's hand, and we moved around the torn-up road, and I tried to imagine how strong something had to be to rip pavement in half like paper. Before I could even begin to figure that out, a fountain blocked our view of the next section of road, only it wasn't a real fountain.

"I think that was a fire hydrant," Springer wheezed as we jogged through the spraying water. Car alarms seemed to be going off everywhere. My hair got soaked. Our shoes got soaked. Here and there, people seemed to be wandering out of toothpick houses that had all been stomped by the same giant that crushed the yellow house and tore up its thirty-seven bushes. One lady had on a blue bathrobe, and she was standing beside a turned-over car, crying.

I ground my teeth together.

Don't count people. Don't count busted houses. Don't count anything. Just move. Just get to Sam-Sam.

Seconds went by. Maybe minutes. I couldn't make sense out of time because nothing looked right, not even the light from the sky. Too cloudy. Too rainy. Weirdly green. And all the *noise.* My chest started to hurt from running so far.

We came to another corner and both stopped at the same time. Springer bent over and heaved a breath as I looked around.

We were at the shutter house, where I would have trespassed to count if I hadn't been with Springer last Wednesday. Maple. Yes. We needed to turn right by the shutter house. But . . .

"It's half gone," Springer said, breathless. "It's just broken wood and turned-over cars."

"And some people." I pointed to a group pulling boards off a leaning doorframe. One was a tall man in green shorts with a cast on his hand. Another looked familiar, with her scarf and short-sleeved blouse. "Is that Coach Sedon and Ms. Jorgensen?"

"I think so." Springer sounded scared now. "I thought

Coach Sedon was supposed to be getting his hand fixed?"

"Why are they at that house?" I mumbled. "Dad said the police—this is all kinds of wrong."

Mom's voice whispered through my mind, like she was standing right next to me. *Trust yourself, Jesse. Trust what you know . . .*

Fear flickered in my chest, too. "Let's go, Springer. Now."

Without another word, we ran to the right, down Cedar. Or what was left of it. The sidewalk had chunks missing. The road looked like somebody had shaved it with a knife and dropped the pieces to either side. My teeth started to shatter. My soaked clothes and shoes squished as we hurried through the drizzle.

In a few minutes, we passed a fallen flamingo statue, and another, and another. The redbrick house was there on the corner ahead, but it had no roof. All the flamingos in the yard were gone. I didn't try to look for the six gnomes. They were heavier than pink birds, I was sure. Maybe they didn't get thrown or busted.

As we got past the house, we wheeled to our left—and stopped again.

My street—

There was nothing on my street but pieces of board and pink insulation and turned-over cars.

I started crying.

"Okay to touch?" Springer asked.

I nodded.

Springer put his arm around my shoulder. "Let's get to your house."

"It's not there." I couldn't breathe. I couldn't feel my toes or my hands or my body. Maybe I was gone, too. "My house is gone."

"Let's get to what's left of it and call Sam," he said. "Dogs are smart, you know?"

Air. I had to breathe. I didn't want to breathe. It hurt. But I had to. "Sam-Sam was in a crate. He couldn't—he couldn't get out."

"Let's go call him." Springer's voice sounded too high, almost like a scream.

We stumbled ahead, and the rain got harder. I still couldn't breathe. Too much water in my face. Too much nothing and broken awful everything, everywhere around me.

Was this my house?

No, wait. There. I recognized the driveway, the part of it not covered up with a door and a sink and a mattress. Were those Aunt Gus's shirts in the oak tree?

Without saying a word, Springer and I picked our way closer and closer to what had been the front of our house. Then we just stood staring at the rubble and I couldn't stop crying because Sam, because my baby dog—the whole house had just fallen down or exploded or something. What chance did a tiny, tiny fluffy white dog have against a tornado?

"Sam?" Springer called. "Hey, Sam-Sam!"

Nothing but car alarms and rain sounds and busted hydrant spraying.

My insides twisted.

Springer elbowed me.

I tried to speak, to say a word, to call out my dog's name, but I just sobbed.

The next thing I knew, Springer's arm settled on my shoulder. "Come on, Jesse. You can do this. Sam needs you to try, right? So try."

It didn't bother me, Springer giving me a hug. In fact it felt kinda good. It kinda helped. I kept crying, but this time when I opened my mouth, I squeaked out, "Sam-Sam?"

We listened.

Alarms. Spraying water. No dog sounds.

"Sam!" we yelled at the same time, and waited again.

Alarms and water, water and alarms.

I got a bigger breath, a huge one I pulled all the way from my toes. With every bit of volume I could manage, I hollered, "Sam-Sam! Here, boy! Where are you? Sam!"

Nothing even remotely dog.

Springer let me go and sat down on the torn-up grass and bricks and glass and wood. His butt made a huge crunch. "I'm sorry, Jesse. I'm so sorry. I thought—"

"Hush!" I shouted, because I thought I heard—

Alarms? Water? Something else?

My imagination.

"Sam-Sam," I whispered, tears and raindrops running together on my cheeks and chin and neck.

And somewhere in that pile of sticks and rocks and pink fuzzy junk that used to be a house, something shifted.

And then, something barked.

14

Thursday, Four Days Earlier, Afternoon

Ryker totally likes Trisha," Springer said.

"What?" The thought almost made me sick. "Why would you even say something like that?"

"Because," Springer said, and I would have looked at him to figure out if he was joking with me, but the two of us were huddled so tight behind a bunch of scrub pines that if I turned my head, I'd poke a pine needle up my nose. We had been there for a while, half an hour maybe, in our green-and-brown shirts and shorts, camouflage like Mom would have worn if she was stationed in a forest instead of a desert. In front of us lay the cul-de-sac where Ryker, Chris, and Trisha lived. We were closest to Chris's house, facing the other two houses, and far enough away that we could talk quietly to each other.

So far, our surveillance mission to see if Jerkface and the cockroaches talked about the stolen money was one big giant bust. The dead-end street seemed so quiet. No cars parked at curbs. No cars in driveways, because they had garages. Nobody was around Chris's house, where we were hiding. In front of Trisha's house, her older sister Meredith sat in a porch swing with some sharp-faced girl I didn't know. They were looking at stuff on the sharp-faced girl's phone.

Springer nodded toward Ryker's driveway, where Jerk-face and the cockroaches were taking turns shooting baskets. "See how Ryker always catches the ball for Trisha and hands it to her?"

I watched them play a round, wishing I had Sam-Sam in my arms to kiss and pet, but no way was I putting my dog in danger. "Okay, you're right, but isn't that because it's her turn after his?"

"He doesn't catch the ball for Chris," Springer said.

"That makes no sense."

After a few long heartbeats, Springer said, "This stuff is hard for you, isn't it?"

"Yeah." And just like that, I felt sort of awful, even if I couldn't quite say why.

Springer shifted his weight from one foot to the other, making pine branches twitch. "I'm sorry, Jesse. I didn't mean to make you sad."

"You didn't." I traced a finger down the branch closest to my face and tried to focus on the rough bark. "The—whatever's broken in my brain makes me sad."

"But your brain isn't broken." He sounded genuinely shocked. "Why do you think it's broken?"

"It doesn't work like everyone else's," I told him.

"That doesn't mean it's broken. Your brain is fine."

This conversation was making me itch inside, not just in my broken brain, but everywhere. "So how come Trisha doesn't look at Ryker like he looks at her? She catches Chris's basketball shots, and she gives him that sort of goo-goo face."

"Oh," Springer said. "Ooooooh. Good observing. Then Trisha likes Chris."

I kept rubbing the branch bark with the pad of my finger, because it felt different and strange and sort of good, and it kept that itchy feeling away. "That's all kinda awkward, isn't it? The wrong ones of them liking each other?"

"Kinda," Springer said.

Just then, a *thump* made us both jump. The branches around us shivered like a breeze had caught them. Ryker and Trisha and Chris looked almost directly at us, and I thought about running—but Coach Sedon came into view from the front yard, wearing basketball shorts and a jersey like always, though these were University of Kentucky blue, not school green. He jogged across the street, heading to Chris as he called, "Hey, bud, where'd you leave the screwdrivers? I need to tighten the legs on your mom's computer desk."

Chris took his shot, made the basket, then turned toward his father. "I left them in the garage next to my bike. I'm sorry."

"Did he sound scared?" I asked Springer, since I didn't always get emotional stuff correct.

"I think so," Springer answered quietly.

That was weird. Why would Chris be scared over screwdrivers? In fact, all three of them, Jerkface and both cockroaches, seemed pretty stiff. They stood, arms to their sides, sort of smiling but sort of not, like people did when they wanted to be nice but they really wished somebody would go away.

The front door of Ryker's house opened, and his mother came out. Ms. Morton had on basketball clothes, too, only hers were University of Louisville red.

Coach Sedon shielded his eyes. "Awful color! I need sunglasses."

Ms. Morton laughed and clapped Coach Sedon on the back. "How's it going?"

Coach Sedon hesitated, then inclined his head toward his own yard.

As they walked back across the road, closer to Springer and me, Jerkface and the cockroaches relaxed, but they didn't start bouncing the ball again. They pulled in close together, watching Ms. Morton and Coach Sedon so intently that I worried they'd see us in the trees.

"Be. Really. Still," Springer whispered.

"No. Kidding," I whispered back without moving my lips.

My heart started to beat harder, and I realized I was holding my breath. Little by little, I let out air and breathed in again as Coach Sedon told Ms. Morton, "I'm doing better."

"Glad to hear it." Ms. Morton stopped about ten feet

away from us. "So that problem—you got it taken care of?"

"I did." Coach Sedon smiled. "Chris gave me a hand. Got rid of some of his old stuff and gave me what he made."

"You have a good boy," Ms. Morton said. Then, with a not-so-friendly look at Coach Sedon, she added, "Don't let him down, okay?"

"I won't," Coach Sedon said. "It's not like that now. I've got everything in hand."

If they hadn't been standing so close to us, I would have asked Springer why Coach Sedon was talking so fast, and why Ms. Morton looked like she didn't believe anything she was hearing. Almost as soon as Coach Sedon took a breath, Ms. Morton nodded, then headed to her house again.

Coach Sedon watched her go, and even with all my problems understanding people, I could tell the look on his face wasn't too friendly. One of his fists clenched and unclenched, and if I didn't know better, I would have sworn he was counting and imagining puppy pictures so he wouldn't have a meltdown.

Meanwhile, as Ms. Morton got to Ryker, she said, "You're working your full-speed dribbling drills, right?"

Ryker stood straighter. "Three times so far today."

"Make it five," his mom ordered. "Make it ten. You've got to improve your ball-handling. That's how you get to be a starter like your brother."

"Soon as we finish this game," Ryker told his mother.

His mother went silent and folded her arms, like she was waiting to see something. Closer to us, Coach Sedon stopped working his fists and walked away from our hiding place. In a few seconds, we heard the *clump* of his front door closing.

I watched Ryker shoot at the basket over his carport while his mother looked on. The shot missed, and Ryker hung his head. His mother heaved a sigh, then went back into their house.

"Should we feel sorry for him?" I asked Springer.

"I don't," Springer admitted.

I frowned. "Does that make us mean?"

"Maybe."

The itching in my brain started back, and I wanted to stop thinking about feeling sorry for Jerkface and the cockroaches. "Ryker likes Trish, Trish likes Chris, and Chris doesn't seem to like anybody," I said, listing what we'd learned so far. "And Ms. Morton wants Ryker to be a star like his brother even though he's not that good, and nobody really likes Coach Sedon."

"Sounds about right," Springer said. "And Coach Sedon looks like he's got a bad temper. And he had a problem he says he's fixed now, but Ms. Morton doesn't believe him. Sounded kinda like a money thing."

"So much to figure out." I bit at my lower lip. "But I don't think questioning any of these people would be a good idea, Springer."

He laughed. "Me neither."

"And I'm sort of tired of staring at them."

"Me too."

"Good. Then let's roll." I moved my fingers off the branches in front of my face and started to back away from our hiding spot, careful not to go too fast.

Springer backed up, too. And put his foot down funny on a rock, stumbled, started to fall, grabbed the closest pine, and launched himself into Chris Sedon's backyard.

My entire body went rigid with shock.

For a count of two, then three, it didn't seem real.

Like slow motion from a not-funny cartoon.

Springer swung his arms, staggered, then fell face-first, splatting on the grass in Chris Sedon's yard, and I heard all the air go out of him in one big huff.

All I could do was watch as Springer lay in the grass trying to breathe.

Across the street, Jerkface and the cockroaches stopped dribbling and shooting, and they turned toward us at the same time. The ball dropped out of Trisha's hands, bounced twice, then rolled into the grass.

Springer rolled onto his back and wheezed, "Run. Run!"

But he was lying there, and they were coming, first Ryker, then Chris, then Trisha.

They walked a few steps. One of them laughed. Then they walked faster.

I threw myself out of the cover of the trees, bent and grabbed Springer's arm with no touch warning, and pulled at him. "Get up. You have to."

He locked eyes with me, and the next time I pulled, he pushed himself up with his other arm, and somehow we got him off the ground.

Jerkface and the cockroaches paused in the middle of their road, staring at us as we stared back at them. They still looked confused.

Then Ryker raised one finger, pointing. "Were you two . . . *spying* on us?"

My legs started moving without my brain talking to them, backing up. I still had hold of Springer's arm, so I towed him with me.

Three steps. Four. Five. Three more, and we'd make the tree line.

At step seven, they bolted toward us, charging off the cul-de-sac road like angry, bellowing rhinos.

My brain and legs connected in a big whoosh, and Springer seemed to get control of his body at exactly the same moment. I pushed him into the trees ahead of me, and together we took off like our eyes and noses and faces depended on it.

15

Thursday, Four Days Earlier, Later Afternoon

We thundered down the main trail into Pond River Forest, Springer and me, side by side. I could have moved faster, but no way was I leaving him. I kept his wrist in my grip. He had to speed up. We had to speed up.

Branches smacked and stung the bare parts of my arms and legs. I didn't have to look behind us to know Jerkface and the cockroaches were coming hard on our tails. Their voices seemed to get closer with each noise they made.

Terror tried to grab me like I had grabbed Springer, fast and hard with no touch warning at all, but I pushed it out of my head. One running step, two, three, four, five, six, seven . . .

When steps didn't work, I counted breaths for a while, each number settling me as much as I could settle with three mean buttheads chasing me and my friend.

"This way," I told Springer, and pulled him with me on a sharp right turn.

Somebody—Ryker, I think—let out a snarl.

Springer kept his balance as I took him left, then right, then left again, off the main trail and the side trails, too, past mounds and rock markers where I had hidden Sam's treats. I knew we were getting close to the pond when we ran through a clearing and plunged into heavy underbrush. Spotting the cover I wanted, I urged Springer down with me, under branches and thorny blackberry vines and leaves, into a covered grassy spot big enough for a few deer to hide on their bellies.

We huddled there together, both breathing hard. Red-faced and sweating, Springer gazed at me with huge eyes. Little cuts scored both his cheeks, and I knew I was probably bleeding in a dozen places, too. Some of my hair was trapped in a blackberry vine, so I reached up and worked it free, poking my fingers another dozen times in the process.

Jerkface and the cockroaches stormed into the clearing, and I brought my throbbing fingers down to my mouth, covering my lips so I couldn't even make an accidental noise.

"Where are you two?" Ryker hollered. "You know you can't hide forever!"

Springer's eyes got even wider. His mouth came open, and I knew he didn't mean to talk or say anything, that he was just scared, so I pointed to my eyes and made him look at me and made myself look at him and ignore the itching jumping itching twitching running across my brain and up and down all my nerves.

"Why were you spying on us?" Trisha yelled. "Is this more of your investigation stupidity?"

"Y'all need to stay out of what isn't your business," Chris added.

My eyes narrowed even though I was trying to keep Springer's attention. My father *was* my business. And Jerk-face and those cockroaches—well. They matched their nicknames.

Springer took a breath in, then let it out slowly and quietly. He did this two or three times, and then he closed his mouth and nodded to me as if to say *It's okay. I'm okay.*

Feeling relieved, I looked away from him, through the twigs and branches separating us from the clearing.

"They have to be around here somewhere," Chris said.

"Dunno," Trisha answered. If I squinted, I could see the green of her knee-length shorts, about thirty feet away from us. "Messy knows these trails pretty good. Maybe she had a shortcut."

"They probably just wanted to see how real winners spend their time," Chris said, way too loud, like he hoped to make us mad enough to say something. "Or maybe the beached whale likes Trisha?"

The sound of the smack Trisha laid on him echoed around the clearing.

"Ow," he complained. "Lay off the shoulder!"

I watched Ryker's legs move to some bushes on the other side of the clearing. He picked up a stick, then jabbed it into the brush, and my heart seemed to quiver.

I leaned back, put my mouth very close to Springer's ear, and whispered, "The pond is behind us. The main path is that way." I pointed to my right. "If you find it, you can get to the clubhouse."

He shook his head.

I got even closer to Springer's ear. "Look, I know the forest really well. I can get away."

Head-shake.

"It's the smart thing to do, Springer. I'm going to get their attention, and you go."

I leaned away from him and picked up some chunks of dirt and rock, and a few pinecones. When he saw these, his jaw clenched and he looked so stubborn I thought about hitting him with one of the pinecones.

Ready? I mouthed.

He nodded.

I shot up from my hiding spot, busting through blackberry vines and pine branches, tearing my shirt and almost dropping some of my weapons. As Springer scrambled out of our cover on his belly, I stepped out of hiding about ten feet from Ryker, Chris, Trisha, and their sticks.

Before they could so much as smirk in my general direction, I launched the dirt clods and pinecones right at their mean, ugly faces.

When they swore and ducked, I took off in the opposite direction from Springer, and I ran as hard as I could toward the bank of the pond.

All three of them charged after me.

I dashed past a thick pine and grabbed the nearest low-hanging branch, pulling it with me, bending it, bending it—

They kept right on running toward me, and I let go of that branch and stumbled to a stop, watching. The branch swept back, smashing Ryker and Chris in the face and knocking them both into Trisha, who had finally caught up with them.

I turned and took off again, but it only took me a second to get to the pond bank. The tangles of vines and branches didn't leave any room to move, so I'd either have to go back the way I came, or go across the water.

The dark, muddy water.

Which was probably full of snakes and snapping turtles.

For a few seconds, I couldn't decide. I glanced back toward the trail and imagined Jerkface and the cockroaches, cut up from that branch in the face and twice as pissed as they had been. Then I looked at the water again. On the other side of the pond lay the path to my clubhouse and Springer, to my house and Aunt Gus and Sam and Charlie and Dad. To everything good in my life.

Okay.

No real choice, right?

I walked forward, sat on my butt, slid down the bank, and waded into the water. Mud smacked and pulled at my sneakers, but I kept walking. It took maybe a minute—a minute that felt like an hour—before I got to the other side and splashed and slogged up the bank.

After I shook gunk and water off my arms, I turned to see what was happening behind me.

Ryker was standing on the far bank, glaring at me. Blood trickled out of his nose, running down across his lips to his chin. Trish and Chris came next, with Chris walking funny and rubbing his eye.

I scrubbed mud off my face with my palms, sort of. More like smeared it.

"That was a pine branch!" Trish shrilled at me. "It really hurt them!"

"Ryker's fist really hurt Springer at the Little League tryouts!" I yelled back. "If you stop trying to smash us, I'll quit smashing you."

"It doesn't work like that," Chris said, his voice a snarl across the surface of the muddy pond.

"Yeah?" Heat bubbled in my chest now, fighting the chill from the pond. "Then how does it work, cockroach?"

"You quit being a freaky little loser," Riker said. "Turn invisible. Stay out of our way."

"Or you get hurt worse," Chris said. "Maybe real bad."

I jammed my hand into my wet, grody pocket, pretending my phone was in there. "Want to send that in one of your mean messages? I'm sure the police would love to see it."

Chris surged toward the edge of the pond, but Ryker and Trish both grabbed hold of him. I realized they were giving him weird looks.

He stopped trying to get in the pond, but he yelled, "I'm serious, Messy! Just let us catch you alone somewhere. Let *me* catch you alone."

And with that, he jerked out of Ryker's and Trisha's holds and stalked off into the forest, back toward the side trail. Trisha and Ryker ran right after him, with Trisha calling his name.

I was pretty sure they weren't planning to loop around the pond and come after me again, but I wasn't taking chances.

I turned and ran toward the clubhouse as fast as my mud-caked shoes and legs would go.

16

Thursday, Four Days Earlier, Early Evening

Y ou ever seen *Swamp Thing*?" Springer asked me as he poured more water on some paper towels and tried to scrub off my face.

"Funny," I told him. "Not."

We were huddled inside the clubhouse, sitting close together with my cleaning tote open, and I couldn't stop shivering from my yucky swim.

"You have a lot of little cuts on your face and arms," he pointed out.

I sighed. "I know that. And now Dad'll be all like, see, it's like I said, you can't keep yourself safe."

"That's not true." Springer dabbed my forehead. "You saved us both."

"After I almost got us both stomped. Stupid idea, observing Jerkface and the cockroaches. Do you think it would hurt if I used spray cleanser on my arms?"

"Yes," Springer said. "Don't do that. And I think your shoes are ruined."

"Nooooooo." I took the paper towels away from him and used the spray cleanser on my poor sneakers. "I'll tiptoe into the house and put my clothes and shoes in the washer. I'll even take a really long bath, even if it makes me itchy."

"At least you were grounded from your phone," he pointed out. "Or that would be ruined, too. And I don't think it was stupid to observe Ryker and Trisha and Chris. We got some evidence, didn't we?"

I scooted away from him and leaned against one of the clubhouse walls. I wanted Sam-Sam, but I was sort of glad he wasn't here to roll around on me and get all muddy, too. I kept remembering swimming through the pond, and the way Chris's voice sounded and all their dumb threats.

"They are such jerks," I whispered, wishing I had better words to express how much I loathed every cell in their bodies. "But I don't know if they seem guilty because I can't stand them, or because they really had something to do with the money being stolen."

"Well, there's one way to find out," Springer said, pulling out his phone and wiggling it back and forth. "OBWIG can keep investigating. Question the other suspects and see if we can rule them out—or in."

He lowered the phone and punched in his security code, then pulled up the photos he had taken in my dad's office.

I blinked at them, then remembered. The initials. The people we needed to look up in the yearbook. The yearbook that was still here in the clubhouse. I pointed to it, and Springer handed it to me, then got out a head lamp and switched it on without strapping it to his head. He handed that to me, too.

"What's the first one?" I squinted at the phone. "I remembered them all when I was talking to Dad, but a lot has happened since then."

"KA," Springer said. "So go to the *A*s."

I held the head lamp in my hand and shined it on the pages until I found the *A* names in the senior high section of the yearbook.

"KA has two senior high matches," I said, pointing at the pictures. "Karen Abelmore and Kevin Aztine. I don't know either of them. Do you?"

Springer shook his head, then used his phone to type the names into a note program. When he was finished, he said, "JS, then MK, then NN."

I flipped pages. "Okay, JS is Josh Sharp. The only JS in the book. He's on the student council—or he was last year when this was made." More flipping, more searching, then, "MK is Maleka Keston. Her, I've heard of. She's captain of the volleyball team."

Springer typed on his phone as I moved to the *N* section. "Got it," he said.

"NN is Nancy Newsom," I said, staring at her picture in the yearbook. "I don't know her, either, but something about her looks familiar."

"You seen her before?" Springer asked.

I gazed down at the dark hair, the sneery sort of expression. "I—yes? But I don't know."

"Maybe it'll come to you," he said.

His phone buzzed, and he looked at it and frowned. Tapped a few buttons. Frowned again.

"Your parents?" I asked. "Do you need to go?"

He shook his head. And then I saw how round and sad his eyes were, and I knew.

"Touch coming," I murmured. I leaned forward and put my muddy hand on his wrist. "Jerkface and the cockroaches are sending you bad messages, too. How did they get your number?"

Springer's lips trembled. "I gave it to Ryker myself, when I first got to town. Before I knew how he was. He asked me, and I thought he was being friendly, and I was such an idiot."

He let out a shaky breath.

"They started sending you crappy messages as soon as they had the number?"

He nodded. "Not right away. Just one or two. I showed them to my mom, and she said she hoped they'd stop once they got to know me, and I asked them to stop, and they sort of did until—"

Everything inside me suddenly felt heavy. "Until you started talking to me. Springer, I'm so sorry."

"Don't be," he said. "I don't blame you. It's them."

"They got my number from some guide the school published a long time ago," I said. "I thought about changing it, but they'd find it sooner or later."

The head lamp lit up the place where my dirty fingers touched Springer's clean skin. I wished Sam-Sam were with us again. I felt sort of halved without him.

"You said ignoring them works best, right?" His lips stopped trembling, but his chin still moved a little when he said, "That's what I'm going to do."

I patted his wrist, and flakes of muck dropped everywhere. "Do you have social media accounts?"

"Nah." He shook his head. "Dad said those are a waste of time."

"Good. One less place they can bother you."

Springer looked me in the eyes, surprising me. "They've been messing with you since you were little, and you don't let it get to you. You're really brave, you know that?"

"I'm not. I just do what I have to."

"I bet you could be a soldier like your mom," he said.

My insides got twitchy in a hurry. No, worse than twitchy. More jumpy-icky-hot-cold. "I'm really not brave. I'm not hero material. Just ask anybody."

"I don't have to ask other people," Springer said.

I thought about Ryker's face bleeding from the branch, and Chris's cold, awful voice, and the threats they made. "I'm not sure I saved anything. Maybe just bought us some time."

"Well? That's something. It's more than I did."

His tone confused me. He seemed pretty set on not hitting people, but now he sounded unsure. Now I really got jumpy-icky-hot-cold-tight-crampy. I counted one of my breaths, then two, then three, and said my three times table to help myself relax, only I couldn't really relax.

"Why won't you hit people, Springer?" I asked.

"Because I don't want to grow up to be a bad man." His answer came out so easy, so quiet, I knew he meant it way down deep, even if he was mad at himself. "I'm big, so I could do a lot of damage, and I don't want to be like—like them, you know?"

"I know," I echoed.

Echoing was better than what I almost said, which was *Well, I don't want to get hit in the nose,* but when I glanced at him, his expression had changed from sad to serious. Even if Springer and I never agreed about whether or not it was okay to hit bullies when they attacked, that was fine by me. I mean, it would have been great if Springer stomped those idiots, but if it bothered him, I was fine if he didn't. I'd just have to look after him. And when necessary, I'd stomp the bullies for both of us.

"Thank you for helping with the investigation," I said, mostly to change the subject. "It's nice, having a friend."

Springer managed a small grin. "Yeah, it really is nice. But you don't have to thank me. Unless you want me to thank you. Then we'll be thanking each other all the time, and that'd be weird."

I grinned, too, and the mud on my face cracked. "OBWIG," I said.

Springer raised his fist. "OBWIG forever!"

17

Monday, After the Train Came

The world shrank to the size of my road.

Bark!

The world shrank to the size of my yard.

Bark!

The world shrank to the size of the pile of planks and bricks and pipes and spraying water and rain puddles and torn-up mud-splattered everything that was my house.

Bark!

The world shrank to the size of my body and Springer's body and that tiny, distant, muffled . . .

Bark!

Springer said something but I didn't hear what it was. "Shhhhh!" I held up my hand.

Bark!

To my left.

I walked forward, stumbling as busted bits of concrete bit into my ankles. The front door should be here, only it wasn't. But if it were and I went through it and tried to get to my room, it would be more to the left.

Ignoring the ache in my ankles, and the hot warm stuff slipping into my sneakers that was probably blood, I climbed on a stack of boards and pink stuff that I figured came out of the attic.

". . . Careful . . ." came Springer's voice.

He might as well have been in another town.

Bark!

Closer than it should have been, not really where my room would be, but that was okay, because a freight train of wind could move a dog cage before dropping a house on it.

A board stopped me. I reached down and grabbed it, and wiggled it free. I pitched it behind me and grabbed another. Got a splinter in my thumb. It didn't matter. I got the second piece of a board loose and threw it behind me, too. A chunk of rock went next, then a big wad of attic pink stuff that prickled at my fingertips.

Bark!

"I'm coming!" I said, and when I heard my own voice, the world seemed to grow and sound came back and my heart started beating again and I started breathing again and my ankles hurt and my thumb hurt and my fingertips hurt and I grabbed the next board anyway, the rain on my face hiding my tears.

Then Springer was beside me, sitting down on a bunch of boards, showing me how he was taking off his shoes and his socks, putting his shoes back on, and sliding his socks over his hands.

I stopped long enough to do that, and with my sock mittens, grabbing stuff and moving stuff got easier. When a board wouldn't come, or a chunk of brick felt too heavy, Springer helped with his sock mittens.

Bark!

Almost there. Almost through some of the pile, maybe making a hole where we could get into what was left of the house, a room, to the cage, and—

I froze with a brick in my hand.

Springer pushed up beside me, slipped on some wet pink stuff, got back up—

I heard it again.

Not a bark.

"That's—" Springer said.

"Not a dog," I finished.

18

Friday, Three Days Earlier, Morning

The office was empty early Friday morning. I had ridden in with Dad, because after the walking-to-school-without-permission and water-bottle-fight stuff on Wednesday, and me showing up home looking like a voodoo doll made out of mud Thursday evening, he said he wasn't feeling *trusting*. So he'd arranged for me to stay in the office until class started.

The only good part about all that was, somehow, Springer had beaten me to the school. His mom brought him, he said, because after I told him I had to come in early, he asked her to do it. And before I got there, he'd been trying to sweet-talk Mr. Chiba into giving us the attendance list for the staff meeting that happened on the day the library fund money went missing from Dad's desk drawer.

Mr. Chiba hadn't cracked.

As we sat side by side, me kicking carpet squares with my freshly washed and very itchy sneakers, and him messing with his phone, he pulled up our list of the senior high students we needed to question. I glanced at the list.

"I don't know where to start," I admitted. "Got any ideas?"

Springer glanced toward the front counter, where Mr. Chiba was leaning over and marking things in a book. "I wonder what their class schedule is."

Before I could say anything about that, he got up and headed back over to Mr. Chiba's counter. Mr. Chiba didn't look up as Springer approached, but after a few seconds, he did—and as I watched the two of them, I realized that sometimes I saw people, right down to the number of hairs escaping ponytails and the exact amount of yellow streaks on their teeth. Sometimes I noticed that their shirts had pointy collars or round collars or no collars, or that boy shirts had buttons on the right and girl shirts had buttons on the left. But sometimes, I didn't see people at all.

I had never really processed that Mr. Chiba's black hair had streaks of silver on both sides. He had lines around his forehead and dark eyes and mouth that made him look grandpa-sweet when he smiled, and he smiled at Springer more than he smiled at most people. That is, when he wasn't scratching that spot behind his ear.

He did that a lot when I was around.

I figured being around me made him nervous. Lots of people got nervous around me, even when I'd never hit them.

"Your eye looks better," Mr. Chiba said. "More green than blue now. It'll be normal by next week, I hope."

"Me too," Springer said. "Listen, we really need to know about the staff meeting attendance." Springer gave a little shrug, like everyone knew how important staff meeting schedules were. "Who was absent—that's the most important thing, for our investigation."

Mr. Chiba kept smiling at him, not looking in my direction even a little bit. "I understand what you're saying. It's just—" He glanced at Ms. Jorgensen's closed door. "I really need to get the okay from my boss."

"Isn't Ms. Jorgensen here already?" I asked, then covered my mouth when Mr. Chiba flinched.

His hand drifted to a thick folder on her desk. "She isn't," he admitted.

Well, that was weird. She had been here yesterday at this time, fussing at Coach Sedon about something outside the senior high entrance. And her work hours covered both junior and senior high, since she was supreme queen mighty principal over both parts of the school, right?

"Something came up," Mr. Chiba added, his words coming out too fast. "Personal business again."

"Again?" Springer frowned. "So is Ms. Jorgensen away from work a lot?"

"More than she should be." It was Mr. Chiba's turn to cover his mouth. He closed his eyes for a second, too. When he opened them again, Springer kept up his campaign.

"I don't want to get you in trouble," Springer said. "I just want to help Jesse so her dad doesn't ever have to go back to jail. She really needs him, you know?"

Mr. Chiba's glance strayed over to me. He scratched behind his ear. I thought about what Springer might do in this situation, and I did my best to smile.

Mr. Chiba looked away.

I held back a sigh and wished I had a mirror to see what was wrong with my face. My friendly looks definitely didn't seem to work like Springer's did. In fairness, though, he had a really nice grin that made his whole face shiny. When I smiled, I mostly looked like I wanted to bite somebody.

"Well," Springer said, "if you really can't help us with the staff meeting, can you tell us which classes Karen Abelmore, Kevin Aztine, Josh Sharp, Maleka Keston, and Nancy Newsom are in today?"

"Kevin Aztine moved away last year," Mr. Chiba said, sounding surprised by the request—so surprised he forgot to tell Springer he couldn't help us. "Karen Abelmore's on homeschool because she's been ill. The other three, I'd have to look—but I shouldn't. Privacy and all."

Springer gave him puppy eyes.

Mr. Chiba sighed. "I really don't think Mr. Broadview will have to go back to jail. I think all this will get worked out when he has his hearing next week."

Hearing next week?

Wait.

My breath went shallow, and the insides of my hands started to itch.

Hearing.

Okay, that was definitely a court thing. Was a hearing the same as a trial? Was that when Dad would have to prove he was innocent or get sentenced to jail where I couldn't see him and he couldn't come home and he'd leave me and Aunt Gus and Sam-Sam and Charlie all alone?

I scratched at my hands. The room seemed to lurch in circles. I quit scratching and gripped the arms of my seat and looked at the thin office carpet squares under my tennis shoes. The squares were green. There were twelve squares between my feet and the wall across the room.

"One, two, three," I whispered, trying to count the longways squares, because if I could get the right number, I could multiply them by the shortways squares and figure out how many green squares made up this part of the office. *Hearing. Guilty. Innocent. Jail.* "Four, five, six." But the front counter got in the way.

I pushed out of my seat and walked around the wooden counter, pushing through the gate part even though a little bell rang and somebody said something. "Seven, eight." There. I could almost see the rest of the squares. I walked past the desk where Mr. Chiba was standing, until I could get a good view of the floor near the office windows.

She does that, said Springer's voice from somewhere. *Numbers and counting things—it helps her not be upset.*

You haven't known her that long, Mr. Chiba answered, like he was in a dream I was having. *How have you figured all this out?*

She told me.

I'm sorry this is hard for her, Springer. And sorry it's hard for you, too.

We'll be okay, Mr. Chiba.

Somebody touched my wrist.

I jumped.

"I'm here," Springer said, and I looked at him, holding both my hands away so nothing could touch them again.

"There's fourteen squares over here," I told him. "That makes one hundred sixty-eight in this part of the room." My palms were still itching. Sweat trickled down the side of my face, and I worked not to breathe like I had been running. "I don't know about the other room. Is a hearing the same as a trial?"

"I don't know anything about legal stuff," Springer said. Then, to Mr. Chiba, "Are the carpet squares in the hall and other rooms the same color as these?"

Mr. Chiba's voice sounded shaky when he said, "Yes."

Springer nodded. "Jesse may have to count them. I don't think she knew about this hearing thing, whatever it is."

"I see," Mr. Chiba said. "Well, a hearing is a preliminary step in the trial process. So it's part of a trial, but not the same thing. Lawyers talk about things in hearings, like evidence and plea deals and diversions, and the judge makes decisions about motions."

I dug my nails into my palms and scratched. "One hundred sixty-eight green squares," I said to Springer, because I couldn't look at Mr. Chiba because if I looked at him, I'd probably yell and scream until somebody took me home to my dog and my aunt Gus and my dad and maybe even Mom on the phone and I wouldn't be faking a meltdown. "One hundred sixty-eight. It's an even number. Twelve times fourteen, that's how I did it."

Springer reached out his hands and turned them both palm up. "Put your hands here so you don't accidentally scratch yourself too hard."

"No," I said. "That'll make my brain itch."

He looked confused. "Do you try to scratch your brain when it itches?"

"I—" My breath pulled in and out, in and out as I thought about that question. "Uh, no. I don't think so."

Springer smiled and his face did that shiny thing, and my chest got a little looser with each breath. "Then it's better than your hands and arms itching, right? 'Cause you won't make yourself bleed."

I put my palms on Springer's and stared at them.

My brain did itch.

I didn't try to scratch it.

I just kept breathing and multiplying to get to one sixty-eight. "Two times eighty-four. Three times fifty-six. Four times forty-two."

More smiling from Springer. "You are way better at math than I am."

"Six times twenty-eight," I said. "Seven times twenty-four. Eight times twenty-one."

When I stopped, Springer bit at his bottom lip. "Nine doesn't work. But twelve does. Twelve times fourteen."

I nodded.

"My brain doesn't itch about math," he said. "It just sort of hurts."

"I'm okay now," I told him. "I think."

I took my hands back.

He let me.

We both looked at Mr. Chiba.

His expression said his brain might be itching now. His fingers drummed on the folder on his desk. He said, "I have to go to the restroom. I'm going to trust both of you to sit right here and stay out of trouble."

He patted the thick folder and stared at Springer.

Springer stared back.

I felt like they were talking without words, but I had no idea what they were saying.

Mr. Chiba left the main room and walked around us, into the office's back hall. A second later, I heard a door close.

Springer hurried over to Mr. Chiba's desk. "Keep watch," he told me as he flipped the folder open.

"For what?" I didn't know whether to watch the hall or the office door or the folder.

"Watch for people," said Springer. "Don't let any of them in the office."

"Okay." I walked toward the office door, then worried about Mr. Chiba. So I walked back to where Springer was pawing through the folder pictures and taking snaps with his phone, went past him, and glanced down the back hall of the office. All the doors were still closed.

"Got it." He tucked his phone in his pocket.

When I just stood there looking confused and probably still a little itchy, he opened the gate between the desks and the chairs. "Jesse, I got the staff meeting attendance records! That's what he left on the desk."

The alarm buzzed until we shut the gate again.

I could still hear it ringing in my head even after it stopped.

"Sit," Springer told me. "Look innocent."

Oh, no. If my *smile* looked like biting, my *innocent* would probably come off like axe murderer.

I looked at my hands. Then the ceiling.

Probably the best thing was to look anywhere but right at Mr. Chiba.

By the time he came back out, Springer and I were both sitting in the chairs where we had been before he mentioned—

Nope. Don't think about Dad and court and hearings. You'll look like a freaked-out axe murderer then and that won't look innocent and don't smile, don't smile, don't smile because you'll look guilty—

Springer did innocent really, really well.

He nodded at Mr. Chiba, and Mr. Chiba nodded at him. When he turned his attention to me, I swallowed and held on to the chair so I wouldn't start scratching my hands again. I strained so hard to keep from looking at the carpet squares that my eyes watered.

Then I got a nod, too.

Why did that feel like I won something? I mean not like, yay, I came in first in a trivia contest or a hard computer game—but at least like winning a hand of cards or a game of checkers.

I couldn't take any more and glanced away, just in time to notice the sea of kids washing through the front doors, since it was nearly time for school to start. Jerkface was dead center in all the rampaging bodies, with Chris on one side and Trisha on the other. Jerkface and Chris gave me sneery looks. Trisha started to, but stopped. As they passed by the office, she turned her face away from me.

For some reason, that felt like a win, too.

At least until Mr. Chiba said, "Okay, you two. Head out, now. Time for class."

Springer and I looked at each other, then out into the

hall again, where Jerkface and the cockroaches were holding court. Chris and Ryker pretended to shoot baskets using crumpled paper, and people made rings with their arms. I could imagine Springer or me getting tossed in the air like those paper wads, so I didn't move.

Springer didn't move, either.

Mr. Chiba narrowed his eyes at us, then glanced into the hall over our heads. The corners of his mouth pulled down in a frown. "I see," he said. "Well. How about I walk you to the library, and you can go to class from there, when you want to?"

"Thank you," Springer said, but Mr. Chiba waved off his appreciation. He came out from behind the counter, then led us into the hall, locking the office door behind him.

"Let's hurry," he said. "I'll have to sign in late students in about five minutes."

"Yes, sir," Springer said, and that got him a wink.

Mr. Chiba led the way to the library, and we hustled behind him, ignoring all the noise behind us. I was almost positive I heard some whistling and jeering, and maybe one *Messy Jesse*, but I didn't look back.

We looped around the main hall, past the biggest set of bathrooms and the line of girls spilling out into the hallway, fixing hair and straightening clothes using mirrors in backpacks, reflections in the windows—whatever they could find. I figured guys did that sort of thing, too, only they could use the bathroom a lot faster, so they didn't have lines too much of the time.

"We need bathroom parity," I told Springer as we got to the library.

"What?" Mr. Chiba asked.

"The bathroom," I said. "It doesn't have enough stalls for all the girls who need to use it. We need more stalls because girls don't pee as fast as boys. Since we have to sit down and all."

Mr. Chiba stopped us at the first library table, an old round one with colored chairs. "Okay," he said, and I noticed he was blushing. Springer was blushing, too. Neither of them looked at me, but seemed like they wanted to catalogue every book on the nearest shelf instead.

I looked at the shelf. The top line of books had twenty-three, but since books came in all sizes and shapes, there wouldn't be twenty-three on the second line, and I probably shouldn't start counting, because it would be hard to stop and I just couldn't figure why talking about peeing made Springer and Mr. Chiba blush. What was wrong with talking about peeing and the fact girls took longer than boys, and needed more spaces to sit down?

Mr. Chiba patted Springer on the head. "Don't let those hooligans bother you, you hear me? If they harass you at all, go straight to the nearest teacher. Those kids are on notice about their bullying, and so are their parents. One more episode from any of them, and they'll face serious consequences."

"Yes, sir," Springer said. He had his phone out, fidgeting with it, but managed not to look at it, which was good, I guess, because sometimes older people reacted to phones like they did to me bringing up peeing.

I managed to keep my mouth shut until Mr. Chiba left, so he didn't have to scratch behind his ear or anything. The second row of books on the shelf in front of us had thirty-two books. They were all yellow and nearly the same size, so it was hard to count them.

"What are you squinting at?" Springer asked.

"The yellow books." I pointed, then put my hand down because I remembered Mom telling me once that pointing was rude. Jeez, people had a lot of rules that made no sense.

"Oh," Springer said. "Yeah. It's hard to count those because they all look alike. It's the yellow, too."

"Pee is yellow," I told him.

This time, he didn't blush. He just said, "It is."

"Why was it wrong to talk about pee, back in the office?"

Springer looked down at his phone and started pushing buttons. "Body functions embarrass most people. Pee, and poop, and farting. All that stuff. They just don't talk about it in front of older people like Mr. Chiba, or in . . . I don't know, certain situations. It's hard to explain."

"So don't mention body functions in conversation?" My eyes went back to the shelf, but I closed them so I wouldn't count.

"It's kinda like trespassing, only not illegal." Springer sounded distracted. He used his fingers to resize something on his phone screen.

"You can trespass by talking about pee and poop?"

"Not really," he mumbled, staring even harder at his phone screen. "It's just kind of gross to talk about."

"So don't do it." My brain started to itch.

"Unless we're alone," he said.

"How alone do we have to be?"

"It doesn't matter, Jesse." Springer sounded really, really worried about something. "Open your eyes and look at this."

I opened my eyes.

He held out his phone, and I took it.

I found myself looking at a grid, or some kind of spreadsheet. It had names on it with black Xs beside them, all but two. Those two had red Xs.

Oh.

Oh, wow.

When I looked at Springer again, his eyes were wide. "You see it, right?"

"Yeah. This is way better than pee, anyway." I went back to the phone, to the attendance record Springer had photographed. On the day the money went missing from my father's classroom, two people had missed the staff meeting. The red Xs glowed like *guilty* brands right beside their names.

Out loud, I said, "Ms. Jorgensen and Coach Sedon. What does it mean? I mean, why were they—and if they were involved with the money going missing—"

I lowered the phone, feeling giddy and freaked out at the same time. "Ms. Jorgensen is supposed to be helping find the real thief, and Coach Sedon, too. All the teachers should be helping, right? Just like the police. Just like OBWIG. Us, I mean."

I sort of had to pee all of a sudden, and wondered if I could say that, or if it would be trespassing right now, here in the library, where mostly only Springer could hear me. My cheeks got hot, partly because I was worried about Dad, and partly because the world had all these strange rules that didn't make any sense to me, and I'd never get them all right.

"All the grown-ups should be helping, yeah," Springer said. "The fact that the head grown-up might be a problem—it's bad, Jesse."

I thought about Coach Sedon and Ms. Jorgensen arguing outside the senior high entrance the day before. Had they been fighting about the stolen money? Did one of them know the other was guilty? Were they in it together and they were just worried Springer and I were going to figure everything out and turn them in?

"My father's in serious trouble, isn't he?" I whispered, and not because I was trying to use a library voice.

"Maybe," Springer whispered back. "But OBWIG can save him."

"OBWIG," I echoed.

"OBWIG forever," Springer said, like it would be automatic now. "We have the initial people from the ledger to question. We have this information about the staff meeting, and I don't need to jump to conclusions. We need a plan, Jesse."

The bell for first period rang.

My stomach lurched, then clenched. I really did have to pee, trespassing or not.

Springer and I looked toward the librarian's office at the same time.

Her door was shut.

I glanced at the clock above her door. In four minutes and twenty-six seconds, the final bell would ring, and Springer and I might be marked absent from social studies if our teacher noticed. Since we were supposed to study battles in the Revolutionary War and I hadn't exactly done the weekend reading, that part didn't bother me.

Springer motioned to me and pointed to a table in the back of the library, half hidden by a partition. It was the place people went to listen to audiobooks or watch stuff on the computer with sound, if they didn't want to use headphones.

It was the perfect place to make a plan, at least until somebody told Mr. Chiba we weren't in class and he called our parents and we both got locked in our rooms until we turned twenty.

I decided I could hold my pee, and trespass or go to the bathroom or whatever later.

We headed toward the table.

19

Friday, Three Days Earlier, Afternoon

I didn't have to pee anymore, at least not at the moment, because I went when we left the library, before we stuffed our backpacks in our lockers. That was good because I kept coughing.

Springer and I stood in the dark spot under the junior high's back stairs, neither of us moving. I wondered if people tromping up the concrete stairs could hear my heart *thud-thud-thud*ding, or the way Springer's throat sort of whistled when he breathed.

We had talked and sketched things and made lists for almost an hour, but in the end, the plan turned out simple enough: question the people on our list from the donation ledger, then question Coach Sedon and Ms. Jorgensen. Or, question as many of all of them as we could before we got yelled at or suspended or sent to alternative classes.

"Or killed," I muttered, because if Coach Sedon and Ms. Jorgensen stole money and they were trying to blame Dad, they might kill us.

"People kill you if you find out about their crimes," I told Springer when I realized he was staring at me.

As the crowd started to slow above our heads, he whispered, "I don't think the library fund is enough money to kill for. And it smells like gym socks under here."

"Worse," I choked back. "Moldy old cheese. Covered with motor oil."

He gagged.

"Shhhhh," I told him.

He shhhhhed.

A few more kids went by. Jerkface and the cockroaches had probably already gone upstairs to the same math class we were about to miss, but I couldn't be sure. I didn't hear them in all the ruckus.

When no more footsteps echoed above our heads, I turned to Springer. "Do you have the paper?"

"It's here." He held up a bunch of papers, not just one.

We had gone to second-period computer science, and then I went to English while Springer went to health, and then we both went to lunch just to keep suspicion down.

Springer handed me one of the papers. "How does it look?" He held up a letter Ms. Jorgensen had sent out last week, something about not selling cookies to support Little League during school hours. It had her signature stamped on the bottom. The other paper was a plain, typed paragraph that read, *Please excuse _____ from class and have them report to the senior high office.* It was signed, too, like Ms. Jorgensen had sent it.

Only . . .

"It kinda looks like a kid squiggled Ms. Jorgensen's name," I said.

Springer frowned. "Does it need to be more squiggly or less squiggly?"

"I don't know. Maybe less shaky? And smaller?"

Springer crumpled up the first note and got down on his knees. He found a mostly not-disgusting spot on the grimy floor, a part where a little bit of light let us see the letters on the printed page, and he tried again with another copy.

Now I understood why he made so many, and I squinted at the result of his second try. "Better. Just, still smaller, or something."

"You want to try?"

"No. It'd be awful if I did it."

Springer handed me the rejected note and made another while I tore up the first one and crammed the pieces in my jeans pockets.

This time when Springer showed me the permission note, the signature looked passable. We printed in *Josh Sharp* in the blank, then made one each for *Maleka Keston* and *Nancy Newsom.*

"They aren't perfect," Springer admitted, staring at the three notes. "But maybe the teachers won't look too close."

He picked up the letters and handed them to me. Then he dusted off the knees of his jeans, but the black streaks from the floor stayed.

I folded the letters and put them in my pocket, feeling . . . weird, somehow. I wasn't scared, because I knew I needed to do this for Dad. Really, that I had to do it, especially now that I knew that the principal and one of the other teachers might want him to look like a thief. I didn't really even feel nervous. More worried, and—

Yeah. Guilty. That was new.

I blinked at Springer, who had stepped back into the stinky darkness under the steps to get his clothes and backpack straight. "You know, we'll probably get detention, or maybe suspended just for going over there again. I can get to the senior high by myself. You don't have to do this."

"Yes, I do," Springer said, like it was no big deal.

I thought about asking him why, but before I could say anything, he added, "Of course I have to do this with you. You'd go with me if it were my dad in trouble, right?"

"Yes," I said. Then, "Well, maybe if it were your mom. I don't think your dad is very nice to you."

"He—Dad's okay. He's just really stressed out about money, and he works too much." Springer stayed in the shadows where I couldn't totally see his expression, but his voice sounded normal-Springery, like that was all the truth.

"But he's mean to you," I said, "like Jerkface and the cockroaches are mean to me. To us."

"They're mean because they're jerkfaces and cock-roaches." Springer eased out of the shadows, and I could see he was actually smiling. "Dad's not really mean at all. Just sort of stern. He pushes me to get ahead in life so I never have the problems he's had."

I really didn't see how stern and pushy didn't add up to mean, but if Springer thought it was different, I was okay with that. Sort of. But I still didn't want to get him in trouble. "I'll feel bad if you get kicked out of school and murdered by your parents for trying to help me."

"They won't murder me." He smiled even wider. "Maybe take my phone and holler a lot, but it'll be okay."

"Will you run away to the clubhouse if it gets too bad?"

"Yeah."

"Okay, then." I glanced at the underside of the stairs. The part I could see had maybe a million wads of gum stuck on it. Ew. "Let's go."

We eased out from the cover of the stairs and hustled down the hall, then hurried straight out the back door we knew was one of the four designated daytime exits that wouldn't set off an alarm in the office.

"Slow," Springer reminded me, and I eased my speed a little. We kept to the sidewalk, not trying to hide, since that would just make teachers notice us more, or at least that was Springer's opinion during our big planning session in the library.

"Slow," he repeated. "But with purpose."

Slow, with purpose. Yeah.

"Slow-with-purpose," I said out loud.

"That's it. Kinda like a marching song."

"Slow-with-pur-pose," I said, like I was military-marching. "Slow-with-pur-pose."

"Don't really march, Jesse. That'll make people look at us."

"We're almost to the back door, though."

"Teachers would still notice somebody marching."

"Fiiiine."

It was last period at the senior high, since the older kids came to school earlier than we did and left earlier, too. Luckily, the teachers tended to leave the back doors propped open late in the day, especially this time of year when it was so hot in the afternoon. That worked in our favor just exactly like I thought it would when we planned at the library table, and as we got into one of the senior high halls, I had that "win" feeling again so strong I let out a little whoop.

"Shhhhhhh," Springer said immediately. "No whooping. No marching. Nothing to make people look. OBWIG is cool. OBWIG is barely visible."

"OBWIG forever," I said, and then I hushed for a fraction of a second, and then I whispered, "Okay, here's the tricky part."

Springer nodded as I pulled a note out of my pocket. It turned out to be the one with Josh Sharp's name on it. Sweat broke out in a line on Springer's forehead, but when he looked up, his jaw had that tight, determined set I had learned meant he was ready to do something even if it was scary.

"I can go first," I told him. "If I blow it, you could run back to the junior high and—"

He shook his head. Turned away from me and walked to the first classroom and knocked, just like we had planned. I hurried to the nearest locker and tried to look busy.

A teacher answered, a man I didn't know.

"Yes?" he said to Springer, then narrowed his eyes. "Who are you?"

"Sp—uh, Sam," Springer said. "I'm new." He thrust out the letter. "I need to see Josh Sharp. He's supposed to go to the office."

"Josh Sharp isn't in this class, Sam."

Springer blinked. Seemed to remember Sam was actually him, for the moment. "I'm sorry, sir. This was the class number they wrote down. Would you have any idea where I should look for Mr. Sharp?"

From inside the class, we heard snickers. Somebody said, "*Mister* Sharp?"

The teacher glared over his shoulder at this students. "Funny. Do any of you wiseacres know which class Sharp is in now?"

"He's in English Three, Mr. Deng," a girl said. "One hall over to the right, with Ms. Dionne."

"There you have it, Sam," the teacher said.

"Thank—" Springer started, but the door closed in his face.

When Springer looked at me, I shrugged. Rude people didn't bother me much, probably because I was rude a lot, too, even if my rude was mostly by accident. Our plan had worked just exactly like we thought. Even though we didn't have any class schedules, we just had to start looking, and somebody would tell us the right way to go.

Springer walked over to where I was standing, and then slowly, with focus, OBWIG headed to the study hub. We turned right, then found ourselves facing another hallway full of closed doors.

No problem. We had planned for this, too. Springer walked straight to the first door and knocked on it.

Another male teacher answered. I'd seen him before, but I didn't know his name. I bent over to work on the lock of my pretend locker, so he wouldn't recognize me.

"Oh, I'm sorry, sir," Springer said. "I'm looking for Ms. Dionne's class. I thought this was it."

"Four down," the teacher told him, jerking a thumb over Springer's head.

"Thank you," Springer said before the guy managed to slam that door in his face, too.

A few seconds later, Springer knocked on the correct

door. Like before, I pretended to be opening a locker, but my hands shook so badly I couldn't even turn the knob.

Ms. Dionne turned out to be a very short lady with big black eyes and dreadlocks. She snatched the note out of Springer's hands, and my heart almost stopped beating. As she studied it, I saw Springer back up a step, like he was thinking about running, which I thought was fine, because I was ready to roll, too. Fifteen running steps would get us back to the study hub. We could haul cookies out the front door, or blast back down the hall we came in.

"Sharp!" she barked, loud enough that Springer and I both jumped. "Office wants you."

She handed the note back to Springer, who took it, dropped it, grabbed it out of the air before it hit the ground, and almost crumpled it in his palms.

"Apparently, you're so bad you need an escort," Ms. Dionne said to a lanky boy with long brown hair, distressed khakis, and hints of a chin beard who came slouching out the door. One of his white shirttails wasn't tucked in, like it was an accident, but I wondered if it really was. He laughed at his teacher, then looked down at us and laughed again as she shut the door.

"What is this?" Josh Sharp wanted to know. "Munchkin patrol?"

"We aren't that short," I said.

He kept right on laughing, and I was suddenly sure, absolutely positive that my uncle Jesse would have looked something like this guy when he was alive, and that he would have laughed at us, too.

"Yeah, you're that short," Josh Sharp said. "And you aren't senior high." He pointed to our jeans. "Out of dress code. What are you doing over here? And who busted you in the eye, dude?"

"It had to do with baseball," Springer told him, steering him down the hall away from the study hub. "This way, okay?"

"But it's shorter to go to the office the other way," Sharp complained, looking over his shoulder but following Springer anyway. "What'd I do, anyway?"

"Nothing," Springer said. "Probably just, um, student council stuff."

"Wait." Sharp stopped so fast I ran right into him from behind.

"Ouch," I mumbled. Then, "Sorry."

"I resigned like three weeks ago," Sharp said. "Why would the office want me for council stuff?"

We were so close to the back door. Like, a body length. And if we got him outside—

"Maybe I had it wrong," Springer covered smoothly. "I just know Ms. Jorgensen wants to see you."

Sharp's eyes shrank to slits. "Okay, seriously. What are you two little goons up to?"

I found myself counting the almost-holes in his pants. Three total. No wait. Four. And I couldn't see the other side—

"Sorry, Josh," Springer said. "Uh, Sharp. Or whatever we should call you. We are up to something. I'm Springer, and this is Jesse. We're from the junior high."

Sharp still looked suspicious, but his posture loosened a fraction. "Yeah, no kidding—oh, wait, I heard about you. Didn't you guys get in trouble over here yesterday? Busted a couple of bullies in the face with water bottles?"

"Springer doesn't hit people," I said. "I threw the water bottles."

Sharp turned his attention to me, and his slit eyes became wide eyes. "You're Mr. Broadview's kid. The smart autistic girl."

"Smart?" I echoed.

"Yeah. The one who's a whiz with numbers." He gave me a giant grin, sweet as any Springer could come up with. "That's why you get to go to regular school and all, right?"

My mouth and brain seemed to be stuck on echo, because the best I could do was "Regular school."

Sharp looked from me to Springer, who translated with "What she means is, do you remember donating to the library fund the day the fund got stolen?"

After folding his arms, Sharp nodded. "Yeah, I bring Mr. Broadview money every paycheck, because he's seriously cool. Did you know that, Jesse? That your dad is seriously cool?"

"He is seriously cool," I said, trying to process that

other kids might see my father as cool and feeling a little jealous. And why was I crossing my arms?

Stop echoing everything!

"So you have a job?" I asked.

"Sure," Sharp told us. "I've worked at Tom's Hardware since my sophomore year. Now I'm doing the work exchange."

"You get a paycheck," Springer said, and I worried he was sliding into echo mode, too.

Sharp nodded. "Yeah."

"He probably doesn't need money, then," Springer said to me.

"Did you steal anything out my dad's drawer?" I asked him, hating how high-pitched my voice sounded. "Because he's gonna go to jail unless I figure out who really took that money."

"Hey, little dudes, I didn't steal anything," Sharp said. "I'm no thief. And even if I were, I wouldn't snatch anything from Mr. Broadview."

He seemed so believable, now that I could see into his Uncle Jesse eyes, and take in his Springer-like smile. But what did I know? I was just the smart autistic girl, or whatever it was he called me.

"He seems legit," Springer said, making me feel a little less out of control and alien to the planet.

I nodded.

"Are you autistic, too?" Sharp asked Springer.

Springer hesitated. "I don't know."

"Why would you think I took that money?" Sharp asked, and he seemed to be talking to both of us.

"Your name was on the list," I told him. "Everybody who donated that day probably saw how much was in the drawer, or read the total in Dad's ledger."

Sharp seemed to weigh what I said, and he gave us two thumbs up. "Not bad. Pretty smart, even. Who are your other names?"

Springer and I shared a glance, and we both seemed to decide Sharp was okay at the same moment.

"Maleka Keston," I said.

Springer said, "Nancy Newsom."

Neither of us said anything about Ms. Jorgensen or Coach Sedon, but Sharp whistled low and long, like we had spilled everything. "Listen," he said. "I'll do you a solid, little dudes. Both of those girls have last-period band—but I wouldn't suggest you march up to them and ask them if they stole money."

"Why not?" Springer asked.

"Because they'll straight-up slap your face," Sharp responded.

"Oh," I said, and my fingers moved to my cheek.

"Am I cleared?" Sharp asked us.

I didn't know what to say, but Springer came up with "Yes, for now. We'll find you if we have any more questions."

"You do that," Sharp said. He bowed to each of us like we were royalty, then turned his back on us and headed off to his class again.

I faced Springer. "Slapping sounds bad."

"We know where they are," he said. He glanced at his phone. "It's still twenty-eight minutes before senior high classes dismiss for the day. We can make it to the gym."

"That boy just said Nancy and Maleka are going to hit us," I reminded him.

"I think that was a figure of speech," Springer said. "I mean, I think what Sharp meant is, we have to be more careful when we question them."

He was backing away, toward the doors, but I didn't move. My joints felt icy, and my brain itched and itched and itched. "You do realize I talk about pee when I shouldn't, right?"

Because I'm the smart autistic girl.

Springer grinned at me. "How about don't talk about pee, okay? We'll keep it simple."

"No pee," I said. "Simple." And then, because Springer somehow made everything feel possible, I said, "Okay."

Springer turned and started to jog toward the open door, aiming for the room attached to the gym, the one with the giant BAND ROOM placard over the door. Even this far away, we could hear the faint sound of tubas grumping and humphing, and every now and then, the crash of a cymbal.

Still rubbing one of my cheeks, I followed him.

20

Friday, Three Days Earlier, Later in the Afternoon

That's not the principal's signature," Maleka Keston said, her voice cutting under squiggly blasts from people playing trombones in the next section.

She stood with her knee on a bench next to her instrument, and she waved our note at us as the other three tuba players seemed to be spitting into their mouthpieces and fiddling with valves as faraway flutes tweeted and saxophones wailed and oboes let out reedy, sad whines. Since percussion instruments were in the far left corner of the band room, grouped together and a little away from the brass and woodwinds, Springer and I had our backs to everyone else. All the instruments seemed to be arguing with each other. My brain twitched and spun and tried to leak out my ear. I crowded so close to Springer that my shoulder rubbed his. He didn't move. A drum boomed from like five feet away, and we both jumped.

Maleka towered over us, glaring down like she planned to call the police, then pick up her big green tuba and stuff it over our heads to hold us until they arrived. Her white blouse had a starched collar, and her khakis still looked crisp and pressed even though it was late in the day. The muscles in her arms rippled and flexed as she waited for us to respond.

"It's not Ms. Jorgensen's signature," I admitted. "We wrote the note because we needed to talk to you."

Trumpets blasted all at once, and Springer and I jumped again.

I closed my eyes and waited to merge with Maleka's tuba.

"Open your eyes, Jesse," Springer hissed.

"Can't," I said. It was like my eyelids had glued themselves together. My ears wished they could stick shut, too, especially when the clarinets really got going.

"What's wrong with her?" Maleka asked Springer. "And who hit you in the face?"

"Probably the noise," he said. "And she's worried about her father. That's why we're here. Oh, and a bully hit me last week, but it's okay because my eye's getting better. All the color should be gone soon."

Pause.

Then, "Who's her dad?" Maleka asked.

"Mr. Broadview."

"Oh! She's—oh." Something in Maleka's tone changed. "And the money getting stolen. You know, it's bogus how they blamed him. Mr. B would never do anything like that."

That unstuck my eyes, and I was able to look at her again, and even use my voice. "We agree. We're trying to find out who would."

Maleka's gaze shifted from Springer to me. "So why do you need to talk to me?"

"You were one of the people who gave money the day the fund got stolen," Springer said. "We thought—well . . ."

He stopped. His cheeks flushed.

Maleka stopped staring at me and studied Springer instead. "I get it. You're being detectives, and I'm a suspect."

"Something like that," Springer mumbled.

She grabbed her tuba and popped out its mouthpiece.

Both of us flinched, and she laughed at us. "It's okay," she said. "I'll play." She glanced at an office door about ten feet from us, with DIRECTOR etched into the frosty glass. "We have ten minutes before Mr. Quo comes out to inspect our cases and trunks and be sure we stowed our instruments correctly."

"He doesn't need to see us," Springer said.

"Or you'll be in a lot of trouble?" Maleka gave us a look.

"You have no idea," I said.

"Best be careful, then." Maleka jerked her chin toward the teacher's door. "That one's a hard-a—um, he's a real rule-follower. Very strict. So go on. Hurry up and ask me all your little investigative question thingees before he comes out here and busts you."

I tried to speak, sort of wheezed, then got the words out. "When did you see Dad—I mean, Mr. Broadview that day?"

"I have his class third period, so around nine forty-five." Maleka kept her eyes on her mouthpiece, polishing it with a cloth.

Senior high classes were an hour and fifteen minutes, so she would have been in Dad's room until about eleven. "Is that when you gave him your donation?"

"Yes."

"Do you give regularly?" Springer asked.

Maleka reached into the nearest trunk and took out a plastic case. As she fit her mouthpiece inside it, she said, "Not that often. We play Shakespeare Trivia on Mondays, and the losing team has to give to the fund, if they can." She grinned at Springer, and he backed up a step. "I don't lose often, so my team doesn't usually have to pay."

"Got it," Springer squeaked.

From over my right shoulder came a lot of oboe-ing. Bad oboe-ing. It almost sounded like somebody trying to blow snot out of one side of a stuffy nose.

It was my turn to make words again, and I did my best to use it well. "Could you tell if the rest of the fund was still in the drawer when you donated?"

Maleka put her finger on her cheek, and she really seemed to be thinking, not just messing with us. "I think so. When he opened the box to drop our donation in, I saw money."

My heart beat faster, but in a good way. So now we knew almost for sure that the money disappeared sometime between eleven and the end of the staff meeting at four thirty. I got so excited, I didn't even think too hard about my next question, which was "What's your financial situation?"

"That's a nosy question." Maleka snatched up her tuba. "You know that, right?"

I leaned away from her, wondering if she'd changed her mind about stuffing her instrument over our heads.

"Did I trespass?" I whispered to Springer.

"Maybe a little," he said.

Maleka gently placed her tuba in the trunk with her mouthpiece. "Did you take the library fund money?" Springer asked her.

"I didn't," Maleka said.

"Are you going to hit us because we asked?" The question popped out before I could stop it.

"Trespassing," Springer whispered loudly. "Trespassing, trespassing . . ."

Maleka rolled her eyes. "I am so not a bully. Seriously, who told you I'd hit you?"

"Josh Sharp," I said, even as Springer said, "Nobody," then glared at me.

I had no idea what I'd done wrong so I ignored him.

Maleka laughed. "Sharp's a suspect, too?"

"He was," Springer admitted, "but he's not as much now."

"Why, because you liked him?" Maleka laughed again.

"Yeah," I said. "He sort of, um, looked like my dead uncle and all, so . . ."

I stopped, because even I realized how strange that sounded.

"Everybody likes Sharp," Maleka said. "But he's a mess. He dropped off student council last month because he got arrested."

Cold chills plunged up and down my neck, and the world seemed to tilt a little. I tried to process what I'd just heard, but I couldn't match that with the Springer grin the guy had given us, and—but my dad got arrested, and he was a nice guy, too, but—

"For what?" Springer asked.

Maleka waved her hand in front of her face like she was shooing a fly. "He tagged the outside gym wall with his lame initials in gold spray paint, like nobody would figure out it was him. Only J.S. in senior high. Idiot."

"He said my dad was cool, and he has a job, so he doesn't need the money, and we trusted him," I said, starting to feel numb on the inside.

"Legal charges can be expensive." She shrugged. "Just sayin'. Who are your other suspects?"

"Nancy Newsom," I mumbled, and almost said Ms. Jorgensen and Coach Sedon and threw in Jerkface and the cockroaches for good measure, but Springer stepped on my toe and I shut up.

Most people had stopped playing instruments, and I heard a lot of paper shuffling and cases opening as Maleka's eyes drifted over our heads, toward the front of the room where the flute players were sitting. "Okay, yeah. Nancy. She's one to look at."

"Because she needs money?" Springer asked.

As the other three tuba players slammed their trunks, Maleka said, "How about because she's plain mean? Come on. I'll give you a hand." She turned around to the guy nearest the teacher's door and said, "James, if Mr. Quo comes out, can you handle him?"

The big guy shifted his tuba and nodded.

Maleka took off walking, and Springer and I had to wheel around to follow her. Maleka swept past the trumpet players and clarinets, right to the front row near the door, to where a girl was sitting in the first chair. She was bent over, putting her flute into a tiny case on the tile floor.

When she sat straight in her chair again, I saw that her white blouse was silky with a lace collar, and her khaki pants seemed smooth and fancy, too. Her brown hair was pulled back at the base of her neck, her dark eyes had a hint of ice at the edges, and her pretty face seemed vaguely familiar, just like it did when I looked at her picture in the yearbook.

Springer pulled up short next to me and gaped at her, and I could tell he thought she looked familiar, too.

Her cool gaze snapped from us to Maleka. "What do you want?"

Maleka pointed at us. "They want to know if you stole that money out of Mr. Broadview's desk."

My mouth came open. I mean, I knew I was tact-free, but Maleka didn't seem to be much better.

"The library fund?" The girl, Nancy—she sounded genuinely surprised. "I donate to that every month. Why would I take anything out of it?"

One of Maleka's eyebrows arched up. "Every month, huh? What, you got a big sense of civic duty?"

Nancy picked up her flute case from the floor and nestled it in her lap. "It's for my little brother. I'm out of here at graduation, but he's got to go to this dump two more years. And he likes to read."

The lines of her face. That not-friendly smile. So familiar. But from where?

"Do we know her?" Springer whispered to me.

I gave him a one-shoulder shrug because I couldn't figure it out.

"I didn't know you had a little brother," Maleka said. "More people like you in the universe. Who knew? Jeez."

"Nobody asked your opinion," Nancy snapped. Her eyes darted to the clock, and to the door. "Look, I gotta go. My best friend and her little sister will be here in a minute. I'm giving them a ride home since their parents had to work."

"Do we know her?" Springer whispered to me again, sounding tighter and more nervous.

"What's your friend's name?" I asked Nancy.

She leveled that chilly stare at me. "What's yours?"

"Don't," Springer said, but I was already talking.

"Jesse Broadview."

A few papers shuffled. A few more cases snapped shut. Then silence seemed to grab the room.

"Ooooh." Nancy's grin turned nasty. "I know who you are. The weird kid. Messy Jesse. Right?"

And then it clicked.

The color of her hair. The sharpness of her face. "Your best friend is Meredith Parks, Trisha's older sister. You were at their house last night, sitting in the swing."

She winked at me, turning my stomach into an arctic ocean of dread.

The band room door slammed open, and in came Meredith and Trisha, followed by Chris and Ryker. For a few seconds, they looked sort of normal, if you didn't count the pine branch scratches all over Ryker's face, and Chris's, too. Then they spotted Springer and me, and mean-masks seemed to drop down, replacing their smiles with smirks.

"Well, look at this," Chris said. "It's the two spies, butting in where they don't belong. Again."

"Jesse," Springer said in his lowest, calmest voice. "We need to go."

Which was true and all, but Jerkface and the cockroaches were blocking the main door.

From behind us, another door opened, and a man's voice bellowed, "Inspection!"

All the band members leaped to their feet or ran to their trunks. The ones with cases held them out.

Springer and I tried to melt in between the band people as they grabbed their stuff so the band director couldn't see us. We couldn't get in trouble again so soon. This time, Springer might really get suspended, and my father would probably have an aneurysm.

The saxophone dude we were hiding behind shifted, and the band director looked right at us. Then he glanced at Jerkface and the cockroaches, too.

"You—uh, driving all these kids home?" Mr. Quo asked Nancy. "Because I only agreed to Meredith and three others meeting you here. I'll need to see passes and notes if they're all missing their study period at the junior high."

I sucked in a breath and held it. Springer said something like "We don't need a ride," but it sounded more like he almost threw up.

Maleka moved closer and put an arm around Springer's shoulders. "Those ones in the door, they're the ones that blacked your eye?" she asked him in a low voice.

"One of them, yeah," Springer whispered back.

Maleka's head whipped to the back of the room, and I realized she was staring straight at the other tuba players—three huge guys. She gestured to the one she had called by name, James, and he got up and cut off Mr. Quo, asking something about his mouthpiece.

Maleka gestured to the other two tuba players, and they headed to us.

It took them one breath to get there. Two breaths. Three breaths.

The bell rang.

"If you want out of here before you get in serious trouble with Quo, go now," Maleka said. "We'll get you past the buttheads in the door, but then you're on your own."

"Okay," Springer said, and with that, Maleka and her two friends surrounded Springer and me. Somebody grabbed my arm. I tried to pull away, but Maleka leaned down to my ear and growled, "Move."

I moved. Or rather, I let her drag me forward, stumbling to keep up.

"Hey!" Mr. Quo shouted, stepping out from behind James, who was still trying to talk to him.

Maleka and her friends hustled us toward the band room door, muscling Jerkface and the cockroaches and Meredith and Nancy out of the way.

All of a sudden, Springer and I were in the hall, and Maleka let me go, and one of the tuba players said, "Better hustle. These three seem wicked mad about something or other, and Mr. Quo's gonna get a better look at your faces if you don't move."

I almost stopped to work out those words, but Springer yelled, "Jesse, run!"

My legs started to churn, even though I had no idea where I was going. Springer's hand found mine, and we moved together, fast, out into the grassy area in front of the gym and band room.

From somewhere behind us, I heard Jerkface holler at the tuba players, then snarl, "We told you what would happen if you bugged us again, Messy. We told you!"

Then I heard the teacher shouting for us to stop, but we didn't turn around and we didn't even slow down.

21

Monday, After the Train Came

Not a dog.
  Not a dog.
  Not a dog!

My heart stopped beating all over again, and I couldn't breathe, and the world shrank into a tiny little spot, a tiny little place where boards and pink stuff and bricks fell inward, where I could see inside my house, a few feet down to the floor, where some boards were still attached to each other in a V shape, like a camping tent made all out of wood.

The wood hadn't splintered even though it had fallen over, and a bunch of stuff had bashed down on top of it— stuff Springer and I had cleared.

Something moved under that tent.

Something definitely bigger than a dog.

Some rocks and wood pieces moved as a leg kicked out from under the wood tent.

A leg wrapped in a pink bathrobe.

"Help me," came the weak cry. "Please. Someone help me!"

The leg disappeared.

We heard stuff moving around under the wood tent. Then stuff at the other end of it shifted, and a hand scrabbled into view.

A hand with fingernails coated in cracked red polish.

22

Friday, Three Days Earlier, End of School

Springer pulled me through the grass between the front of the gym and the band room, and then I pulled him. For a few seconds, we ran toward the senior high back entrance, and then I turned us toward the junior high. Because I knew it better. Because it seemed safer.

We hit a puddle and splashed.

People shouted behind us.

"Where?" Springer yelled.

"I don't—"

But then I sort of did.

I ran for the door we had come out of when we snuck away from our side of the campus, dragging Springer behind me. I knew I needed to do something to confuse the people chasing us, so I hollered, "Upstairs!" as loud as I could. "The chemistry storeroom!"

Springer started to slow down, because he had no idea what I was talking about, but I pulled him with me as air rasped out of my lungs, as we got to the doors, as we glanced at our reflections and saw Jerkface and the cockroaches coming for us, fast. They were halfway across the grass already, looking just as mad as they had looked when they caught us spying—or even later, after I hit them with the branch. That was the kind of mad that didn't care about rules or teachers or anything else except getting even. That was the kind of mad I didn't want any part of.

Trying not to slow down too much, I jerked the door open. Springer and I threw ourselves into the back hall of the junior high and the door swung shut behind us. He didn't resist as I pulled him the few running steps to the stairs, and back under them into the hidden spot where we had finished our plan to go to the senior high.

Into the stinky darkness we went, as far as our bodies would fit, hunching down, then crawling.

Don't think about rotten plastered gum on stair bottoms.

Don't count rotten plastered gum on stair bottoms?

Was that a sock?

Gross, that was definitely a spiderweb.

"They'll go upstairs because of what they heard me yell," I whispered. "They'll try the chemistry storeroom door and an alarm will go off. I set it off last year by mistake—it's really loud. We'll be able to get away while everybody's paying attention to that, okay?"

"I don't think I can do this." Springer pressed both hands into his face. "It smells so bad, and they're mean, and—"

"OBWIG," I said. I touched his knuckles with my finger-tips. "OBWIG forever."

"OBWIG forever," he muttered. His hands shook against his face, but he stopped freaking out.

Then we pressed ourselves into the corner where the stairs joined the wall and the floor, so close together I could feel Springer's breath on my face.

Don't count the breaths.

One. Two. Three. Four . . .

The doors near the stairs banged wide open and light shot across the shadows.

Both of us didn't breathe at all.

Jerkface and the cockroaches charged right in front of where we were hiding without ever looking in our direc-tion. Their feet slammed onto the stairs, and it sounded like a herd of wild mustangs stampeded up to the second floor. More feet went by. Kids following them to see the fight. Maybe Mr. Quo. I didn't know.

Springer breathed and choked a little.

I breathed without choking. But neither of us could quit shaking. I didn't know what to do next. If we ran away again, would they hear us? Could they catch us if we got a big head start?

Where should we go?

My fingers tapped against Springer's knuckles. I could barely see his face in the dark, but I knew his eyes were closed.

I closed mine, too, and tried not to imagine what would happen if they caught us. I didn't want Springer to get another black eye. And he definitely would, because there were three of them and only two of us, and Springer didn't believe in fighting, and I was all out of water bottles.

The storeroom bell rang. Three quick bursts, all over the school. So loud.

We both opened our eyes.

I wondered if I looked as terrified as Springer did.

I got to my feet, smacked my head on the gummy concrete, staggered, and reached for Springer. "Come on. Let's try to get to the office."

Springer eased up on his knees, then his feet, and then he grabbed my fingers, folding them into his sweaty fist.

"I'm scared," he whispered.

"Me too," I said.

We lurched out from under the stairs, right about the time we heard the thundering herd coming back down, right over our heads. My muscles tried to lock.

No.

One, two, three, four, five, six—

Nothing to count but steps. Short at first. Then bigger. I heard Jerkface yell something that sounded like *Messy*.

I pushed Springer ahead of me, through a set of double doors and into the junior high's main hall. He tried to stop and turn around, but as I half ran, half fell through the doors, I hollered, "Go to the office. Get help!"

He jogged backward and almost splattered himself on a doorjamb. "I'm not leaving you, Jesse."

"Move!" I shouted to him, and he started running again, and so did I, but somebody grabbed my arm and jerked me to a stop. Fingers dug hard into my muscle, frogging it, making me grind my teeth from the pain.

Anger shoved all my scared away, and I breathed, and I breathed, and I counted in my head as blood pounded through my veins, flooded my face, my chest, and I ground my teeth harder.

"Where you going?" Ryker asked.

His voice *wah-wah*ed into my ear, distorted like he was some kind of movie demon.

"Office," I told him. "Then home."

I stomped his foot with all my strength.

Ryker howled and turned me loose, but Chris jumped in front of me before I could get up any speed. I tried to pull away from him, but he spun me around and pinned my arms behind my back, and when I tried to stomp his foot, too, he danced from side to side.

Kids seem to come from everywhere. Some of them chanted, "Fight, fight, fight!" It echoed in the hallway as I tried to get away from Chris.

"No way, Messy." Chris laughed at me. "Now just hold still. Stop moving."

Ryker hopped around, swearing and holding his foot.

I couldn't see Trisha, but I heard her say, "Let her go,

Chris. We'll get expelled if anything happens after that lecture we got Wednesday."

She actually sounded nervous.

"So?" Chris laughed again, forcing my elbows together until my shoulders popped. Pain burned across my neck and shot to my fingers.

I yelled and tried to jerk away from him.

"Chris," Trisha said again.

"Quit fighting, you freak," Chris ordered, his voice dropping lower, almost a growl. "Knock it off!"

"I'm not afraid of you!" I lied. "I hate you!" Not a lie. "You're a horse's butt!" Definitely not a lie.

He squeezed my arms so hard I lost my breath. Could shoulder bones break like arm bones? Elbows? Tears blurred my eyes, and I couldn't see any lockers or cinder blocks or floor tiles to count. My stomach clenched. I bit my lip so hard I tasted blood.

"Chris," Trisha said. "Stop."

"Let her go, man," Ryker said from somewhere. "You heard what your dad said Wednesday about zero tolerance on bullying. Jorgensen'll roast us if you hurt her."

"This isn't bullying!" Chris hollered. "She just broke the rules again. We're holding her until the teachers get here. Plus, she spied on us yesterday, and hit us with that branch. Besides, nobody cares what happens to—"

I threw myself backward, ramming my skull into his mouth and nose so hard I felt his teeth bite my scalp.

He fell backward like a tree hit by lightning.

I fell forward, my whole world nothing but hot pain in my arms.

Before I hit the floor, Ryker caught me around the middle. "He didn't mean it," Jerkface was saying as I ripped away from him and slammed against some lockers. "He's just—Messy, we joke around too much, and he took it too far—"

"Yes," said Ms. Jorgensen from somewhere. "He did."

I doubled over in front of the lockers and pressed my butt against them to hold myself up. My arms burned like somebody had lit them on fire. My shoulders hurt. Hot liquid ran down my neck and I was pretty sure my head was bleeding.

A hand came to rest on my back and I came up swinging. "Don't touch me! Don't touch me!" My fists connected with solid flesh.

Somebody *oof*ed.

"Don't touch me! Don't touch me! Don't touch me!" I kept yelling it over and over and I was counting each time I said it and not seeing anything and whatever I hit, whoever I hit got away from me and that was good. Swinging my arms made them feel better so I kept doing it. "Don't touch me!"

"Jesse?" Springer's voice cut through me echoing myself and listening to it bounce off lockers and bricks and tiles and people I didn't care if I hit or not. "Hey, Jesse. It's me. I'm here, okay?"

"Don't touch me! Don't touch me!" I wanted to stop. I wanted to breathe. I sort of wanted to sit down and relax and let somebody put Aunt Gus's stinky muscle rub on my shoulders, but my body kept getting hotter and hotter and everything got louder and louder and hotter and hotter and meltdown isn't really a metaphor and I didn't want to keep melting.

"OBWIG forever, right?" Springer's voice shook like his hands had been shaking under the stairs and under the stairs there was old gum and spiders.

"Don't touch me! Don't touch me!" Shrieking now. It hurt my throat.

"That was one, two." Springer sounded so worried. "Let's see. I think that's twelve *don't touch me*s so far."

"Don't touch me!" I hollered, helpless.

"Thirteen," Springer said.

I didn't want to worry him. I really didn't.

"Thirteen!" I echoed.

"Yep, thirteen. Does your brain itch, or is this different?"

My mouth came open to yell *thirteen* or *don't touch me* or something else but instead I took a breath and looked up and put my arms down and focused in on Springer's sweet, really nervous face. "Different!"

Still yelling . . . but better.

Springer nodded. I thought he was shaking all over. I didn't want him to shake.

"It's hot!" I said loudly, but it wasn't really yelling.

"There are fifteen lockers behind you," Springer said, sounding a little less worried.

"Thirty if you count top and bottom." I rubbed some blood off my neck.

"You bleeding?" Springer asked me, worried again.

I became vaguely aware of a ring of people. Jerkface and Trisha, eyes wide, standing next to Ms. Jorgensen. Chris, seeming woozy, sorta hanging in Coach Sedon's grip. Mr. Chiba standing right behind Springer.

The heat in my face turned down a few degrees. I couldn't hear blood pounding in my brain anymore. "It's not an itch," I told Springer. "It's like a fire. A flameout, only not just in my brain. All over."

He nodded. Breathed. Breathed again like he was counting in his own head, and maybe imagining puppies, too. "Is the flameout done now?"

I nodded. "I think so." Then, so he'd know I wasn't going to smash him in the face, I added, "OBWIG forever. And thanks."

"You're welcome," Springer said. He pointed at the blood on my shirt. "But you really are bleeding."

"Chris bit my head," I said. "I hope I don't get rabies."

Mr. Chiba's mouth twitched. He cleared his throat and said, "Jesse, please come with Springer and me. Let's get you to the nurse."

"The boy's bleeding, too," Ms. Jorgensen said, indicating Chris's nose.

"I'll get him an ice pack," his father grumbled. "He doesn't need a nurse."

I left with Mr. Chiba and Springer, heading toward the office. Behind us, the others followed. I could hear them walking, and sometimes mumbling stuff to each other, but I ignored them.

"OBWIG," I said to Springer, to keep myself calm.

"Should I count OBWIGs?" he asked.

"No, just say it back."

"OBWIG," Springer said.

"One day, you'll have to tell me what that means," Mr. Chiba said.

"No, sir," Springer and I said together.

23

Friday, Three Days Earlier,
After School

After the nurse finished putting some sort of weird cream on my head that didn't smell menthol-y like Aunt Gus's stuff or even set my skin on fire, I sat in Ms. Jorgensen's office with the pop-and-squeeze kind of ice packs on my shoulders. They weren't very cold, and Aunt Gus's muscle rub would have helped a lot more.

Springer sat beside me as we waited for my dad to get his classroom locked up and come get us. Coach Sedon and Mr. Chiba were in the office next door, babysitting Jerkface and the cockroaches. Ms. Jorgensen sat behind her desk in front of a bunch of framed pictures of her playing volleyball in college. She had her chin on her hands and was gazing at us. Her short, dark hair had gotten messed up, and she had her glasses on. They were crooked.

"What were you two doing at the senior high this time?" she asked. "Investigating again?"

"Yes, ma'am," Springer said.

"When this happened before, I didn't suspend both of

you because I understand Jesse is stressed about what's happening with her father, and you were being a good new friend and helping her."

"Investigating again was my idea," I said. "Springer just went to the senior high to be sure nothing happened to me."

"That's not true," Springer said. He sounded hurt.

Ms. Jorgensen held up one hand, and my gaze fixated on where her arm came out of the short sleeve. People weren't as scary when I looked at them in pieces, even principals.

"Your elbows need lotion," I said.

Ms. Jorgensen stopped talking and tried to look at her elbows, but looking at your own elbows is hard, unless you're double-jointed like Mom. So she stopped, then frowned. Her elbows went back to her desk, and her chin went back in one hand.

"What, exactly, were you checking out in South Hall and the band room?" she asked.

"We were questioning suspects," Springer said.

"Suspects." Ms. Jorgensen stared at us.

I shifted my ice packs and glanced at Springer. "I didn't know principals echoed, too."

"I think everybody does when they're confused," Springer said.

Ms. Jorgensen rubbed her elbows. "Why are we talking about echoing?"

"Because you echoed," I said.

"I echoed?" Ms. Jorgensen's eyebrows pulled together like Dad's did when he got confused.

"See?" Springer pointed at her.

"Yeah," I agreed.

Ms. Jorgensen rubbed her eyes. "Okay, let's try this again. Who did you question, and why?"

The room got too quiet. Even with all the people in offices all around us, the only sound was the *whick-whick* of air coming through vents. I realized the office smelled like old carpet, but I wouldn't let myself look down to see if this office had squares I'd have to count.

"If you two don't want to be suspended, I really need you to help me understand," Ms. Jorgensen said.

Springer opened his mouth to answer and so did I, but both of us seemed to remember at the exact same moment that Ms. Jorgensen was a suspect, too. We both closed our mouths.

"You know I'm going to find out anyway," Ms. Jorgensen added.

I had no doubt Nancy Newsom and Meredith Parks would sell us out in a heartbeat. But I had my doubts about Maleka and even Josh Sharp, even though Maleka had let us know that he might not be that trustworthy. I still sort of liked him.

Thinking about all that made my shoulders tighten, and that hurt. I wished I could find a switch in my brain and just flip it to Off.

"Can we trade questions and answers?" Springer asked Principal Jorgensen, and I had to work not to gape at him.

"Trade—" Principal Jorgensen started to echo, stopped herself, and sighed. "Okay, if that'll work. You go first, though."

"We questioned Nancy Newsom," Springer said.

Ms. Jorgensen eased back in her big leather principal's chair. "Trisha's sister's best friend—the one who gives them rides when their parents have the cars at work. Why?"

"It's our turn," Springer said. "Um, our turn, ma'am."

Ms. Jorgensen seemed to think about getting mad, but she didn't. Instead she gestured with one hand. "By all means. Ask away."

Springer glanced at me.

I nodded. "Okay. Let's start with, where were you during the staff meeting on the day the money was stolen out of Dad's desk?"

Ms. Jorgensen sat up straight so forcefully that I actually leaned back in my chair. The ice bags slid off my shoulders and plopped onto the ground.

Principal Jorgensen's calm in-charge expression melted right off her face, and her cheeks got red streaks on the tops. Her nostrils flared like she could smell the old carpet stink, or maybe even the funk under the back steps where Springer and I had hidden.

When she spoke, her voice was quiet, but so cold it made me shiver. "How did you know I wasn't at that meeting?"

Springer curled his fingers into a fist. I knew he was worried about getting Mr. Chiba in trouble, and so was I, so I didn't say anything.

We just looked at her.

"It's still our turn," I reminded her. I meant to sound like a real detective, but my voice came out like a doggy whine. "I mean, you didn't answer our question, so you don't get to ask one yet."

Ms. Jorgensen took a turn of not saying anything and staring at us.

Finally, she said, "I had an emergency."

Springer nodded. "We questioned Nancy because she was on our list."

Oh. He'd answered the first question Ms. Jorgensen had tried to ask when it wasn't her turn. And he gave exactly as much information as Ms. Jorgensen did with her answer. Wow. Springer was good at this game. I gazed at him with new appreciation.

Ms. Jorgensen jumped right back to "How did you know I wasn't at that staff meeting?"

"It's our turn again, ma'am," Springer said.

"I'm through playing games, Springer." Ms. Jorgensen got that weird look again, that pinch-faced one I had seen Wednesday when we talked about the stolen money. "Answer the question."

"I want a lawyer," I said to Ms. Jorgensen. To Springer, I whispered, "Look out, she's got the pinch-face again."

Springer nodded.

"What?" Ms. Jorgensen yelled.

"Suspects get a lawyer if they ask," I said.

Some of the red left Ms. Jorgensen's cheeks. "You aren't a suspect in anything, and I'm not the police."

I folded my arms. "Then I want my dad."

Ms. Jorgensen sucked in a breath. Let it out slowly and looked at Springer.

"I want her dad, too," Springer said. He echoed my arm-folding.

Ms. Jorgensen didn't look mad anymore, and the pinch-face went away until she looked mostly normal again. "How you found out about my staff meeting absence—it's a simple question. Just answer it."

"If it's simple, why did it make you mad?" I asked. "And why didn't you tell us where you really were?"

She stood up suddenly.

I grabbed my ice packs off the floor. They weren't as heavy as water bottles, but if she tried anything funny I'd chuck them at her face, grown-up or not.

"You can't hit a principal," Springer whispered way too loudly.

"I can if she tries to touch me." I squeezed the packs in my shaky fingers. "And I will."

Ms. Jorgensen held up both hands. "I'm not going to touch anybody."

"Why have you been gone from school so much?" I

hollered at her, keeping tight hold on those packs. "Do you need money for something?"

She kept her hands up, chest-level. "You think I took the library fund."

"We think you're a suspect," Springer said.

I didn't know people could roll their eyes, sigh, and get a pinch-face all at the same time, but somehow Ms. Jorgensen managed this.

A few seconds later, she pointed at me, then at Springer.

"Look, you two just—just—stay here."

And she walked out of the office, leaving us all alone with the old carpet stink and the *whick-whick*ing vents.

"Do you think she's guilty?" I asked Springer as I sat in my chair again and lowered my weaponized ice packs.

"She acts guilty," Springer said.

"Yeah," I said, staring at the door until it opened and Coach Sedon came into the office.

For a moment, he just stood inside the room. There was blood on his green basketball shirt and his green basketball shorts. His whistle hung around his neck, and my brain noted that no blood had gotten on the bright silver. His hair had gotten messed up, and a bald spot was showing near the front, just off the line of his forehead. For the briefest second, I looked into his eyes.

Brown and cold, like Chris's.

"Where's Ms. Jorgensen?" I asked, almost on reflex, as my muscles tightened.

"Staying with my son and his friends," Coach Sedon answered.

Silence.

One second. Two seconds. Three seconds . . .

Coach Sedon kept standing just inside the door. He let it shut behind him, and my breathing moved to my chest.

"Why did Ms. Jorgensen switch places with you?" Springer asked, proving he was a lot braver than me.

Coach Sedon glared down at Springer. "You two were trying her patience. She asked me to take a shift." His gaze shifted to me. "I think you broke my son's nose, Jesse."

"He tried to break my arms." My voice sounded squeaky, and I thought about kicking myself.

"I'm sorry about that, Jesse. I really am." Coach Sedon's tone was like a winter weather front moving through the office.

I moved in my chair, even though I wanted to stay still. "Why don't you make him stop being awful to people?"

"Why do you set him off all the time?" the coach asked. Louder now. But still cold. "Spying on him. Throwing dirt and pinecones at him in the woods—even hitting him with a branch in the face?"

"Your son's a bully, Coach Sedon." Springer's fingers moved to my chair arm, like he might need to grab my shirt if I jumped up to swing at a teacher. His other fingers went to the edges of his still-healing black eye. "Chris is a bully, and so are his friends. It's not my fault, and it's not Jesse's, and she's allowed to defend herself when he attacks her."

Coach Sedon walked toward us too fast, and I clamped my teeth together. He pushed past my legs and stopped in front of Springer, taking up all the space between Ms. Jorgensen's desk and Springer's legs. Then he pointed his finger right at Springer's nose and said, "You need to be more respectful to adults."

Everything inside me went so still I didn't even think my blood was pumping anymore. I wanted to get up and move away from the coach, but I couldn't leave Springer all alone, staring at that finger.

Springer kept his head up, his nose inches from Coach Sedon's chewed fingernail.

I tried to keep my head up, too, but my chin trembled.

"Please don't stand over me like that, sir," Springer said, so quiet it was almost a whisper. "You're scaring me."

Coach Sedon's mouth came open, and he leaned even closer to Springer. Another millimeter and that ragged nail would chew into Springer's nose. "Little boy, you don't get to tell me what to do."

My jaw clenched so hard my teeth hurt, but Springer managed to keep talking. "I am speaking up respectfully about something that makes me uncomfortable, and I'm asking you to stop."

Coach Sedon stared at him.

He stared at Coach Sedon.

I stared at both of them.

Coach Sedon moved his finger, put his arm to his side, but kept looming, right in front of Springer. "You think it's fine to be a smart-mouth, to speak to teachers like this?"

Springer's throat worked as he swallowed, but when he spoke, he still sounded steady. "I think it's fine to ask you politely not to stand over me like you're doing right now."

Every muscle in my whole body hurt. I was so scared Coach Sedon would hit Springer and really, really hurt him. Could a grown-up kill a kid with a punch? I was pretty sure they could, and I was scared Springer would die, but as far as I knew, Coach Sedon had never hit a kid ever, at least not at school. He needed to move, though. Why was he so close to us?

Coach Sedon's voice dropped low, and meanness dripped off his words as he said, "Why'd you let a girl fight your battle for you, Springer? Something wrong with your own fists, you little coward?"

"Don't call him names," I said at the same time Springer said, "I don't hit people, sir."

"Move," I said to Coach Sedon, forgetting about the please and thank you and everything polite. He smelled like soap and sweat and anger, and with the old carpet stench, too, my nose wanted to close up. My fists wanted to close up. My good sense was starting to close up, and I could barely hold on to it.

Coach Sedon ignored me.

"Why don't you hit people?" he asked Springer. "You a chicken, or something?"

"Move!" I said again, louder this time.

"I don't want to be the kind of person who stands over smaller people to scare them." All the color had drained out of Springer's face, but he kept right on looking Coach Sedon dead in the eyes.

I spun in my chair and climbed over the back of it, almost turning it over to get to my feet, to get something between me and Coach Sedon, to get—away. Just, away.

Neither Coach Sedon nor Springer moved.

As I turned to face them, Coach Sedon's hands curled into fists. He bared his teeth.

"Where were you during the staff meeting when that money got stolen out of Dad's desk?" I yelled instead of screaming, loud enough to hurt my own ears.

He turned on me, face purple-black like the old beets that had made Aunt Gus gag when she found them in the vegetable bin last month. The second he shifted his position, Springer got up and came around behind his chair, too.

"Take it easy," he said to me, but it was Coach Sedon who yelled next.

"You little—are you accusing me of taking that cash?"

"You know it was cash, not checks?" Springer asked, so quiet it came out nearly a whisper.

Coach Sedon spun toward him and grabbed his chair

like he was thinking about picking it up and tossing it aside. "I'm not a thief. And what I do with my time is none of your business!"

"Why are you yelling at us?" I hollered.

"Because you're obnoxious little brats!" Coach Sedon hollered louder.

The office door smacked open, and my father strode into the room. He walked straight to me and Springer and put himself between us and the chairs and the coach.

"You can stop speaking to my daughter and her friend like that," he said. "Right now, Sedon."

Coach Sedon walked away from all of us, straight over to the wall next to the office door. He drew back his fist and bashed the concrete block so hard I thought I heard knuckles crack.

Ms. Jorgensen came hurrying into the office, turned a circle, then went to Coach Sedon. She grabbed the coach's wrist and pulled the man's still-clenched fist toward her. "I heard yelling. What are you doing? Did you hit the wall? What the—did you break anything?"

Red-faced, sweating, Coach Sedon admitted, "I don't know."

Dad cleared his throat as he moved from behind the chairs and gestured to Springer and me. "Hey, you two, come on. Let's go."

Silent, Springer and I filed away from our safe spot and followed him.

As Dad passed Ms. Jorgensen, he stopped and said, "I'm not signing off on her suspension. It's not right or fair, and you know it. Those three next door, yes. But her, no way. She's the victim here."

Ms. Jorgensen kept hold of Coach Sedon's swelling fist and didn't look at Dad. "Chris Sedon's nose didn't break itself."

"He would have pulled her arms out of their sockets," a man's voice said from the hallway. "He was trying to hurt her, and you saw that as clearly as I did."

Ms. Jorgensen hesitated. Her head lowered. "Mr. Chiba. Please go back to your desk."

Instead, Mr. Chiba came all the way into the office. He folded his arms and stared at her, and at Coach Sedon. "I'm not being quiet about this anymore. Fire me if you want, but I'm through with 'let me handle this,' because neither of you are handling anything and this is out of hand. Somebody's going to get hurt a lot worse than a broken nose if you don't put a stop to it."

Coach Sedon pulled his wrist out of Ms. Jorgensen's grip. "Are you letting him talk to you like that?"

"Actually, yes. Please stay out of it." Ms. Jorgensen ushered Coach Sedon over to his chair and made him sit down. Then she turned back to Dad, Mr. Chiba, Springer, and me. "Can we agree to just give it the weekend?" To Dad, she said, "Please, just take Jesse home. We need to let things settle down."

Dad didn't respond. He just gave Ms. Jorgensen his dad look.

Ms. Jorgensen sighed. Without looking behind her, she said, "I know those three have crossed the line. They're getting three days of formal. It's got to stop, what they're doing. All of them."

Coach Sedon didn't say anything. He just rubbed his hand and stayed that awful red color.

"Not Springer," I said to Dad, pulling at his belt. "He didn't—"

"No, not him," Ms. Jorgensen said. "Springer followed the rules and came to get an adult."

I glanced over my shoulder at Springer, relieved.

But he didn't look relieved. He looked miserable.

Before I could ask him what was wrong, he hurried out of the office, passing Mr. Chiba without saying a word. I heard the gate at the front counter bang and figured Springer was headed straight out the front door of the school.

Dad and I headed out, too. With every step, I kept thinking Springer had just needed air, that he'd be waiting for us.

When Dad and I got outside, though, Springer was nowhere to be seen.

"I guess he decided to walk home," Dad said.

"I guess he decided to walk home," I echoed, feeling shaky and strange and hollow, glancing around and counting cars and people but not seeing anything remotely Springer-like.

"Get in. I'll go let Mr. Chiba know he's not with us, so he can check in with Springer's parents."

I nodded and got in the car.

And then as Dad went back into the junior high, I put my face in my hands, and I cried.

24

Friday, Three Days Earlier, Late Afternoon

Sounds like some good detective work, Private Broadview," Mom said. Then she yawned, because it was somewhere around midnight in Mosul.

"But Dad didn't even ask me what we found out," I told her as I sat on my bed taking turns between painting my nails purple and gazing at the screen on the iPad Aunt Gus had delivered to me.

Sam-Sam lay right next to me, staring at Mom's image just like I did.

"I think he's a little overwhelmed," Mom said. She had on a sand-colored T-shirt and sand-colored pants, and her hair lay against her shoulder in a sweaty ponytail. Shotgun sat next to her in front of the tent wall, tongue lolling out, panting faster than I could breathe.

"Why is Dad overwhelmed?" I asked Mom as I finished all the easy nails on my left. "Because of the money and the hearing?"

She smiled. "Maybe because you and your friend are

turning out to be better detectives than the police, and because of one of those brats biting you in the head. He was so upset you got hurt at school. That's why he made the emergency call to me."

I reached up with the hand I hadn't started on and patted the back of my head. "I didn't really get hurt. No stitches or anything. My arms are just sore." A lump seemed to jump into my throat, and I choked, then coughed, then managed to squeeze out, "But I'm not sure Springer's still my friend."

Mom's expression turned horrified. "Oh, honey. What happened?"

I barely managed to get the lid on the polish before I choked again, and the tears came, and Sam started licking my face, and I told her. Everything. Every detail about what happened after we questioned our suspects. Even the parts about our observation session that went wrong, and the pine branch, and swimming across the pond, and bashing Chris's nose with my head and cutting myself on his teeth, and how the coach treated us in the office. When I finished, I had my arms around my dog and my face in his fur as he frantically licked my throat and chin.

"Good move with that kid who grabbed you," Mom said. "You remember our self-defense lessons, Private. I'm impressed."

"I bet Dad didn't think it was a good move. I bet Springer didn't, either. Maybe that's why he left like that—because I hit people yesterday and today, too, and he thinks it's wrong."

"Maybe," Mom said. "But he probably just needs some time. That was an intense situation today, Jesse."

"Intense," I echoed, and Sam licked my teeth.

Mom let out a loud breath. "Did that boy really talk you out of a meltdown? In the hallway, after the fight?"

I pulled Sam gently away from my face and kissed his nose. "Springer was great. I can't wait for you to meet him, except I think Shotgun would terrify him and I don't think he'd ever shoot at people, even if they're bad guys."

Mom smiled again when I looked at her, then got a more thoughtful look on her pretty mom face. "Some people don't see the world in terms of good guys and bad guys."

That made me focus a little more, trying to sort through the confusion of those words. "But if they don't—I mean, how do they see it?"

Mom shrugged one shoulder and leaned closer to her screen. "They see a world full of imperfect, troubled people. They see everyone as more equal."

"Okay," I said, trying to take that in, but I couldn't quite get my head around it. "Do you think Springer's mad at me for fighting?"

"I don't know. He may be mad at himself because he didn't fight."

I felt better enough to shake the nail polish and start on my hard hand as I thought about the way Springer faced down Coach Sedon without ever getting out of his chair or raising his voice or saying anything ugly at all. "I don't think Springer's mad about not fighting," I told Mom as I finished my thumbnail. "Springer's brave and he got help when I asked him to. I mean, I understand why he doesn't fight. He's like Dad. Springer could have beaten the snot out of all of them, but he chooses not to. Is it wrong that I hit back?"

"Everybody has their wars, Jesse, and everybody fights their wars in different ways. You and I, we hit back. Springer and your dad don't."

It was my turn to frown. "Are we protecting them, or are they protecting us?"

"That . . . is a very good question, Private Broadview." Mom's eyes seemed to dance in front of me. I could even see the tiny drops of sweat in her eyebrows. "Anything else on your mind tonight?"

"Dad's still mad at me for investigating." I finished the last couple of nails, put the lid on the polish, then blew on my fingers to help everything dry.

"Those are seriously purple," Mom said.

I smiled. Then I stopped smiling. "Doesn't he know how important he is to me?"

"He does," Mom said. "He just doesn't want you in trouble or hurt."

"Well, I don't want him in jail." I waved my hands around to increase airflow, and Sam ran around trying to lick my elbows. "But I didn't really figure anything out, except it's probably not Josh and definitely not Maleka. It's probably not even Jerkface or the cockroaches, even if I wish it had been one of them, because I don't think they could have gotten in the doors, or been over at the senior high without somebody knowing, except they might ride with Trisha's sister's friend a lot, since their parents always have to work late and they have study period at the end of the day. And, speaking of Trisha's sister, it could have been her friend Nancy, or Ms. Jorgensen, or Coach Sedon." I stopped listing suspects long enough to groan. "I guess it might have been anybody."

"Who do you really think it is? Not just your head thought." Mom moved away from the screen so I could see her whole face, and she touched her temple. "But your gut thought." She touched her tummy. "What do your emotions tell you? Your heart? Your instinct?"

I stared at the pad on the bed in front of me, feeling like Mom had just punched me in the stomach. Even though my nails might still be sticky, I wrapped my arms around my middle and rocked, trying to handle the huge rush of heat in my chest and face.

No meltdowns in front of Mom. No more meltdowns at all. Too old for meltdowns. Too strong for meltdowns . . .

"Jesse?" Mom sounded worried. "Honey? What is it? What did I say?"

The words wouldn't come. Just the rocking. So I rocked. Then I rocked some more.

"Come back to me," Mom said, her voice tinny in the pad speakers. "Please."

I tried, and Sam-Sam helped by standing on his tiny back legs and pawing at my sore shoulder.

"Jesse?" Mom said again. And then more army-stern. "Private Broadview."

My head snapped up at her tone.

The world inside me slowed down a little, enough for me to count to twenty and back down again, fast at first, then slower.

"That's it," Mom said. "Take it easy."

It took a few more seconds before I could stop moving, stop the heat, and glance in Mom's direction.

She waited, her expression intense and worried, but not mad.

I paid attention to my breathing, getting air all the way in, then all the way out. When I thought my voice would work, I said, "All those things you said. Emotions and heart and instinct." Deep breath. Bigger breath. "Do you really think I have those things the same way normal people do?"

"Of course you have them." Tears glistened in the corner of Mom's eyes, turned sandy-colored by reflections and the tent lighting. She leaned toward the screen again. "If I were there, I'd ask to hug you."

"I'd let you," I told her.

"Why would you think you don't have emotions and

heart and instinct the same way normal people do, Jesse?" she asked.

"Because whatever's broken in me, I sort of thought those were the things that got most messed up."

"Nothing's broken in you," Mom insisted. "You see and experience the world differently. There's nothing wrong with that. It's just harder on you, trying to live in the society we've set up."

"I want to believe that, but—"

"But what?" Mom asked.

"Do you ever regret naming me after your brother?" The words came out so fast I couldn't stop them, even though I sort of wanted to as I started saying them. "Since I'm not . . . well, exactly like everybody else, and all?"

Mom's serious face got even more serious. "I absolutely don't regret it. Your uncle would think you're the most perfect thing in the universe."

I looked at her eyes for just a few seconds, her brown eyes, so like Uncle Jesse's in the picture, and mine, too. "How do you know that?"

"Because my brother saw the truth of people," Mom said. "He'd know how strong you are."

"I don't feel very strong." I tried to smile but couldn't. "I don't ever do anything important. Not like you do. Not like Uncle Jesse would have done if he lived."

"Private Broadview, I order you to see your own worth." Mom reached her hand toward the screen again. "What you do doesn't matter. Who you are is enough. It's more than enough, Jesse."

"But, Mom, what I do *does* matter." Why was my voice so quiet? I didn't mean to be whispering, but I was. "Because it matters to me."

Mom's hand lowered to her lap, and now she was the one who looked like she'd been punched. Only, Mom had never been one for the whole freak-out-and-rock thing. "All right," she said. "I hear you. If that's the case, then get out of your own way, Private. Stop treating yourself like you're broken and tell me, in that heart you really do have, in that gut that really knows things your mind isn't seeing, in those beautiful emotions you really do feel in your very own way—who stole your father's money?"

I thought about it, and felt it, and thought about it some more, and held my dog, and kissed my Sam, and finally, I said, "Coach Sedon or Ms. Jorgensen."

Mom scratched her chin. "Explain."

"Ms. Jorgensen keeps not being where she's supposed to be, and her reactions to stuff have been . . . weird. She makes a pinch-face every time we bring up anything about the money."

Mom blinked. "A pinch-face?"

"Like this." I mashed my hands against my cheeks and squinted my eyes.

"I see," Mom said. "And Coach Sedon?"

I stopped mashing my face and sat very, very still on my

bed. The thought of the Sedons, Chris and his dad both—yuck. "Jerkface and Trisha, they're mean buttheads. But Chris and his father, it's more than that. Coach Sedon, it's like he's—well, something's really wrong with him, Mom."

Mom's face tightened, and her eyes got a flinty, stern look. "Then stay away from him, Private. Investigate all you want, but don't go one-on-one with Chris or his father."

I nodded.

"Promise," Mom said.

"I promise," I told her.

Mom sighed and reached her fingertips toward the screen one more time. "When you go back to school Monday, just be careful and stay away from that whole bunch of people. Your dad and I, we're through letting this play out on its own. We're making a school board complaint about the bullying—and about Coach Sedon for how he acted in the office, and Ms. Jorgensen for not putting a stop to all of this."

I thought about arguing, but every time I moved my arms and felt how sore they were, I knew I was done with Jerkface and the cockroaches.

"I'll stay away from them," I told Mom. "Or I'll make them stay away from me."

Mom gazed at me across sand and oceans and trees and miles and miles, one warrior to another. Then she gave me a single, quick thumbs-up that meant just . . . everything.

After that, she stretched out her arms, and I had to smile as she said, "I love you this much."

"And I love you this much." I blew her the big slobbery kiss she was waiting for.

Then, across those same sands and oceans and trees and miles and miles, Mom punched a button on her screen, and left me in Kentucky, without her.

"Here." I nudged Sam-Sam toward the pile of leaves and dirt in front of the clubhouse, where I'd buried his container. We were at one of fifteen on tries so far. Not much improvement. But I kept lying on the ground beside him, doing my best, because I absolutely was not giving up on this, even though it was getting close to dark.

Sam dug at a leaf near my hand.

My eyebrows lifted, and a tiny bit of hope surged in my chest. "That's it," I whispered. "Keep looking. You can find it. I know you can."

Sam looked at me. At the leaf. At me.

He picked up the leaf and offered it to me.

I sighed and dropped my face into the dirt.

Stretching my neck felt good on my sore shoulders, so I just stayed still for a minute, letting my muscles rest.

Sam darted around and around my stretched-out arms and legs, bouncing off my head as he searched for my face like he never seemed to want to look for the hidden containers. After a few laps, he gave up and tugged at the leg of my jeans, growling as he pulled.

I smiled into the dirt.

Sam suddenly stopped tugging and started growling for real, a loud throaty rumble too big for his fuzzy little body.

I sat up so fast I got dirt on my lips and had to scrub it off before I reached for him.

He darted away from me and the clubhouse, toward the main path, barking like a maniac. Scrambling to my knees, then my feet, I lurched after him, barely able to catch my breath. What if it was Jerkface or Trisha? Worse, what if it was Chris—or his dad?

"Sam!"

His barks rattled the leaves.

"Sam-Sam!" I called, running now.

And then Sam stopped barking.

Before I could start screaming, Springer walked into view in the gray-blue twilight, carrying Sam in his arms.

I stumbled to a stop, mouth open, drooling dirt onto my blue shirt.

Springer looked from my drool to my hands to my dog as he got closer. "Working with the containers again?"

I nodded, brain buzzing but not itching, which was good, but I really didn't know what the buzzing meant.

Springer handed Sam to me. "Maybe he's just not going to learn to do that."

I wiped my mouth on Sam's fur, then made myself look at Springer. "Are you still my friend?"

"Of course I am." He sounded genuinely shocked. Looked shocked, too. "I figured you and your dad were really mad at me—I mean, Chris hurt you. He bit your head and I didn't even try to fight. So I deserved you being mad, and I thought you wouldn't want to ride in the car with me."

"We weren't mad at you." I handed dirt-drool Sam-Sam back to him, because he looked like he needed a dog. "You probably only thought that because of all the mean stuff Coach Sedon said to you."

Springer kissed Sam's head, away from the dirt-drool, and he nodded.

"He's a bigger Jerkface than Jerkface, and an even huger cockroach than his kid," I said. "We'll call him Jerkface Cockroach, enemy of OBWIG."

Springer laughed, but he was still hugging Sam tight and close. "You . . . you really aren't mad? I was hoping we could talk when I came here, but I was ready to apologize and everything, if I needed to."

"Come on," I told him, jerking a thumb toward the clubhouse. "I've got cold Cokes and some Twinkies. And I thought you were really brave, when you stood up to Jerkface Cockroach, enemy of OBWIG."

I started walking, and Springer followed behind me. "I made him hit a wall," Springer said. "Mom says she heard he broke a bone and has to get it operated on."

"Well, he kind of deserved that. Hitting a wall is pretty ridiculous."

"Yeah."

A minute or so later, as I pulled open the clubhouse door, Springer asked, "Did you get in any trouble?"

"Nah. Dad called Mom and went to grade papers. Aunt Gus says he's burning off negative energy. And Mom said I did the right thing. And Aunt Gus asked if I wanted chili for dinner again, and I said yes, so she's making some."

Springer seemed to consider all of this as he lowered Sam-Sam to the clubhouse floor, found a head lamp and switched it on so we'd have a little light, then sat on a rock beside Sam. "But you think I did the right thing, too, by not fighting?"

I handed him a Twinkie and a Coke. "I think you did the right thing for you and I did the right thing for me."

He held his food as Sam sniffed at the wrapped Twinkie. "How can both ways be right?"

I told him what Mom said about people having wars and fighting their wars in their own ways. Then I got my own Twinkie and Coke, and I sat on a rock close to Springer and my dog.

Springer rubbed behind Sam's ears, then picked up one of Sam's little balls and tossed it for him. As Sam darted after the toy, Springer took a bite of his Twinkie. He had to throw again before he got it chewed and swallowed.

"So maybe Sam-Sam isn't a bomb-sniffing warrior," he said. "Maybe he's a fetching warrior."

I lowered my Twinkie. "I don't think they have bomb-fetching dogs in the army. That wouldn't work."

"Well, yeah." Springer pitched the ball again. "But maybe digging stuff up isn't his best thing. I mean, he fetches great. And he does pretty good at noticing when people are around. Maybe he could find lost people?"

I shrugged. "Not sure if they have people-finding dogs, but I could ask Mom. When we talked, she asked me which of our suspects I thought was guilty."

"Ms. Jorgensen maybe." Springer ate and threw the ball. "But more Coach Sedon."

"Yeah, that's what I thought, too. Remember how we saw him fighting with Ms. Jorgensen outside of the senior high?"

"Yeah. And they were both absent from the staff meeting."

"Something's up with them," I agreed. "But they might not be acting weird about the money. Could be some other reason. And somebody else could have taken the cash, and—I just don't know." I quit eating my Twinkie and put the rest on my knees. "I made Aunt Gus tell me when Dad's hearing is supposed to be, and it's next Wednesday. I'm afraid he's going to jail, and there's nothing I can do to save him."

I coughed and hiccupped, because I didn't want to start crying.

Sam-Sam stopped running back with his ball and

stood at the door of the clubhouse. He put the ball down and stared at me, then turned his head to the side like he was trying to hear what I wasn't saying.

I couldn't keep looking at his silly dog face, or I really would cry, so I stared at my half-eaten Twinkie instead, at how the yellow crumbs blended in with the dirt on my legs.

"Jesse, can I hug you?" Springer asked. "Or would that not help?"

I thought about that. Tried to imagine it. Couldn't. But I felt pretty awful, so I said, "It might help."

Wrappers rustled as Springer moved his food. Then I felt him sit on my floor rock, right beside me. Next, I felt his arm around my shoulders, and a gentle squeeze.

Sam-Sam ran forward and ate my leftover Twinkie in two bites. Then he licked my fingers and my hands and my knees and Springer's knees.

That helped.

And Springer's hug kind of helped, too.

25

Monday, After the Train Came

I stared down through the hole we had opened in the house rubble as rain slowed to drizzle, then became a foggy sprinkle.

A few feet below me, fingers felt around the edges of the wood tent, then grabbed the top of the V shape.

I reached through the hole with my sock-hands, grabbed a hunk of plaster propped against the side of the wood tent, and pushed it off to the side.

Springer came to the other side of the hole in the rubble and looked down. "Wow," he said. "It's like part of the closet just fell over and kept the rest of this mess from crushing her. We need to get her out of there, Jesse."

"Help!" Aunt Gus yelled.

"You're supposed to be getting your nails done!" I yelled back as I sat up and grabbed more boards on the big heap underneath me, pulling them and digging at pink stuff. I kept pulling and digging until my muscles screamed like I wanted to scream.

"Oh," Springer said as he pulled at boards, too. "Oh. Oh!"

Aunt Gus pushed more rubble away from the boards that had sheltered her. Now she had her head and arms and shoulders out from under the wood that had saved her. Springer and I dug harder and faster, trying to clear her a path to climb out of the collapsed house, once she got free.

"You aren't supposed to be here," I said again. "Why are you here, Aunt Gus?"

Rocks and insulation fell and bounced off the wood tent. Aunt Gus let out a groan. My heart skipped at the sound, and I stopped digging.

"Aunt Gus?" I yelled. "Are you okay?"

"There's a house on my head, Jesse." She coughed as she scooched the rest of the way out from underneath the protective boards. "My favorite bathrobe is ruined. I don't have a smoke and I really want one, and I could use a bottle of water." She looked up through the hole we had opened. "But other than that, yes. I'm okay."

Springer and I worked together to shift aside a big board with bricks stuck to it on one end as Aunt Gus got slowly to her feet. Little by little, she stood, her shoulders and head rising out of the house wreckage, through the hole Springer and I had widened.

That's when she started barking.

No, wait. Not her.

Sam-Sam and Charlie!

Both dogs wriggled out from under the wood tent. Aunt Gus stooped and picked them up, putting one under each arm.

Sam yapped and squiggled and I pulled the socks off my hands and crammed them into my pockets, and as my aunt stood again, lifting the dogs free of the rubble, I reached for my dog. I took my sweet little Sam-Sam from Aunt Gus and buried my face in his fur and kissed him and kissed him and kissed him, then let him lick my face until I smelled stinky doggy spit in both nostrils. Then I handed him to Springer and leaned toward my dust-covered, bleeding aunt.

She gave me a half-smile. "Glad to know where I rank in your world, niece of mine."

I hugged her without asking, careful not to fall into the hole she was standing in, and she hugged me back with one arm while Charlie jerked and grunted in her other arm.

"What in the world are you two doing here?" Aunt Gus asked. "How did you even get to the house so fast?"

"We walked," I said into her dust-coated shoulder. "Or sort of ran. I thought you were at Nails, Nails, Nails so I wasn't worried about you."

"Weather scared me off." She turned her head left, then right, taking in the devastation on our road. "Might have done better if I'd gone."

I straightened up and studied her face. "Your forehead is cut. It's bleeding."

She let me wipe it with my sleeve, then handed me Charlie. With a bulldog-sounding grunt, she pushed herself out of the hole and sat on the debris pile. I handed Charlie to Springer to hold along with Sam, because that bulldog stank like puppy sewage and weighed almost more than me.

Then I edged over to Aunt Gus and helped her get up again.

As soon as she stood, she tottered on the loose boards and started to sway, and I had to grab hold of her waist to keep her on her feet. Springer put the dogs down and helped me steady her, then held her hand as I kept hold of her waist. Together, we stepped her down off the pile of rubble, out of the chaos of the stuff that used to be a house, and moved her all the way to the curb, where we sat her down.

Her fingers fluttered to the cut place on her head. "Made me woozy. Sorry."

Springer was on his phone, and I figured he was calling 911, but he pulled the phone away from his ear and stared at it, then listened again.

Sam-Sam licked my ankles.

"Where's Charlie?" Aunt Gus asked. "Charlie? Charlie!"

"I called Emergency, but it just rings and rings," Springer said. He punched at his screen. "Let me try again."

I heard a bulldoggy woof and looked back toward the house wreckage. Charlie was sitting on some boards, gazing toward us but not trying to come to where we were, even though Aunt Gus was calling him.

"Sit," I told Sam. "And stay."

Sam panted at me and smiled and bounced, but he sat and he stayed as I made my way up the rubble to Charlie. As I got to his boards, he pulled himself toward me with his front paws but didn't stand.

"Come here," I said. I clucked my tongue like Aunt Gus usually did, and Charlie inched forward, then stopped.

"Seriously, you big lump, come here. Your mom wants to hug you."

Charlie scooted some more. His butt wiggled like he was trying to wag his nub tail, but then he flinched and whined, and he stopped coming toward me.

Frowning, I leaned over the board and picked him up—and he yelped.

"Charlie!" Aunt Gus cried from the curb.

Charlie struggled and cried out again, and I had to work to settle him in my arms. One of his back legs didn't feel right. He wuffled and whimpered against my chest, drooling down my already-wet shirt.

"It's okay," I whispered to him as I eased us forward off the boards, then carried him to my waiting aunt, who was probably only still sitting down because Springer had quit trying to call 911 and had his hands on her shoulders.

"His leg," I told Aunt Gus as I handed him over. "It's hurt. I think it's broken."

"Oh, no, oh, no, no, no," she said, kissing his head. "My poor little baby."

Charlie kept whimpering and cuddled into my aunt, actual tears rolling out of his bulging bulldog eyes.

I blinked to keep myself from tearing up, then snatched Sam off the ground where he had waited on me like the good boy he was. Inch by inch, I checked all four of his legs and paws. They seemed okay. He licked my fingers as I turned to Springer, who was trying Emergency again.

"Do they have a 911 for dogs?" I asked. "We need to get Charlie some help, too."

"Nobody's answering," he said, lowering the phone. He glanced around at the destroyed street and wiped his eyes with one hand. "Not 911, or the police, or the fire station. I guess they're all busy. We'll have to take care of ourselves, at least for now."

"Not good," I said.

"My poor dog," Aunt Gus said over and over, and I could tell she was crying, and that nearly made me cry all over again.

Despite people right next to me and my dog in my arms and distant horns and alarms, the world seemed wrong and quiet and empty.

"Okay." I hugged Sam-Sam. "It's okay. We just wait here. Dad'll come. He'll know what to do."

"My folks are on the way, too," Springer said. "I texted them your address and told them I'm okay."

I was about to ask Springer if his dad would be hard to deal with, but Sam alert-barked and tried to get out of my arms.

"No," I told him, but he barked again, and thrashed harder, more than he ever usually did.

With a sigh, I lowered him to the ground. "Fine, but you'll have to sit right here, and—"

My dog took off like a shot, running straight across rubble and grass to the pile of boards and bricks that had been our neighbor's house. He ran around to the back section, stopped, looked around at me, then alert-barked.

"Come here!" I shouted, moving toward him, feeling my heart in my throat, terrified that he'd climb on that pile of mess and fall in and hurt himself or get killed.

"Jesse, don't you leave us," Aunt Gus said. "Just call for him."

I stopped at the edge of our yard and clapped and whistled. "Sam. Hey, buddy. Come here like a good dog. Sam-Sam?"

Sam wagged his tail and turned a circle, like he really wanted to do what I asked, but he stayed in his spot. Then he turned back to the rubble and barked.

"Jesse," Springer said, his voice low and worried. "I think you need to go over there and see what's bothering him. I'll stay with your aunt and Charlie."

"Oh, no you don't!" Aunt Gus hollered. "Jesse, you come back here right this second!"

I kept walking, and I heard Springer talking to Aunt Gus, settling her down as I made my way to my barking dog.

"What is it?" I asked as I got to him and reached down to pick him up.

He danced away from my hands and barked, and that's when I heard voices. Soft at first, then louder.

"Help! We're trapped in the closet. Help! Please help!"

I wheeled toward Springer. "It's my neighbors. They're stuck in their house!"

And then I was pulling my sock mittens out of my pockets and stuffing my hands inside, and looking to see where I could move boards to make a path to where I heard our neighbors shouting.

"We hear you!" I told them, digging through a pile of splintered siding.

"Jesse!" Dad's voice from behind me. "Wait for me, honey. I'm almost to you."

I turned around, and Dad was there, running toward me. At the same time, a man and woman I didn't recognize came jogging from behind what was left of our house, as if they had come through the woods.

The woman stopped and grabbed hold of Springer, smothering him in a hug and kissing his head.

The strange man jogged past me and met Dad. I saw Dad nod, then shake the man's hand. After that, Dad came straight for me. He opened his arms and I ran into them.

"You rescued Gus?" he asked.

"Charlie has a broken leg," I told him. "And Aunt Gus gets dizzy when she stands up."

"Don't try to stand up," Dad called back to Aunt Gus.

I didn't quite hear her answer, but I wasn't sure it was polite, because Springer told his mother, "They aren't mad. It's just how they talk to each other."

When I let Dad go, I turned to the strange man, who looked like an even taller version of Springer, only without the smile.

He offered me his hand.

I shook it for a second, then let go.

"I'm Dan Regal," he said. "Springer probably told you I work in construction."

I nodded, still wondering if he was going to be a nice man, or Mr. Jerkface.

He pointed at the rubble. "Let me look at this and be sure we're pulling out the right boards, and not doing anything that will make the pile collapse more."

That made sense to me, so I moved.

As Mr. Regal reached for a board, I said, "You might want to use your socks as gloves if you don't have real ones. That stuff cuts and burns after a minute."

Mr. Regal and Dad both glanced at me.

I held up my sock-covered hands. "It was Springer's idea. He helped me get Aunt Gus out of our house."

Mr. Regal glanced toward Springer, and he seemed

to straighten up a little. "That's a pretty smart idea."

"I'm coming to help," Springer yelled. "Mom's going to stay with Charlie and Miss Gustine."

"Miss Gustine?" I asked Dad.

Aunt Gus said something else that might not have been polite.

"Sit," I told my dog, pointing to the ground where he danced.

Sam-Sam sat.

Meanwhile, Mr. Regal took off his shoes, pulled off his socks, covered his hands, and looked at Springer.

"Good work, son," he said. "Thinking of this for our hands—and helping to save Jesse's aunt."

Springer's cheeks flushed, but he smiled.

Then his father put his shoes back on and got to work.

So did my father and Springer, and so did I.

26

The Weekend Before

Dad and Aunt Gus and I sat around the kitchen table Saturday night, digging into Aunt Gus's famous Smoked Chipotle Meatloaf, and Dad's famous Skin-Still-In Mashed Potatoes. I heated the peas, but peas didn't amount to much. I mean, nobody would be too interested in Jesse's Over-Nuked Green Pea Husks. Still, I poked a few in my mouth. They were passable if you just chewed and didn't think too much.

Dad flourished his fork between bites, and after he swallowed, he asked, "Why do you think Coach Sedon stole that money?"

From the living room on the other side of a stretched-out baby gate, Sam grumbled and whined, and Charlie snuff-snuffed. The gate rattled but held.

I breathed in the tangy tomato of the meatloaf, and the buttery potato smell. "You heard him in the office, how he was treating us."

"Point," Aunt Gus said, talking with her mouth full, which Dad ignored.

"That makes Sedon an ass, not a thief," Dad said.

"I think *ass* counts as a swearword," Aunt Gus told him.

"Does not." Dad gave her a quick glare, and then he was looking at me again and waiting for me to get down the huge hunk of meatloaf I'd just tackled.

"Something's wrong with him, Dad." I wiped the corners of my mouth with a paper napkin. "Mom said to listen to my belly, and my belly says Coach Sedon isn't right."

Sam-Sam yapped from the other room.

Dad ate for a minute or so, then said, "I guess I can't disagree with you on that."

"Miracles!" Aunt Gus announced, tucking a piece of meatloaf into the napkin in her lap, no doubt to save it for Charlie.

"I think Ms. Jorgensen's covering for him, too," I added.

Dad gave this some consideration but shook his head. "Ms. Jorgensen might be trying to help him, honey. You know, with whatever's gone wrong for him. When people work together for a long time, they can become friends."

I put down my fork. "Well, are you friends with Coach Sedon?"

Dad paused mid-pea-hull bite. "Um, no."

"Why?" I asked.

Aunt Gus nearly choked trying to get down some potatoes before she said, "Honesty is good for the soul, Derrick."

"Enough." Dad gave her a fork point. "But okay. I'm not friends with Sedon because he's a loudmouth and a bully, just like he was in high school. Never got over his glory days."

I nodded. "I think it's either the two of them, or Trisha Parks's older sister Meredith's friend Nancy. But I guess Josh is still in the running, because Maleka said he couldn't really be trusted. And there's always somebody we haven't even considered, but I think we've considered the most important people."

"Nancy, Josh, Maleka," Dad echoed. "Total strangers, the principal, Coach Sedon. Wow. You've really dug into all this."

"I told you I would," I said. Then I drew in a breath and got ready for the lecture, for Dad to tell me how all this was silly, how it would just blow over.

Instead, he looked deeply into my eyes from across the table, and before I could look away, he said, "Thank you."

Aunt Gus really did choke this time, and I jumped up to bang her on the back because I didn't really know how to do the Heimlich maneuver we learned about in first aid last year.

She waved me off, though, so I ended up standing there listening to dogs whine and watching Dad as he watched me. I had no idea what to say, so I just went with "You're welcome. I love you."

He smiled at me. "Maybe tomorrow, we can try to get a call with your mom together. A family minute or two. We haven't talked to her together in months."

I sat back down and went after my meatloaf again. "I'd like that."

For a few minutes, I didn't focus on anything but eating and tallying what Aunt Gus was hiding for Charlie so I could match it for Sam-Sam. Dad told some silly jokes and Aunt Gus groaned a lot, and we all seemed to finish at the same time. I helped clean the table off, and then Dad and I got the dishes into the dishwasher and turned it on. I snuck Sam's scraps into a baggie when everybody's head was turned, and tucked the baggie under my shirt.

When Dad moved the baby gate, Sam almost bowled me over, trying to jump to my waist, where he obviously could smell his hidden treasures. Charlie, more used to this routine, ambled over to Aunt Gus's favorite recliner and sat, drooling and wiggling his nub tail and waiting for her to sit down and start dropping him bites.

I kept Sam at bay, and as we got to the living room, I said, "Dad?"

He looked up from fishing across the table for the television remote. "Yes?"

"Can I have my phone back?"

Well? It was worth a shot.

Dad tapped the remote against his palm and asked, "Will you tell me what OBWIG means?"

My heart sank a little, and I shook my head. "No. Sorry. That's a secret."

Aunt Gus heaved a dramatic sigh and took the remote away from Dad. As she plopped into the recliner, she said, "Just give her the phone, Derrick. If she and Springer can communicate, they might have this case cracked before you ever have to go to court."

"All right, all right. I know when I'm outnumbered." Dad headed back through the kitchen toward his bedroom to get my phone while Aunt Gus flipped channels to her favorite local news.

She started giving Charlie his nibbles as she watched for a few seconds, then whistled. "Look at the size of that front." She leaned back in her chair, giving Charlie more room to stand up against her knees and beg. "Bad weather's coming, Jesse."

I worked a pinch of meatloaf out of my baggie, made Sam sit, and gave him a bite. "When?"

"That's always hard to predict," Aunt Gus said. "Weather isn't a perfect science."

Dad came back with my phone and my charger, and I put them in my pocket. Then I picked up Sam and snuggled him under my chin while he tried to turn upside down to get to the baggie.

"I'm not scared of bad weather," I told him. "Are you?"

Sam-Sam smiled at me.

Of course he wasn't scared.

My fuzzy war dog of fury never got scared of anything.

27

Monday, the Night After the Train Came

I don't think it's a good idea," Dad said. He sounded as tired as I felt, which was why I was sitting on a pile of boards Springer had brought to the curb so I wouldn't get muddy. The darkness over our heads seemed so total, so absolute, like even the stars didn't want to come out and look at the disaster below.

Bright lights blazed from metal poles set up by the few emergency workers who had made it into our neighborhood. I couldn't look at them. I sat on a curb five houses down from mine—actually five piles of stuff that used to be houses down from mine—leaning against Springer's shoulder and keeping my eyes closed and holding my dog and kissing his nose because he'd led Dad and Mr. Regal and me to another trapped person, an older lady visiting from out of town who got stuck in her daughter's garage.

In front of me, Dad and an Emergency Services worker wearing a name tag that said JOSIAH LINDERS argued like I wasn't sitting right next to them.

"Please, sir." Josiah Linders turned both hands palm up, pleading. "We don't have any search-and-rescue dogs here yet, and this little guy is doing awesome. It's almost like he's been trained."

"He has been trained," Springer said. "Only more for sniffing bombs—er, I mean, hidden treats."

"My mom's dog Shotgun finds explosives in Iraq," I said without opening my eyes. "Dad and I talked to her yesterday. And Sam-Sam's not going anywhere without me."

Even with my lids closed, I could see more blinking, swirling, lights headed toward us, and I knew sireny vehicles were filling up our roads.

About time.

But I really wished I had some earplugs.

It'd probably be months before a store even opened to sell them, though. Maybe I could order them online— but wait. Had to have a mailbox for that, right? I kissed Sam's nose again. Dad and Springer and Mr. Regal and I had been digging people out for hours. Or it seemed like hours. Long enough for it to be this dark, anyway. And cold enough that one of the firefighters had draped his jacket around me and Springer.

"Squads are on the way with at least four dogs," Josiah Linders told my father. "We also have specialized cameras and audio detectors coming in by helicopter. That stuff can pick up body heat and even a baby's breath—but it'll be hours yet. For now, Sam's nose and our ears are all we've got to find people."

After a few seconds of not hearing Dad, I opened my eyes. Springer's dad stood in the center of our street, talking to a crowd of men and women dressed in yellow rescue jackets and hats. He had on real gloves now, and he was pointing to different piles of rubble that used to be houses in our neighborhood. Springer's mom was helping to set up a tent in the yard across the road. Aunt Gus was busy swearing at a medic who kept trying to dab her head with something that she said "burned like hellfire," and demanding that the man splint Charlie's leg instead.

"We've got a call in to the emergency vet, ma'am," the man said. "He'll be over here with his mobile van as soon as he finishes with the horses at the fairgrounds."

"Jesse." Dad knelt beside me on one knee. "What if I take Sam and—"

"No!" I gripped my dog. "He can help, but only if I get a leash for him, and only if I go, too. I don't want him away from me. I don't want him to get hurt!"

Dad lowered his head. When he raised it again, I thought he'd start fighting with me, but he looked like he had a couple of days ago, when he suddenly thanked me for investigating who really stole the money out of his desk.

"You know what?" he said. "Okay. You're right. He's yours, and you'll take care of him better than anybody. So how about you look after him, and I'll look after you? We'll do this together."

Springer straightened, and I lifted my head.

"Acceptable," I said.

"I'll help," Springer said. "I'm more good with you guys than with Mom, because I can't do tents worth anything, and Dad's too busy."

"Done," Dad said. Then to Josiah Linders, Dad said, "Can you find some sort of leash? We'll go with you if we can keep the dog safe."

The guy nodded and jogged off into the mayhem of people and noise.

I got to my feet, and so did Springer. Then I leaned into Dad's arm as he stood beside me. "If we're both helping search for people who need help, who's going with Aunt Gus to the hospital?"

"Hey," Springer said. "I could do that." He held up his phone. "I can text you if you need to come. You know, to get her out of jail or something."

"Just don't let her spit on anybody," Dad said. "Or smoke in the bathroom and set off fire alarms." He gestured to the sea of people, and the ever-growing number of people in uniforms rushing around everywhere. "These people are busy."

"She won't go until the vet comes to X-ray Charlie's leg and fix it up," I said. "You know that, right?"

Dad sighed. "Let me go talk to her."

After he walked away toward Aunt Gus, I snuggled Sam-Sam and said, "Thanks for being willing to take care of my aunt, Springer."

He shrugged. "I like her. I wish my grandparents were still alive—and that I could get to know my own aunts and uncles, but Mom's people live in Rhode Island, and Dad didn't have any brothers or sisters."

I kissed Sam's wet nose and thought how weird and neat it was, learning something new about Springer in the middle of a disaster area, with emergency lights strobing blue and yellow and red all over everything, and a tent getting set up to "triage the wounded and organize the first responders," and Sam and Dad and I about to go on a mission like Mom usually did. Was that what friendship was like? Always finding out more and being happy about it, even in the middle of a great big bunch of mess?

Dad came back frowning. "You're right, Jesse. She's not budging until that dog gets attention."

"I'll stay with her," Springer said. "I'll get her to go to the tent at least."

"Thank you, young man," Dad said.

"You're welcome," Springer said, sounding almost cheerful as he headed out to face the fire-breathing dragon who was currently screaming for a cigarillo and threatening lives over lighters.

Dad watched him go. "He might be a keeper, Jesse."

"Okay," I said, even though I had no idea what that meant.

Then, "Oh, wait. You're talking about boyfriend-girlfriend stuff, aren't you?"

"Maaaaybe," Dad said.

"Why do parents always think about boyfriend-girlfriend stuff? He's my friend, Dad, okay?"

"Got it, got it," Dad said as Josiah Linders came jogging back toward us. As he got closer, he held up a pink leash. It was attached to a pink jeweled collar that looked big enough for Sam-Sam, if I threaded it through his fur.

"Chihuahua," the guy explained as he got to us. "Lady says she can keep the dog in her purse for now."

Sam and I eyed all the pink. We looked at each other.

"Sorry," I told Sam. "I wish it were purple, too, but pink it is—just for tonight."

Josiah Linders fished a baggie out of his pocket. "She sent these, too."

I smiled.

"Bacon treats. Thanks. That'll help."

An hour later, we left the third collapsed house two streets away from mine. By my count, we had searched seventeen houses. Dad walked Sam-Sam on his pink leash. I rode on Dad's back. My arms hurt. My legs hurt. My hands stung from all the cuts I got rescuing Aunt Gus before Springer thought about the sock mittens. I was hungry enough to eat a bacon treat, but just then, Sam pulled on the pink leash and started alert-barking.

"Okay, then," Dad said, letting go of my legs. "You're up again, honey."

He put me down.

I took the leash and let Sam lead me forward.

A group of Emergency Services workers crowded in behind me.

Sam led us to a house where one side had been flattened and the other side seemed mostly okay. He went to the crumpled part and headed to the left, sniffing. His fluffy tail wagged. As we turned where the corner of the house should have been, Sam froze and poked his nose farther into the rubble. Then he pulled back.

Bark! Bark! Bark!

"Good boy," I said. "Now, shhhhhh."

Sam-Sam shhhhhhed and sat, waiting for his treat.

As I gave it to him, the nearest rescue worker shouted, "Anybody in there?"

We all strained and listened.

Sam's head turned as a worker leaned to one side, turning his ear to the rubble.

There.

I heard it, too.

A faint voice, croaking, "I'm here. I'm here!"

"Got something!" the worker cried, motioning with his arm.

"Good boy," I told Sam, and gave him another bit of bacon treat.

He snarfed it up, his wet tail flopping on the ground.

An emergency crew descended on our spot, and the planning to get the trapped people out got started in a hurry. My stomach rumbled, and I wondered if anybody had a sandwich, but then I figured nobody was thinking about sandwiches but me, and maybe that was selfish. My stomach rumbled again. The flashing lights and yelling and rock smells and water smells and burning stuff smells and dirt smells dug into my brain. I made myself think about Mom again. Really, I had thought about Mom pretty much nonstop all night. That her life at war was sort of like what we were doing, only it never stopped. Mom lived like this all day. Every day. I didn't know how she stood it.

"Do you think she knows we're okay?" I asked Dad as I leaned against him, holding Sam's leash. "Mom, I mean. She'll see about the tornado, right?"

"I marked us safe on Facebook, and I sent a message through the network, and left one with Base Command at Fort Campbell, too."

Confusion fluttered through my insides. "You sound confident and worried, too. Why do you sound confident and worried at the same time?"

Dad ruffled my hair. "Because I am."

"Both things at once."

"Yes."

"People are so weird." I bent down and picked up Sam-Sam and held him close. "Dogs are way better."

Hours later. Some other house, streets away from mine. I couldn't even count anymore. My brain kept getting stuck, and I'd forget where I was and have to start over again. When I started trying to count start-overs, I sang songs in my head to make myself stop.

Emergency crews worked where Sam had pointed and barked.

My dog hadn't been wrong yet.

I ate a paper bowl full of pineapple that somebody stuck in front of me.

I don't even like pineapple.

Sometime later, I woke when Dad shifted me in his arms.

I held on tight to his neck, because we were still moving.

A man said, "Sir, I can carry her for a while if you'd like."

"No thanks," Dad said. "My daughter and I made a deal to do this together. We'll see it through."

The next time I woke up, Dad was carrying Sam-Sam, too.

My poor dog looked like a wet mouse, but he smiled at me and licked my face.

I licked him back and burped pineapple in his face.

"Gross," my father said, and I fell asleep again, before I could even laugh.

28

Tuesday Morning,
the Day After the Train Came

I sat in the front row of the courtroom, between Springer and Aunt Gus. Dad sat a table in front of us, on the other side of a wooden fence with a gate in the middle. He and Stan talked to each other in hushed voices.

My heart seemed to be beating in my throat.

"It'll be okay," Aunt Gus whispered. "Easy. It'll be okay."

Springer offered his hand, and I took it.

"All rise!" the bailiff shouted, and we stood.

A judge came in from the side door and headed to the bench. When he sat, we sat. I expected a speech, or a discussion, or something—but he just looked at Dad, said, "Guilty!" and banged his gavel.

Police seemed to close in from everywhere at once.

I jumped up and tried to climb over the wooden fence. "Dad!"

He saw me and reached for me.

I reached for him.

"Dad!"

. . .

My breath left in a wheeze as I sat up, fighting blankets, my aunt's hands, and a suddenly wiggling and licking Sam.

"Easy," Aunt Gus said. "It'll be okay. You're okay, Jesse."

I blinked at her, hearing the echo from my—my bad dream? Sam-Sam tucked himself under my chin, and I hugged him, counting his breaths until I could count my own and slow them down.

My galloping pulse slowed a fraction, and the world came to me slowly, in bits and pieces of light and motion and voices and people, and the strong smell of coffee. Gray light told me it was morning, or maybe rainy daytime. I couldn't tell. I realized I was under a big tent, a green one, not like Mom's sand-colored version. A lot of people seemed to be close by, talking and moving around. I heard them talking, but so many voices it all ran together like one big loud murmur.

Aunt Gus was sitting beside my cot in a fold-out chair. She had a bandage on her head. Charlie sat beside her panting into a cone of shame, his back leg in a little blue cast.

"Where's Dad?" I croaked.

Aunt Gus jerked a thumb toward a tent wall. "Out there with Mr. Regal. They're drinking coffee. Springer's with them, but I don't think he's the coffee sort."

"You're okay?" I squinted at her bandage. "Not going to fall out or anything?"

She gave me a snort. "Spent the night in the emergency

room for concussion observation, but they discharged me when I threatened to use my bedpan as a Frisbee." Her hand dropped to her side, and she scratched her dog's ears. "Place is boring as heck. Plus, there were a lot of people there who needed help a lot more than me."

"Charlie's wearing a cone," I said.

"He'll get all that off in a few weeks with the cast," Aunt Gus explained. "The mobile vet said he'd be fine."

"We're okay," I said, still hugging my dog.

"We're okay," Aunt Gus echoed.

"But we're not," I said. "We're not, Aunt Gus. Dad's hearing is tomorrow, and I never found out who took the money."

Aunt Gus made an effort at smiling but didn't quite get there. "Sweetheart, Avery is nothing but toothpicks and peeled roofs. I doubt they'll even have court tomorrow."

"But what if they do?" I had to hold my breath between sentences not to cry. Hold, release. Hold, release. "We don't have a house anymore, and they could take Dad, and—"

Hold, release. Hold, release.

"Hush, Jesse. Don't do this to yourself." Aunt Gus kept her hand on Charlie but her eyes on Sam and me. "It's just a hearing. We'll get through it."

I had let my father down, even though I had tried so hard to find out the truth. I felt like trash. I felt like dirt. I felt like—I felt like—

"I need to go to the bathroom," I said.

Then I got terrified about something totally new, that there wouldn't be any bathrooms, that I'd have to hike into Pond River Forest to do my business.

But Aunt Gus took Sam from my arms, and with Charlie thumping and snuffling behind us, she led me through the gigantic, sectioned tent, then out one of the open flaps into the gray, misty morning. Every one of my muscles complained when I moved. I felt like I'd run ten marathons, or how I'd imagine that would feel.

Behind the tent, I found a giant row of plastic, square things, blue and no bigger than a closet.

"Knock yourself out," Aunt Gus said, pointing to them. "But you might want to hold your breath."

I opened the door of the first blue closet, which was labeled JOHNNY'S JOHNS, EVENTS AND EMERGENCIES.

Okay . . .

A few gaggy minutes later, I managed to pee into some unspeakable blue liquid and stumble back out, never wanting to see anything blue again.

Aunt Gus had gone back inside with Sam, and I wished she hadn't. I could have smelled his fur to get that . . . *blue* out of my head. My brain itched and twitched as I hurried back into the first open flap I saw. Instead of finding Aunt Gus and Sam on the inside, though, I ended up at a table stocked with pastries and cups of coffee, with people standing all around it talking and eating. Most were dressed in rumpled and torn clothes, streaked with dirt and black stuff. I knew some of them from my neighborhood. Others were strangers, and there—oh, great. Three familiar cockroach faces, and one of the police officers who arrested Dad, the dark-headed one, in his wrinkled uniform, standing next to the two people I least wanted to see, other than Chris and Trisha and Ryker.

Jerkface and the cockroaches noticed me but didn't say anything awful, probably because grown-ups were standing beside them. Ms. Jorgensen nodded at me. I had never before seen her look dirty and so . . . unpressed. Coach Sedon saw me, too. He didn't nod. He held his splinted hand to his chest and looked down instead. I noticed his whistle was missing from his green basketball uniform, and that his arms had cuts all over them.

I rubbed my hands together, then winced from all my own cuts, the ones I had gotten rescuing my aunt. I wondered if Coach Sedon had helped rescue people from that house where I saw him and Ms. Jorgensen, when Springer and I had been running to save Sam-Sam—

Oh.

Wait.

I froze in place as my mind shifted through sights and sounds from the last day, and I thought hard about going past the place that used to have AJS-green shutters on the front, and no flamingos anywhere in the yard, and shutters in the back that I couldn't trespass to count. The house

Dad had told me to stay away from before, because of illegal businesses like . . .

But . . .

Ms. Jorgensen and Coach Sedon had been standing around outside that house, even though Coach Sedon was supposed to be at the hospital getting his hand fixed.

My own hands stung, and my muscles ached, and my nose was still full of blue nastiness, but I started walking. Right past Jerkface and the Cockroaches I went. Then I passed the officer who'd tried to steal my father, and I went straight up to the bad guys.

Coach Sedon kept his hand cradled and his head down.

"Good morning, Jesse," Ms. Jorgensen said.

From somewhere back in the tent, I heard Aunt Gus say, "Oh, no. Derrick? Hey, Derrick? Better come in here."

Then I heard her coming, stomping on the grass, Charlie making his bulldog-snarkling sounds with each step she took.

Sam got to me before anyone else. He danced on his back feet and scratched at my legs, and I picked up my baby even as I kept my eyes on Coach Sedon's hurt hand, so my brain wouldn't itch any more than it already did.

I pulled Sam close, imagined myself made of as much steel as Mom, and said, "So do you have a drug problem, or a gambling problem, Coach Sedon?"

The background conversations in the tent snuffed like

one of Aunt Gus's cigarillos when she stepped on it. People started moving away from us in a hurry, clearing space until it was just the seven of us standing in the area.

"And there it is," I heard Aunt Gus say from somewhere behind me. "Too late again."

"You can't talk to my father like—" Chris started, but Coach Sedon silenced him with a single look.

Then Coach Sedon faced me, took a slow breath, held his hand even closer, then let the air out just as slowly. "Since you asked, Jesse, I have a gambling problem."

"Good for you," Ms. Jorgensen murmured to him.

"That's why you were at the bad house during the storm," I said. "You went there instead of getting your hand fixed like you were supposed to." My gaze shifted to Ms. Jorgensen, and I stared at her elbow. "And you—you went to get him."

"I did," Ms. Jorgensen said.

"All those times you haven't been at school when you were supposed to be," I said to Ms. Jorgensen. "You were out trying to stop Coach Sedon from gambling, because you're his friend, and you wanted to help him. You went to that house to get him the day of the staff meeting, didn't you?"

"Yes," Ms. Jorgensen said. "I really was trying to help. To give him a chance."

"Go away, Messy," Trisha said.

"Don't call her that," Springer said as he came jogging up beside me. "Ever, ever again."

Aunt Gus stepped up beside me, too, holding Charlie in her arms. She said, "I'll second that. No name-calling, or the dogs start biting." Her tone turned chilly. "And I don't mean the four-legged ones."

Trisha closed her mouth and looked miserable, and also like she hated me and maybe Sam-Sam and Aunt Gus and Springer, too. Ryker wouldn't look at me, a lot like Coach Sedon. Trisha did, though, and so did Chris, who said, "You three and those nasty dogs need to move away from us."

"That's enough," his father snapped.

When Chris looked at the officer who'd arrested my father, the officer swallowed his bite of donut and said, "Hey, it's a central disaster response tent. Everybody can be here until other shelters are set up. You're free to leave if you want, though, seeing as you and your dog didn't spend their night helping save people." To me, the officer said, "Want some juice and a pastry, Jesse?"

"No, thank you," I told him. Then I glanced at Springer.

"Morning," he said.

Taking strength from my friend and my aunt standing right beside me, and the fuzzy war dog of fury in my arms, I made myself focus on Coach Sedon again. "My father has a hearing tomorrow. Can't you just tell this officer here how you took the money out of Dad's desk during the staff meeting, then took it to that house to pay your gambling debts? Don't let him have to go back to jail. Please."

"He won't go to jail." Coach Sedon finally looked at me. Well, more at my dog, but close enough. "Fines and community service, maybe. I didn't take the money, kid. Sorry."

Ms. Jorgensen turned to Coach Sedon and cleared her throat.

"What?" Coach Sedon adjusted his injured hand. "I didn't take that cash."

Ms. Jorgensen frowned at him. "When I took you to square up with the bookie Monday evening, you paid an amount very close to what was stolen. I've been waiting for you to come clean about it."

Coach Sedon shook his head. "No. The cash I paid was our money. Chris got it from selling that motorbike he didn't use anymore. Boy wanted to help his family, so I let him."

All eyes shifted to Chris, including mine.

My father made it over to us. Dad was about to say something to me, but Aunt Gus stopped him with a "Shhhhh," and she pointed to Chris. "Not now. I think he's about to confess."

"No," Trisha said. "He's not."

But she sounded shaky. She sounded like she was starting to cry. Chris blinked at her. A cloud of feeling seemed to cross his face, but I couldn't tell what feeling it was. The police officer stood a little straighter, sipping his coffee, eyes laser-focused on Chris.

Chris ran his fingers through his hair, then sighed. "Okay, yeah, it was me. I wrecked that bike months ago, Dad. But I heard you and Mom yelling about the gambling stuff, and how much you owed, and how it had to be paid right away. I knew you needed the money."

My heart thumped against my chest, once, loud and hard, and I almost woozy-swayed like Aunt Gus had done the night before.

Sam-Sam chose that moment to wiggle like crazy, but I held him as Springer's shocked voice said, "You stole the money out of Mr. Broadview's desk, Chris?"

Trisha started to cry for real. Ryker tried to put his arm around her, but she punched him in the shoulder. Coach Sedon gaped at his son, and Ms. Jorgensen seemed to be in shock. She just stood there, fidgeting with the button on her torn, raggedy blouse.

"Are you confessing to the theft, young man?" the police officer asked.

"Yeah, I'm—" Chris started to say, but Trisha stepped between him and the rest of us.

"No, he's not," she said. "Because he didn't do it."

"Yes, I did." Chris tried to come around her, but she held out both her arms and blocked him.

"Chris didn't take the money," she repeated. She lowered her arms, and when he came up beside her, she smiled at him. Like, a real smile that changed her whole mean face into something softer, more peaceful. "But he is trying to take the blame." She swallowed so hard I could hear it even feet away. "Thanks for that."

Then, before anybody could say anything else, Trisha looked at my father and said, "I took the money out of your drawer."

Nobody seemed to be able to speak.

Except, of course, me.

"Your sister's friend saw the amount and said something to you and Meredith, and you knew it was there, right?" I asked.

Trisha nodded. "It was one of the days we were waiting in the band room for Nancy to drive us home. I got to your dad's room during the staff meeting, before the doors got locked at the end of the day." She shrugged. "It was easy. I thought if Chris's dad could get out of trouble, then he'd stop being so tough on Chris, and Chris would—I don't know. Be himself again. Settle down and quit being a butt." Her eyes flicked to me for a hot second, then to Springer, and back to Dad again. "I didn't know you would get blamed for it, Mr. Broadview."

"Touch coming," Dad said to me. Then I felt his hand rest on my shoulder, and he squeezed it gently. I was glad, because I still felt dizzy.

"I'm sorry," Trisha said, sort of to everybody, but mostly to Dad.

"Thank you," Dad said, but he didn't tell her it was okay, what she did, stealing stuff and letting somebody else get in trouble for it, no matter how good her reasons might have been.

Chris just stared at Trisha. He looked sad. Then mad, like the guy that helped Ryker smack people for fun. Finally, he said, "You think I'm a butt? I just confessed to save you and you called me a butt?"

Trisha gave him a pained look.

Ryker ignored Chris and put his arm around Trisha's shoulders. "Do you have to arrest her?" he asked the police officer.

I realized the officer had put down his coffee and donut when he dusted his hands off and asked Trisha, "Where are your parents?"

"They work at the hospital," Trisha said. "They've been there all night. My sister's there, too, helping out with paperwork."

"It's why she's with us," Coach Sedon said. He nodded at Ryker. "His dad's a lineman and his mom's on the city council. They've been at it all night, too."

"Why don't we head over to the hospital to chat?" the officer said to Trisha. To Coach Sedon and Ms. Jorgensen, he said, "One of you got a functioning vehicle? It might be nicer if you drove her."

Ms. Jorgensen raised a hand, then fished keys from a pocket in her slacks. "My car's two streets over. Come on, kids. Let's do as the officer asked."

Coach Sedon immediately walked Trisha and Ryker and Chris out of the tent, with Ms. Jorgensen bringing up the rear. She stopped at the tent flap and glanced at Dad.

"Derrick," she said.

Dad nodded his head once, like he understood whatever Ms. Jorgensen meant to say.

The police officer stopped in front of Dad and stuck out his hand. As Dad shook it, the officer said, "Looks like we'll get this cleared up soon, sir. You and your daughter get some rest and take care of yourselves."

"Thanks," Dad said.

Next, the officer stopped in front of me. "Good job in that apocalypse last night, Jesse." He smiled at Sam-Sam. "And you, too. He's what kind of pup?"

I started to say Pomeranian, but Springer beat me to it with "War dog of fury."

The officer laughed. "You bet. War dog of fury it is."

He turned to leave the tent, then lifted his hand to shield his eyes against the sunlight trying to break through the crowds outside. "Looks like some news vans coming." He turned back long enough to give me a wink. "Suspect they'll be wanting to talk to you."

Then he headed on out, like that was just the best thing ever.

I stood like a frozen statue, holding my wriggling dog in arms that suddenly felt a lot like concrete. Heat rose from chest to my neck to my cheeks, and that dizzy sensation in my head got even worse.

"News," I echoed. "Talk to me?"

"Oh, crap," Aunt Gus said.

"I'll handle it," Dad told us. "Be right back, Jesse."

"But why do they want to talk to me?" I called after him.

After a few seconds of silence, Aunt Gus said, "Honey, you and Sam and your father helped save thirty-two people before the search-and-rescue teams got here with their big dogs and equipment."

My woozy feeling doubled, then tripled. I really did sway on my feet.

"Help?" Springer asked.

"Yes," I said.

He steadied me with hands on either side of my waist.

"Thirty-two?" I asked Aunt Gus. "Like, three tens and two ones?"

"Sixteen plus sixteen," Springer said.

"Four times eight," Aunt Gus agreed.

I took myself out of Springer's steadying grip and sat down on the damp grass floor.

Sam-Sam stayed in my arms, then shifted himself to my lap. I picked him up and went nose to nose with him, gazing deep into his liquid black eyes, feeling absolutely no brain itch at all. "Springer was right," I told him. "You were never a bomb-sniffer. You were search and rescue all along."

Sam wagged his fluffy tail and licked my nose.

"You okay, honey?" Aunt Gus said. "You know your dad won't let those people talk to you with all their flashy lights and microphones, if you don't want it."

"I don't want it," I told her. I shut my eyes and hugged Sam, and realized I didn't want to open them. My arms and legs felt so heavy. My brain felt heavy. Snips and snaps from the night before zipped through my mind. People being pulled out of broken houses. Dad carrying me. Sam barking.

We had done that. Helped those people. Sam was a warrior. I had been a warrior, too, with my father's help.

And we knew who took the money.

Dad wasn't going to jail.

My heavy muscles turned all floppy, and I said, "I really need to go back to bed."

"Sounds like a plan," Aunt Gus agreed. "Want me to carry you?"

"No, thank you," I managed, and somehow, I got my dog and my shaking self to the far side of the big tent where the dividers were, and into the little cot where I had spent some of the night.

After helping to save thirty-two people.

I covered Sam-Sam up with the sheet, then pulled it over my head.

I heard Aunt Gus come into the little section behind me and sit in the folding chair.

I heard Charlie grunt.

I heard Springer say, "I'll stay right out here, Miss Gustine. They'll have to come through me first."

Sam settled under my chin, and seconds later, I tumbled into deep, blessed nothing.

Epilogue

After Sam-Sam and I Handled the Apocalypse and Helped Save Thirty-Two People

Sometime later on Tuesday, I had a vague memory of Dad carrying me into a home that smelled like fresh sheets and vanilla, with a hint of pot roast. It smelled so good I dreamed about potatoes and carrots and thick roasty gravy on fresh bread. Every now and then, Sam licked my ear and woke me up, but I went straight back to sleep.

When I woke Tuesday night, I finally got some of that roast. Ms. Regal had made it, and I found out we were staying with them until our insurance company could process claims and help us rent a place while we rebuilt. I sat at their dinner table with her and Dad and Springer. Mr. Regal was out working, and Aunt Gus was out walking the dogs.

"Aunt Gus has her own room," Springer explained. "In the back, on the sun porch that faces the forest."

"Does it have windows?" I asked. "Because Charlie farts so bad it'll fog up the whole house."

Ms. Regal laughed. "Yes. It has windows. But she promised not to smoke inside."

"Yeah." Dad sighed. "About that—I might end up owing you for fumigation and repainting."

"School's out for a few weeks," Springer said. "I'll watch her and chase her outside."

"She'll beat you with her shoe," I warned. "Just check the closets. If she finds a store open to buy stuff, she'll try to hide it in the closet."

"Got it," said Ms. Regal, looking as stern as Mom could get.

As soon as I finished eating, I felt sleepy again, but when I complained, Dad said, "I think that's normal, honey. We've been through a lot lately. Go on back to sleep, and I'll bring Sam to you when Gus gets back with them."

He didn't have to offer twice, and I was out before I could even count to ten.

I didn't sleep all of Wednesday morning, but I kept taking naps across the day.

It was during one of those that I heard Dad say, "Gus is still sleeping, and Jesse's been up and down. She was amazing when it happened, though, Camila. You should have seen her."

"I'm so happy she has a friend," Mom said. "And so glad she believed in herself about solving that theft."

I smiled in my half-awake stupor, glad Dad was letting her know we were okay, even if we didn't have a house.

"I should have trusted her sooner," Dad said. "I know she's older, and smart—"

"And strong," Mom reminded him.

"And strong," Dad agreed. "Those kids who've been bullying her, they'll be in alternative school for a while. Not sure what's happening with the one who stole the funds, but she'll probably have to stay on that track a bit longer."

"I hope it helps them," Mom said. "Something needs to, before I have to go all war-zone on their little butts."

I laughed into my pillow.

My mom, army to the core.

She yawned. "Twenty-two hours, plus four on the drive. A record."

Dad's laughter made me feel relaxed and normal. I loved hearing my parents' voices and pretending Mom wasn't oceans away from us.

"You need to sleep almost as much as Jesse does, Cam," Dad said.

"Later," Mom told him.

"I need to walk over to the school and what's left of my classroom," Dad said . . .

And then I fell back to sleep, and . . .

SUSAN VAUGHT

Sam wiggled against my face, his tail brushing my nose.

"Well, if it isn't Private Sleepyhead." Mom's voice. "And the little war dog of fury. I hear you're straight-up SAR now, Sam."

SAR. The military abbreviation for *search and rescue*. I felt so proud. I rolled over in my bed to take the pad from Dad—

But instead—

Dark brown eyes gazed down at me. Eyes from that picture in my room that was probably lost forever, of Uncle Jesse and—

And—

She smelled like cucumber-melon lotion and cinnamon gum.

She smelled like . . .

"Mom," I whispered, so stunned I couldn't even move. I hadn't seen her in person in more than a year. Four hundred sixty-three days. That was 11,118 hours.

I didn't get to the seconds in my head before she asked, "Hug?"

"Yes!" And then I was in Mom's arms, and she hugged me so tightly, and my brain didn't itch, and Sam licked our cheeks and noses and ears.

"I'm so proud of you," she whispered into my ear. "Your uncle Jesse would be so proud of you, too. Way to carry that name, my perfect daughter. Way to do it proud."

I held on to her, and loved her voice, and the way she smelled, and her. My mom. Right here. With me.

When Mom finally let me go, I saw tears in her eyes. "Standing up to bullies, dog training, making friends, surviving a tornado, search and rescue—oh, and let's not forget catching a thief and clearing your father—impressive work, Private Broadview. I might have to give you a promotion."

"Can I be a general?"

Mom laughed. "Let's go with private first class for now. We'll talk about general after you bring down a crime syndicate with a pack of rabid detective Chihuahuas, okay?"

"Nah." I shook my head and hugged Sam-Sam. "I prefer Pomeranians."

Mom petted Sam's head. "But they're so . . . fluffy."

Sam stretched up and slurped her nose.

"They don't stink as bad as bulldogs," I said as she wiped off the dog drool.

"Well," Mom said. "I guess that's something."

I chewed my lip for a second, then made myself ask, "So how long can you stay?"

She stroked my hair, pushing strands behind my right ear. "I got three weeks. So not bad."

"Not bad at all!" I said, even though I wished it could be three months or three years, or maybe forever.

"Soon," she told me. "I've only got a year left on this tour. Then we can make decisions."

"Okay," I said.

But in my heart, I knew Mom was a soldier, and if the army still needed her—well. We'd have to see. But I couldn't imagine asking Mom to be anything other than what she was best at being. I shifted Sam-Sam upward and kissed the top of his head. There were bomb-sniffers and SAR dogs, and everything in between. My mom, she was a bomb-sniffer. And that was that.

When she went back this time, and if she decided to stay in the army next year, I'd find a way to be okay with Dad and Aunt Gus and Sam and Charlie and Springer—oh.

"Is the sun still up?" I asked Mom, glancing at the windows—but the curtains were all pulled. "Is it still raining?"

"Yes," Mom said. "And no, I don't think so. Why?"

"Will you help Springer and me with something?" I asked as I climbed out of the bed. "It's important."

Mom got to her feet, then slowly came to attention. "Absolutely, PFC Broadview. Lead the way."

"I wasn't sure it would still be here," Springer said. "The tornado's track was just a little ways off the main path."

Mom whistled. "Not in the best shape, but it held up pretty well."

Mr. Regal unloaded the few salvaged scraps of board he'd brought off his shoulder, tilted his head, then felt around the roof line of the clubhouse as I put Sam down with a pile of chew toys. "This is pretty well done, Jesse. How did you know to build it like this?"

"YouTube has videos for everything," I told him, feeling pretty awesome that Mom was here in Avery and not in Iraq, that she was at my clubhouse, and that Springer's dad was with us, too, still acting proud of Springer and making him so happy.

"YouTube." Mom laughed. "Okay. Brave new world, right? Everything's online."

"It is," Springer agreed. "But I probably would have broken my thumbs trying it, videos or not."

"You and me both," Mom said.

"Nonsense," Mr. Regal said. "I can show you both how to wield hammers like pros. No broken fingers, I promise."

And true to his word, he did.

For a few hours, Mr. Regal directed us on where to patch and prop, and he taught Mom and Springer both how to hammer. Mom remained impressed that I already knew how to do it without smashing anything important.

After we finished, we used blown-down branches to camouflage it again, so it couldn't be seen from the path. Then I went inside and got the tote we needed to put on the finishing touches.

Since we couldn't get to any stores to buy paint, and there probably wouldn't have been any paint even if we had, I passed out the nail polish. We got busy, Mom at the top, Springer on one side, Mr. Regal on the other side, and me at the bottom.

It took a while to cover up the original door sign, but as the sky started to go orange with the sun setting, we finished. I put up the polish box and got Sam out of the clubhouse, and Mom and Mr. Regal and Springer and Sam-Sam and I stood back and examined our work.

Instead of JESSE'S PLACE. STAY OUT AND STAY ALIVE, the door now carried the following message, in lots of different nail polish colors:

OBWIG-DA HEADQUARTERS

STAY OUT IF YOU DON'T WANT TO BE INVESTIGATED

A little less bloody, maybe, but impressive.

Mom had even added THIS MEANS YOU! on the top right corner, with the outline of an eagle head, staring with one eye, like she wore on her sleeve.

Mr. Regal had hung the door properly, with hinges and everything. He nodded like he approved, and said, "Better. Even if I have no idea what most of that means."

"OBWIG," Mom said, shaking her head. "I still think that's a strange word, guys. And now it's OBWIG-DA?"

Springer and I looked at each other, and for the first time ever in my life, I felt like I was the one who got to talk to somebody without saying anything out loud.

As I scratched Sam's head to keep him happy, Springer lifted his finger to the painted word on the clubhouse door, and he touched each letter as he said, "Observant but Weird in a Good Way Detective Agency. That's what it's always been, only now we've really earned the detective agency part, so we wanted to add it."

Mom tilted her head like Sam did when he was listening hard to something. "Shouldn't it be OBWIGW-DA?"

"Don't go overboard, Mom," I said.

Mr. Regal stuck his thumbs in his tool belt, and then he nodded. "OBWIG-DA. Yep. That works. And you did earn it."

Springer beamed.

Mom gave me a thumbs-up, then said, "Okay, troops. Gustine will be awake, and Ms. Regal doesn't need to deal with her and that bulldog all by herself. Plus, Derrick will be coming home from his trek to the out-of-town stores for groceries. We better get back."

She motioned to us, then headed out, toward the main path, marching at a pretty good clip. Mr. Regal followed her. Springer and I hurried along behind, with me keeping Sam in my arms to avoid any early-evening squirrel-chasing nightmares.

As he jogged along beside me, Springer whispered, "I like your mom."

"Me too," I whispered back.

"She's scary," he admitted. "But fun. Kinda like you."

And that made me happier than just about anything anyone had ever said to me.

This whole having a friend thing, I decided I could get used to it, and maybe even like it almost as much as having such a wonderful fuzzy war dog of fury, with all his fluffy SAR talents and happy nose-licking.

"OBWIG-DA," I said as Sam-Sam polished my nose one more time.

Springer smiled at me, and he answered just like I hoped he would, with "OBWIG-DA. OBWIG-DA forever!"

Author's Note

Neurodiversity: Brains and the way brains work and the thoughts brains think can be as different as people themselves. There is no "normal brain." And how boring the world would be if all brains worked exactly the same way!

Neurotypical: A lot of people do have some things in common, and society values some abilities and traits more than others. This changes over time, and different places and different cultures may choose different skills to teach and train. People who have these skills will be considered "neurotypical."

Neurodivergent: Some people have fewer things in common with other people, or have skills that aren't the ones most of society thinks are important.

Since the late 1800s doctors have been attempting to describe and classify developmental issues and find names for all the ways people can be neurodivergent. In the 1940s the diagnoses of "Early Infantile Autism" and "Asperger's syndrome" came into being, and in 1964, doctors began to understand that people with these diagnoses might have differences in their nervous systems. In 2013 terminology shifted to "Autism Spectrum Disorder (ASD)," an acknowledgment that people who are neurodivergent are individuals, with unique experiences and challenges.

The problem with all of these concepts is that they assume a "standard normal" that everyone should meet. Many people diagnosed with ASD do not view being neurodivergent as a disorder or a disease or anything else that might need a cure. It is not simple or easy to live in a world designed for neurotypical folks, but being neurodivergent is part of who they are as people. It is part of who *we* are as people, and many of us prefer to find our own ways of dealing with a world that invests in ableism, and often pulls for everyone to be more similar than we can be.

I asked author Mike Jung, who is neurodivergent, if he has ever written characters who are not neurotypical. He answered:

> *You know what, none of the main characters in my first three books are neurodivergent, which is partly because I didn't truly know I'm autistic until I'd finished writing them. That's going to*

change, though. In October 2018 my essay about being autistic appeared in Kelly Jensen's nonfiction anthology (Don't) Call Me Crazy *(Algonquin, 10/18). In October 2019 my short story about an autistic boy who practices aikido will appear in the We Need Diverse Books anthology* The Hero Next Door *(Crown, 10/19). And I've started writing what will be my fourth novel, which has no title yet, but is about a family of superheroes that includes an autistic child and an autistic parent. Autistic characters as heroes, am I right?*

I asked author JB Redmond (my son, and coauthor in the Oathbreaker books) how he experiences being neurodivergent, and he described these experiences:

I don't remember being diagnosed with autism, but I know I had that tag when I was little. I remember playing with keys. They relaxed me. The way the light moved on the metal helped me focus, and I liked the jingling sound, and how they felt when they moved in my hands. When I was older, I held figurines from Star Trek like I used to hold keys. I literally wore the faces and arms off of them, squeezing, then tapping them in my hands. Finally, when I was a teenager, I found Slinkys. I have one with me all the time. When I hold them, I feel relaxed and like myself. When I don't have one I feel nervous, and like my hands need them, and like I'll lose my mind if I don't have one soon. Sometimes my hands actually hurt to hold a Slinky. My moms used to not let me take them into restaurants or doctor's appointments or movie theaters, and I didn't want to, because of "how it would look." But a few years ago, we realized I should do what made me feel best, and most like myself. Now I take them everywhere. I just try to move them quietly in theaters so other people can hear the films. There are a lot of things I don't eat or drink because I can't stand how they feel in my mouth, and I can't make myself swallow them, and if I try they actually make me throw up. I can't stand being in bright, noisy places for too long. I feel like my brain will melt. I don't mind leaving home and doing stuff—but usually I am glad to get back. I'm happy with my world and the routine I made for myself—as long as there's a Slinky!

As for me, I have this to say:

Jesse is not my first neurodivergent character, but she is my first character who identifies as hav-

ing Autism Spectrum Disorder. I tried to honor some of my own experiences through her, which feels like a big personal step. People and feelings were always puzzles to me, things I knew I needed to understand, but just didn't. I had to learn the details of people, and that's probably why I became a psychologist. It was the only way I could deeply study what I needed to know, what my own mind didn't naturally tell me, and still does not. My thinking tends to be straightforward and without nuance, and that's probably why I became a writer—to learn the intricacy of human beings and life.

Mike is finding his way and his place in the world. JB is finding his, and I am finding mine. We're learning to move away from the suffocation of how we "should" be, and into the freedom of who we are. So if you are neurodivergent, know that you have authors writing for you, and characters and stories waiting to speak to you. I believe that more and more, we will be able to make spaces for ourselves, and be heard, and be who we are, and be how we are.

Stay safe, and find calm-happy where you can. It gets better. It really does get better.

—S V

BOCA RATON PUBLIC LIBRARY

3 3656 3034912 8

J
Vaught, Susan,
Me and Sam-Sam handle the apocalypse
/

May 2019